DAEMON AND THE ANGEL

"Milady?"

She tensed at Daemon's voice, which sliced through her thoughts. "Aye?"

"Why do you weep?"

Arina licked her lips, tasting the salt on her face. She wiped her eyes, amazed by the wetness. When had her tears started?

The moment she'd realized Daemon intended to leave. The moment she'd realized that all her dreams were nothing more than fantasies that could never be hers.

"I am merely happy that milord is well," she whispered, unwilling to tell him the truth. Nay, she would not beg him to stay. His life had been hard enough without her adding any more guilt or pain to it.

He rolled her onto her back and kissed away the dampness. "I would never have milady shed a single tear on my behalf," he whispered, his voice bringing a flood of bittersweet joy to her breast. "I would never cause you pain."

His lips covered hers and she reveled at the taste of the warrior, the taste of wine on his tongue. Chills shot the length of her body and she prayed for a piece of him before he left. If she could have one wish it would be to carry his child. To give that one precious child all the love he had been denied.

Daemon's Angel

Sherrilyn Kenyon

LOVE SPELL **NEW YORK CITY**

LOVE SPELL®

May 1995

Published by

Dorchester Publishing Co., Inc.
276 Fifth Avenue
New York, NY 10001

The name "Love Spell" and its logo are trademarks of Dorchester Publishing Co., Inc.

Printed in the United States of America.

For Cathy-Max, Debbie, Kim, Lorraine, Rickey and Tanya—the cooks who sampled the soup!
As Max so often says, "I am truly wealthy in friends."
For my editor, Alicia Condon, who gave me the chance to do something different.
Laura Cifelli, for all her encouraging words.
And as always, for my parents, family, and Ken. Without their love and support, I'd never have come so far.

Prologue

She drifted out of the billowing smoke from between the fallen bodies like the Angel of Death come to claim their departing souls. Her pale flaxen hair blew in the strong breeze reminding him of a battle standard.

Daemon blinked at the sight, his eyes burning from the smoke and sweat, and the stench of death that surrounded him. A shadow from the right caught his attention. He turned in his saddle with his sword raised just in time to prevent the Saxon's seax from slicing his thigh. With two swift, clean strokes, he finished his attacker and dared a quick look back at the eerie form.

All Saxon males who remained able-bodied drew around her in a protective cloak as if they would now rally to her favor. Daemon shook his head at their effort. Their number would scarce frighten a babe, let alone the Norman army that had cut through them with little difficulty.

The sounds of battle settled to a raspy silence, broken only by the occasional neigh of a horse, or moan of the dying.

"M'hlafdie, why do you come?" one of the Saxons snapped in their coarse native tongue, his voice carried on the wind to Daemon's ears.

She lifted her chin with a courage to rival even the bravest of the men and turned away from the Saxon soldier. "Who leads this army?" the woman asked in the pure dulcet tones of an angel as she spoke in Norman French.

"Milord!"

Something grabbed Daemon's arm. With a curse, he swatted at the pest, but contacted only air.

Angered over the interruption of his dream, he blinked open his eyes to see his squire standing next to his cot.

" 'Tis a messenger from your brother, the king," Wace said, his youthful face beaming in the cheerful manner that always annoyed Daemon first thing in the morning.

His lips curled in a snarl, Daemon pushed back the blanket and rose. "I shall be right out," he said, reaching for his breeches and tunic.

What the devil could William want with him now? He'd quelled the Saxons as promised, and now all he sought was freedom to return to the continent, where he intended to search until he found another army or cause to fight for.

Daemon tossed his hair out of his eyes and reached for the tent flap. He saw William's messenger, a frightened-looking youth who paled considerably when he faced him. Daemon shrugged the reaction away, a bitterness burning raw in his gullet. He was too used to people's reactions to him, too used to the stark terror shimmering in their eyes as if they feared for their souls. As if he ever had any use for anyone's soul, including his own.

"What does my brother want with me?" Daemon asked, his voice gruff to even his own ears.

The messenger's eyes widened as he glanced up and noted Daemon's mismatched eyes. For a moment, Daemon feared Wace would have to bring the man a towel and oil cloth. The man looked about like a cornered rabbit. "His Majesty the King sends this for you, milord," he said, extending a bound parchment.

Daemon took it from his hands and broke the seal. Curiosity riding him hard, he scanned the contents. His mood darkened with each word he read. William had given him lordship of Brunneswald Hall, the demesne lands, and all outlying territories.

By hell, he'd kill William for this!

His grip tightened on the letter. He looked up at the messenger, his breathing hard. "Tell William I'll take care of the rebellion as he requested, but I want him to find a permanent castellan for the manor. I have no use for such."

The messenger nodded furiously. "Aye, milord. I shall tell him forthwith."

Daemon shook his head, his stomach knotting over William's humor. What was the man thinking? He had served his brother well; why would William do such a thing to him?

"Bloody bastard," he said as he entered the tent, unsure of whom he intended the insult for, himself or William.

He reached for his armor.

"Who leads this army?"

Daemon whirled at the sound of the voice in his dream, but saw nothing. An ache spread through him, an ache whose source he couldn't name. 'Twas always the same, though. Ever since he'd landed at Hastings with William, he'd been haunted by the dream of a fair maiden coming for his soul.

Grunting, he realized it was more than likely a warning of his death. Aye, he would welcome the moment and the peace it brought with open arms.

Chapter One

"Look homeward, Angel, now, and melt with compassion."

Arina screamed in agony, the words languishing in her mind like a serpent, twining about her limbs, making them heavy, unbearable. A foreign weight dragged her from the heavens in a violent whirlwind, down toward earth. She reached out, trying to stop her descent, but found only rushing air that bathed her body in a strange pelting storm. The savage winds whipped at her hair, her wings, and howled in her ears like the vicious beasts that guarded the pathway to Hell.

What was happening? None of it made sense. Every part of her ached and pulsed in waves of crashing sensation. No primary angel had ever experienced the scar of original sin. 'Twas meant for mortals to bear. Yet she experienced it now. Pain ripped down her spine, and took the breath from a body that needed no breath, made a chest heave that should not heave, a stomach churn that had never churned before.

Blackness surrounded her in a swirling funnel. Deprived of her sight and hearing, Arina reached out with her other senses, trying to find the answers to her questions. A mixture of odors assailed her—the charred stench of fear, the sulphur of Hell, and worse, the bittersweet smell of human flesh. Before, all these had been muted; now they assaulted her in a pungent bouquet that almost overwhelmed her with a primitive vitality that didn't belong to her world, or understanding.

Suddenly, she slammed against the ground, her body aching and throbbing in such a way she couldn't fathom. Dear saints, what had happened to her?

The buzzing in her ears gave way to the gentle call of birds and beasts frolicking in the forest. But the sound soon dulled until all she could hear was an occasional bird's cry, and the rustle of a breeze through bright, late autumn leaves.

Arina pushed herself up, but quickly fell again, her limbs shaking with unfamiliar heaviness. Her hair tumbled around her shoulders, hanging in her face. She tried to breathe through the heavy weight, but her breath caught in the strands and almost suffocated her.

A hand snatched back the mass of hair.

Arina looked up into the face of hatred and she knew the source of her misery. "What have you done to me?" she asked, her throat stinging from the use of vocal cords that hadn't existed ten minutes ago.

The old woman glared at her with dark, dilated eyes. "You stole from me my most precious possession. I begged you for mercy and still you took my son. 'Tis time you learned what it means to be mortal, what it means to suffer loss."

Her body trembled from rage, and Arina wondered at the sensation. She was an angel and angels had no feelings save love. Yet her body responded to the woman's presence with a burning fury that made her yearn for retaliation.

"Return me to my original form!"

The old woman's laugh echoed around her, into the trees of the forest surrounding them. "I cannot undo my spell. Only you can."

Arina stared at her in disbelief. She couldn't stay here. Mortals were brutal and cold. She knew nothing of survival in Man's world. A prayer came to her lips, but she knew there would be no answer. The Lord gave all beings sovereignty over their own existence, and He allowed nature, even evil nature, its course.

But she couldn't stay here. This was not her home. Looking up at the clear gray sky above them, Arina knew she must return to her domain before the taint of mortalness damaged her eternally. "What must I do?" Arina asked in desperation.

The smile that curved the crone's lips sent a shiver down her body. "You must love, then watch your mortal lover die. Hold him in your arms while he struggles for breath and life. Only then will you be free."

Arina shook her head in denial. "I love all mortals. I grieve for your loss as if it were my own, but I have no choice about whom to take from this world. 'Tis the will of the Maker!"

"And now you dance to my command." The woman walked a small circle around her, dried, fallen leaves dragging crisply under the full hem of her skirt. "You do not truly understand grief, nor the bonds of love. But you will, angel. You will."

Then she was gone.

Arina looked around the forest. No trace remained of the woman. If she could dream, she'd call her situation a nightmare, but she never slept. Nor did she feel stiff, dry grass beneath her hands, the cool breath of air on her cheeks, nor the heat of the sun on human skin. Yet she felt those things now and she knew she was awake.

"Nay!" she screamed. She must return home.

On trembling limbs, she pushed herself up. Lifting her arms above her head, she commanded herself to rise. What had always come so effortlessly was impossible now.

Her wings were gone. She was mortal. The thought shot through her mind with a fright that spun her head and brought tears to her eyes.

She couldn't stay in the mortal world and fall in love. Angels were not made for such. But how else could she regain her place?

"Surrender yourself to the curse."

She spun around at the words and faced a white wolf. Its eyes glowed red and she knew it for a manifest demon. "I am not Eve to fall to your wiles, demon," she said. "Return to your master and tempt me no more."

It moved forward. With each step, its form changed until it became a winged shadow. Only the glowing, red eyes remained the same. "You are no longer in my world, angel," the demon said. "You are in their world. They will fear you, beat you, destroy you. Then where will you be?"

Arina lifted her chin with a confidence she didn't feel. "If they kill me, I will return to my place. If I surrender myself to the curse, you will drag me to yours. I am of Heaven, not Hell, and I refuse to damn myself."

His evil laugh rang out. He touched her chin with his icy, chafed fingers. The coldness of Hell burned her skin, causing her to flinch. "My master will give me much for the soul of a primary angel. Come, pet, be nice and sacrifice yourself for me. I promise you a cooler spot to bathe in if you come now."

She glared at him, her new body trembling in fear and fury over his offer.

Belial. The name flashed through her mind, and she realized some of her powers still remained. But not enough to combat this particular demon who delighted in mischief and discord, whose evil power was second only to that of Lucifer himself. A cold tremor of panic shook her hands. She clenched them together, knowing her fear gave him strength.

"I deny your call," she said. "Leave me in peace and return to your hole."

His eyes flashed, radiating heat and malice. "You will be mine, fair angel." He curled his shadowed form up into a ball and drifted around her head. The odor of burning flesh and sulphur choked her. "How long can you remain true to your heavenly form now that you're corrupted by the temptations of human sensation?"

She opened her mouth to deny him, but as soon as she did, the cloud encompassed her head, choking her with its stench. The black thickness filled her body. Arina fought for breath. Her lungs burning, she fell to her knees.

Still the demon remained inside her, blotting her thoughts, her will.

With one last gasp, she collapsed on the ground.

Daemon watched his men training in the list. The sound of clashing steel filled his ears, making him yearn to leave this place far behind and yield to the familiar call of battle and war. Upon his arrival several months back, he had driven out the few remaining Saxons. Most of the rebellion's leaders had reached London under the escort of his men, and there they had met their final fate.

What few rebels remained now hid themselves from his wrath, and for the last few weeks peace had reigned in the valley of Brunneswald Hall. And Daemon despised peace, the extra time it brought—time to think, to remember. He needed to find another war to occupy himself, but William still refused to free him from his duty.

"Milord?"

He turned away from his men to see his squire running toward him. The blush of youthful exuberance covered Wace's cheeks. Daemon couldn't remember ever feeling that excited about anything.

"What is it?" he asked as Wace came to a huffing stop beside him.

Wace took several deep breaths before he

could finally respond. "The men you sent out scouting have returned. They found a woman in a field and brought her here."

Daemon frowned at his words. "Why would a wench have you—"

"Nay, milord. 'Tis no wench, but a lady."

His frown deepened. A lady? "From where did she come?"

"They know not, milord. They merely sent me to fetch you."

Daemon closed his eyes, agitation riding him fiercely. What imbeciles. Could they not even take care of a woman without his direction?

Nodding to Wace, he headed toward the hall.

Daemon wondered how his brother had managed to conquer England with the fools who fought in his army. Surely they could return the woman to her home without disturbing him. After all, dealing with the fairer sex was not something with which he had much experience, or for which he had much tolerance. Indeed, he fully intended to find her lord and get her out of his hall as soon as possible.

Daemon pushed open the heavy wooden door, its hinges squeaking like running mice. The odor of baking bread wafted toward him, twisting his stomach. How he hated manors and castles. He'd spent too many years of his life inside places such as this, listening to the echoes of foul rumors that resounded off the whitewashed walls, of people laughing in mockery. Clenching his teeth, he snarled in fury. He wanted to quit this place. He was a warrior, not a lord.

The group of men gathered in the center of the hall pulled back at his presence, displaying a body lying on a bench. His anger dissipating, Daemon hesitated. Deep, dark red cloth hugged the woman's voluptuous body, spilling onto the floor like a puddle of blood. Her flaxen hair lay atop part of the kirtle, its paleness highlighted by the dress's richness. Never before had he seen a kirtle, nor hair the color of hers.

A golden cross lay in the hollow of her throat, pulsing with each beat of her heart. Its shape glinted in the dying sunlight that still illuminated the room. His hands clammy, Daemon wondered at the way his heart raced, the way his body burned out of his control. Not an eager youth in the first bloom of manhood, he'd never before met a woman who stirred him so. Whose form begged for his touch.

Yet he wanted this woman. Against all his years of strict denial and discipline, he reached out and touched the softness of her cheek. He marveled at the texture of the cool white flesh, then turned her to face him.

His breath caught in his throat. Instinctively, he took a step back, releasing her. 'Twas the face in his dream.

Sweat broke out on his forehead as Daemon stared in awe. Had he summoned her up? Was this some trick of the light?

A low moan escaped her lips, and her chest heaved with a deep breath. His men stepped back in unison, some crossing themselves as if they feared her.

Regaining control of himself and forcing away his initial shock, Daemon scoffed at their superstition and his own. She was a woman, no more, no less. How she had infiltrated his dreams, he didn't know, but he refused to believe for one moment that she had any more supernatural power than he did. Indeed, too many years of people crossing themselves when they looked upon him had left him skeptical over the presence of demons and witches.

Her long, dark lashes fluttered opened, displaying a beautiful pair of deep blue eyes. Aye, the wench was as lovely as the Virgin Mother, and he could imagine how angry her lord must be over her loss.

A frown creased her brow and she sat up. "Where am I?" she asked in flawless Norman French, rubbing her forehead as if an ache beat inside her skull.

His body inflamed by the sound of her rich voice, Daemon stared at her. How had a Norman lady come to be stranded in the middle of Saxon lands? And she was no doubt a lady. Her dress and manner could never belong to serf or merchant. "You are in Brunneswald Hall, milady," he said quietly, waiting for her to look at him and cringe in terror.

Instead, she turned toward him and met his gaze unflinchingly. "Do I know this place?"

Now he frowned. "Do you not know who you are?"

"Aye," she said. "I am Arina."

"Then why did you ask—"

"But I can't remember aught else." To his surprise, the terror in her eyes was not directed at him, but at an inner horror. "There was a shadow," she whispered, staring at the floor. She looked up at him with a sad, vulnerable gaze, and a wave of protectiveness blasted away all the layers of hardness he had erected around his heart.

Angered over the sensation, Daemon took another step back, unsure of himself. He ached to touch her, but he knew he mustn't. A woman such as this had a lord looking for her, no doubt. She belonged to her husband, not to him, and he must find her husband and get her out of his hall and his life. Before it was too late.

"Do I belong here?" she asked in a whisper.

The question tore through him like a lance severing his heart. For a moment, Daemon wished he could answer aye. He clenched his teeth at the stupidity of his wants and desires. By now, he should be used to deprivation, especially when it involved something as precious as the woman before him. "Nay, milady. You were found in a field."

More sadness darkened her eyes, and he wondered what memories plagued her.

Daemon turned, calling to one of the serving women who watched on. "Take *m'hlafdie* to my room and attend her needs," he said in English.

The woman nodded and moved to help Arina rise.

Arina looked up at the woman. Terror filled her eyes and she screamed. Daemon barely had time to react before she scrambled from the bench and grabbed onto his arm, using his body to shield her from the woman.

No one had ever dared hold him, not even when he was a child.

Uncertain how to react, he stared into her terrified face, his heart pounding. "What is wrong with you, milady?" he demanded in a sterner voice than he'd intended.

"Don't let her touch me!"

Her entire body shook and he instinctively wrapped his arm around her, drawing her closer to his chest. He had never held a woman in such a manner, and he found it somehow comforting and deeply disturbing. "Why does she frighten you?" he asked, looking from the top of her head to the face of the old crone.

"She is death."

He frowned at the words. Was the woman mad? Had she been abandoned by unsympathetic relatives?

"There is nothing wrong with my mind," Arina said as if she could read his thoughts. "I can't explain my feelings. But I know she means me harm."

The old woman's eyes widened at Arina's words. "I mean her no harm, *hlaford*," she said in English. "I could never harm so fair an angel."

Arina stiffened in his embrace. "Angel," she whispered. She looked up at him and all the agony in her eyes tore through him. "She's called me that before. I remember it, b-but I can't . . ." Her voice trailed off, and her eyes glazed as if she drifted back into her past.

"It's all right," Daemon said, releasing her. "I've seen a number of men fall during battle after receiving a blow to the head. Many times they lose their senses for a brief time, but it always returns." He looked at the crone, his gaze stern. "Until milady remembers herself, I want you to stay away from her."

The crone nodded.

Daemon turned to Arina and held his hand out for her. "Come, milady, I shall show you to your room."

Her warm, soft hand closed around the emptiness of his palm, soothing his rough calluses. She looked at him as if he were her savior. His blood ignited. Daemon knew better than to imagine the thoughts that suddenly leapt into his mind, thoughts of her supple form in his arms, of her sweet lips opening for his taste.

He closed his eyes and released her hand, disgusted over his body's betrayal. He musn't hold such thoughts.

Ever.

Leading Arina past the lord's table, he entered the small foyer and pushed open a door. He stepped back, waiting for her to enter his chambers.

She looked up at him with a shy smile that sent even more blood to his nether regions. Daemon clenched his teeth. How could he burn so for something he could never have?

Without a word, she walked into his room.

She wandered around the room, touching various items as if she'd never seen such a place before. Where had she come from to be so enthralled over his meager furnishings? When she stepped to the window, she gave a small squeak.

"Oh, my," she said, a hint of laughter in her voice. "What are you doing out there?"

Daemon moved forward, curious about whom she addressed.

She reached outside the window and pulled to her chest a tiny, black blob. "Come inside," she said softly. " 'Tis a chill in the air I'm sure you don't need."

Daemon paused as she turned around with his kitten held tenderly in her arms. He stared in awe at her gentle hands stroking the soft black fur while Cecile nuzzled against her shoulder.

"Are you not afraid?" Daemon asked, moving

to stand close to her. Mayhap a little too close, his mind warned.

Arina looked up at him with a frown. "Afraid of a little kitten? Nay, why should I be?"

Daemon just stared at her. Ever since he'd saved the tiny cock-eyed creature, women and men alike had shied away from his unorthodox pet in fear and suspicion.

She bent her head toward the kitten and stroked her ears. "Do you have a name?"

"Cecile," Daemon told her.

She smiled, and once more he felt his control wane under the beauty of her features, the happy glint beneath the sapphire hue. When she looked back at him, his stomach wrenched as if someone had struck a fierce blow just below his heart. "And what of you, milord?" she asked. "Do you have a name?"

"Daemon," he said, waiting for the familiar mockery to darken her gaze.

Instead, her smile widened. "It suits you."

His gut twisted. Her face might not show it, but she did mock him and his cursed looks.

"Nay," she said, setting Cecile on the bed. She took a step forward, her hand raised as if to touch him. "I meant no offense to you."

He moved away from her, his lips curled. "You cannot offend me, milady. 'Twould seem fate itself has already done so."

His anger raging inside, he turned around and left her, slamming the door behind him to vent some of his fury before he abused a more sentient creature.

Arina stepped forward, then stopped as Cecile meowed. She looked at the kitten and shook her head. "You think I should leave him alone?"

Cecile nodded slightly, then rushed from the bed, only to collide with the small chest under the window.

Deciding Cecile might be right about Daemon, Arina picked the kitten up and helped her find her food bowl. The poor little creature's eyes were so badly crossed, it couldn't walk straight. Stroking the kitten's neck, she watched Cecile eat the carefully cubed meat left on the floor. What a pair the two of them made—Cecile couldn't find what she needed anymore than *she* could.

Arina sighed in disgust. Why couldn't she remember anything? She knew her name, she knew how to talk, how to do everything except recall herself, her past. Just who was she?

The fleeting images that kept passing before her eyes made no sense whatsoever. She saw hundreds of strange people and places, and yet she knew deep inside she understood all of it. But what would it take to find her way back to her memory?

After finishing her meal, Cecile set about cleaning herself. Arina pushed herself up from the floor and walked to the window, where she saw Daemon cross the yard.

She smiled at his confident stride, then looked back at Cecile. A cross-eyed kitten was a strange companion for a warrior. Yet somehow it suited him.

A strange warmth flooded her breast at the mere thought of Daemon. When she'd first opened her eyes and seen his concern, she'd been certain she belonged to him. The knowledge that she didn't brought an ache to her chest she couldn't quite understand.

But she could understand wanting him. He was the most handsome man she'd ever beheld. His long, white-blond hair reminded her of the brightest snow-covered field, and she was sure it was just as soft as the powdery crystals.

And his eyes . . .

Aye, they belonged to him alone—one the bright green of the deepest sea, the other the rich brown of cinnamon. He stood tall and well muscled with the arrogance of a mighty warrior. And deep inside him, she knew he carried honor and honesty next to his heart.

Her blood raced through her veins. Too easily, she could remember the heated strength of his arms holding her to him, hear the solid thump of his heart under her cheek. Aye, he was a man to warm any maid's breast.

A knock sounded on the door. "Enter," she said, her cheeks scalding. Even though she knew the person outside couldn't hear or see her thoughts, she still felt as though she'd been caught in the midst of indecent behavior.

Slowly, the door opened to reveal a youth of no more than 15 summers with short dark hair and a beaming smile. He shifted the platter in his arms and kicked the door closed with his foot. "Good day, milady."

She returned his smile. "Good day, my young lord."

As he neared her, the platter tilted dangerously to the left. With a gasp, Arina grabbed it, helping him to right it before all the dishes spilled to the floor.

He looked up at her with a shy smile, his cheeks as red as the fading sun. Warm honesty, intelligence and friendship glowed in the rich brown depths of his eyes, and in that instant, she formed a strong liking for the boy.

"Thank you, milady," he said, setting the platter on the table. "Lord Daemon thought you might be hungry."

In response to his words, her belly rumbled. "I suppose I am."

He removed the sliced cheese and bread, and placed them before her, then quickly poured a goblet of wine. "My name is Wace," he said, propping the platter against the wall. "I'm Lord Daemon's squire. If you have any needs—"

"Daemon's squire?" she said, interrupting him.

He nodded.

"Do you know your lord well?" she asked before picking up a piece of cheese.

Suspicion darkened his eyes and he watched her like a mother hare guarding her young from a circling kestrel.

"Calm yourself," she said, taking a bite of the cheese, amazed at the sharp taste of it. "I mean your lord no injury. I merely want to know why his own name bothers him."

Wace gave a small laugh. "You haven't heard of Daemon Fierce-Blood?"

She shook her head. "Should I have?"

He pulled a chair up next to her and took a seat. "Well, most people have. Even when we came to England, it seemed most people we met knew him on sight."

"And this disturbs you?"

He frowned at her. "Aye, how did you know?"

She shrugged, no more sure than he. "Why would his fame not inspire your joy? I thought all boys wanted to serve well-known masters."

Pain filled his eyes and for a moment, she thought he'd leave. Instead, he took a deep breath. "He's a good man, milady, but I fear people do not understand that. Cannot see that, more like." Wace looked around the room as if afraid someone might overhear him. "Behind his back, they whisper horrible, ungodly things."

Arina lifted her brow and leaned closer to catch all the syllables of Wace's low tone. "Such as?"

"That he is the devil's son."

Sitting back, she laughed aloud at the thought. "Devil's son, indeed. Why he doesn't look a thing like him."

A strange light darkened Wace's eyes and he shifted nervously. "What do you mean? You speak as if you know what the devil's son would look like."

Chills crept along Arina's spine and she had the distinct feeling she did know. She banished the foolish thought. "Nay, I've never met him, but my guess would be that he's dark and sinister with the face of a gargoyle."

Wace's humor returned. "Aye, and has pointed ears, no doubt."

Stifling her smile, Arina drank from her goblet. Wace opened his mouth to say something more, but the door swung open, crashing against the wall. With a gasp, Arina looked up into Daemon's stern face.

"Milady, there is a lord outside who claims you as his."

Arina gripped the goblet, her hand trembling. Uncertainty filled her. She didn't know who waited for her, but she had a strange impression that she didn't belong anywhere other than here.

Wace gave her an encouraging smile.

Forcing herself to her feet, Arina followed Daemon back into the hall.

A tall, flaxen-haired man stood in the center

of the room, eyeing the soldiers around him as if they made him uncomfortable. Arina hesitated. Something about the stranger seemed so familiar, yet she couldn't quite place him.

Suddenly, he turned around and faced her. His pale handsomeness startled her and a sharp wave of warning coursed down her spine. An affectionate smile curved his lips. "Dearest Arina!" he said, rushing toward her. "I was so afraid I'd lost you too."

He grabbed her into a bone-crushing hug that frightened her. Frantic, Arina looked at Daemon, hoping he would intervene on her behalf. But he just watched them with a bemused look that puzzled her more than the odd man holding her.

Pushing against the stranger, she couldn't banish her misgivings. She didn't know this man and she had no idea how to escape him.

"Do I know you, sir?" she asked.

He released her. Stepping back, he cast a hurt look at her. "What game is this? Surely, you've had your sport with me. Why, I ought to beat you for straying this far and troubling these good people."

Arina pulled away from him, suddenly terrified. "I don't know him," she said, moving toward the one person she knew she could trust—Daemon.

Before she could reach him, the stranger

grabbed her by the arm and turned her to face him. His rough, cold fingers bit into her flesh, burning her arm. "Stop this, this instant!" he growled.

Arina opened her mouth to speak, but quickly closed it as Daemon stepped forward and removed the steel grip from her elbow.

"She's had enough frights for one day," Daemon said, his voice hinting at violence. "I know not what happened to her, but she no longer remembers herself."

The stranger shifted his horrified gaze from Daemon to her. "You truly don't know me?" he asked in astonishment.

"Nay, I do not."

He held his arms out to her, his features a becoming mixture of affection and tolerance. "Arina, dearest, I'm your brother, Belial."

Chapter Two

The name stung Daemon like the acrid bite of an adder. "Belial?" he asked, unsure if he'd heard the man correctly.

And Daemon knew the arrogant look that crossed the man's face. 'Twas the same look he held when others reacted to his own name.

"Aye, Daemon Fierce-Blood," Belial said, emphasizing each syllable of his name. " 'Twould seem our fathers had a similar sense of humor to name us both for demons."

Belial's eyes darkened to a vivid blue and he raked Daemon with a cold glare Daemon might have found amusing had his own anger not surfaced. "But I would think my father thought more of me to name me for the fiercest of demons," Belial added.

Daemon gripped his sword. The smooth, leather-covered hilt bit into his palm and he yearned to hear the blade sing an exit from its scabbard. It had been a long time since anyone had dared insult him to his face. The reminder of his past, and his father, did little to curb the roiling heat in his belly, or appease the need in his soul to beat the *simpkin* before him.

But Daemon had hurled the first insult. He, of all men, knew the bitter taste of superstition.

Suddenly, Belial's laugh rang out. "Come now, don't look as if your strongest wish is to call me to arms. 'Twas a jest," he said, clapping Daemon on the back.

Daemon stared at him in disbelief. Were all members of their family lacking in sense?

"Forgive me for insulting you," Belial said before turning to face Arina. He ran a long, thin finger down her cheek and Daemon noted the rigidness of her body, the control she exercised not to cringe in response. "I fear my worry for my sister has overshadowed my common sense. And manners. I'm sure you can forgive me?"

The words carried enough emotion to sound sincere, but something in Belial's manner belied his voice. Daemon had the distinct impression Belial toyed with both him and Arina. Aye, the look from the corner of the man's eye. It reminded him of a cutpurse trying to remain inconspicuous as he carefully watched the soldiers around him. Though what Belial wanted with him, Daemon couldn't guess.

Arina shifted nervously, and looked at him. Her eyes beseeched him for protection.

Daemon stiffened. Could her brother be abusive? The thought struck a familiar cord inside him and he instantly knew if that were indeed the case, he couldn't allow her to leave with Belial. If there was anything he could not tolerate, it was the abuse of innocents.

"So tell me, Lord Belial, where are the two of you from, and where are you headed?"

Belial faced him with a tired sigh, his back to Arina. "Our home lies to the south. We are from the Brakenwich Valley. My father and his lands fell to the Norman yoke, and once I realized our cause was lost, I grabbed Arina and left the battlefield. I thought we would travel north to our relatives who live in Hexham." Sadness darkened his gaze and he held his arms out like a supplicant at prayer. "Provided, of course, they still retain their home."

Such was the result of war. Daemon knew it only too well, but it couldn't be helped. Innocent victims always suffered, even in peace. Indeed, life itself scarred the souls of all who traversed its brutal path.

"I won't apologize for my brother's actions," Daemon said. " 'Twas your own people who started this war when they denied my brother the throne he'd been promised."

Belial smiled at his words. "Ah, loyalty. Such a noble trait that leads so many into the dark abyss of Hell." A small laugh surfaced, and Daemon couldn't suppress a brief shiver. "I admire loyalty; it facilitates my job," Belial added.

"What's that?" Daemon asked, not quite certain he had heard the low tone correctly.

"It eases my jaw," Belial said louder. " 'Tis an old Saxon saying my father used to quote. You know, loyalty makes life easier to live."

Daemon nodded, accepting the explanation, but not quite certain it was the truth. "So tell me, how is it two English nobles speak French like they were born to it?"

Belial shrugged. "Our mother. She came from Flanders."

Daemon glanced at Arina and the strange look on her face. Her brother scared her and until he knew the cause of her fear, he would refuse to let her leave his protection. "Well, then, we are almost cousins, and as such, I invite you to stay and partake of our hospitality as long as you wish."

Belial cocked a suspicious brow. "Why would you help us, the defeated?"

Daemon sensed direct confrontation in Belial's voice. Aye, the look in Belial's eyes left no doubt; a challenge hovered in the light depths. Daemon had never been one to back down, and he had no intention of starting now.

His gaze hard, he stepped toward the Saxon noble. "I offer you protection for the sake of your sister. 'Tis obvious she knows naught of suffering." He raked Belial with a cold glare. "I care not what you do, but I will not see the lady harmed."

A mocking smile curved Belial's lips. He gave a short laugh. "So be it. For the sake of my sister, I shall stay."

With a misplaced arrogance that told Daemon much about the man, Belial strode from the hall, out into the cool evening.

Arina moved forward, her head bent in maidenly modesty. "I cannot thank you enough for what you've done, milord," she said, looking up at him with gratitude shining in her eyes.

Then, to his utmost amazement, she raised herself up on her toes and planted a kiss on his cheek. Shock almost sent him to his knees.

Blushing a becoming shade of pink, Arina excused herself and headed to his chambers.

Daemon watched her flee, his cheek still tingling from the warm softness of her lips. He dropped his gaze to the gentle sway of her well-rounded hips and clenched his teeth.

A longing ache spread through his chest that robbed him of his breath, and desire shot through him, igniting his blood, his loins, and for one single moment, he allowed himself to think of her in his arms, of her tender voice whispering in his ear while he held her beneath him.

Daemon closed his eyes in an effort to blot out the image. Don't, he warned himself. And he remembered the last time someone had dared show her gratitude with a chaste kiss.

Anger simmered in his gut at the memory. Nay, he couldn't allow Arina to touch him again. No one must ever touch him.

Arina sat at the raised table, listening to the myriad of conversations that buzzed around her. The last course had been served and still Lord Daemon remained absent. She couldn't fathom what kept him away from the table and his dinner.

Belial sat next to her, but he had remained silent all throughout the meal. She noted the way he looked about the room as if he were a predator stalking game. Something about him warned her of danger, of death, but she couldn't quite find the source of her concern. He seemed friendly enough to her, but still the feeling persisted until she feared she would go mad.

People began excusing themselves from the tables. Grateful for an end to the awkward meal, Arina smiled to her brother. "I should like a walk outside."

He lifted his brow, a look of censure on his face. "Careful, Arina, the hour grows late and I would hate to have anything happen to you."

The hairs on the back of her neck raised at his words. His face appeared sincere, but an air of falseness hung between them. If only she could remember her past, mayhap then she could put her suspicions and fears to rest.

"I won't be long," she said, rising from her bench.

Arina pushed open the heavy oak door of the manor, the wood scraping gently against her palms. A chill wind blew against her, freezing her cheeks. She almost turned back, but she didn't want to face her brother, or anyone else, just then. All she needed was a little time alone, time to think.

Clenching her jaw to keep it from chattering, she made her way out into the dark yard. Rushlights had been lit and they provided a modicum of cheerfulness to combat the eerie shadows of night and the hidden fears lurking in the dust of her memory.

She could hear the sounds of grooms talking to each other in the stable, and various animals settling down to sleep. With no thought to destination, Arina followed a worn path around the wooden hall and into a small garden.

An icy rose scent clung to the air while the flowers fought against their inevitable surrender to the approaching winter frost. And yet the beauty of the garden, the out-of-place cheer of the flowers, warmed her breast.

"Milady?"

She jumped at the voice coming out of a darkened corner. Facing the sound, she watched Daemon push himself to his feet and tower over the bush that had blocked him from her earlier notice. "Milord, what are you doing here?" she asked, walking closer.

He didn't say anything. Instead, he watched her with the steady intentness of a wary fox that had been trapped by a hunting party.

Arina stopped at the side of the bush, and looked down to the pallet Daemon had made on the cold ground where a leather-bound manuscript book lay opened. His intent to sleep out in the cold night obvious, she fought against the sudden pain in her breast over the solitary nature that kept him so distant.

Cecile slept wrapped in a thick woolen blanket next to a small tallow candle. A wooden platter of cheese, bread and half-eaten fruit left no doubt that Daemon had taken his meal out here. Alone.

She looked up at him, taking note of the suspicion in his eyes. What she saw reflected there stole her breath. His were the eyes of an old man, someone who had known untold suffering. No spark of life glowed in the hollowed darkness of his soul, and in that moment she knew he sought the welcomed relief of death.

That look haunted her, scared her more than anything else she could imagine. The familiarity of the look tore through her, and she knew somewhere in her past she had been more than acquainted with it.

"Why are you here?" he asked, his voice heavy with need.

"I-I'm not sure."

Sudden fire sparked in his eyes. Arina stared at him, entranced by the sight. Before she could say another word, he pulled her into his arms. His gaze drifted over her face as if he committed every line and plane to memory. Hesitantly, he reached a hand up to touch her cold cheek. The warm calluses of his palm soothed the chill and sent a shiver over her.

She desired him, she knew, and with that desire came the knowledge that she didn't belong with him.

"Was it not enough you haunted my dreams?" he asked, capturing a strand of her hair and rubbing it between his fingers.

"I know not what you mean."

"Don't you?" A frown lined his brow and his arm tightened around her waist. He brought her up against the strength of his chest and before Arina could move, his lips covered hers.

Her head spun at the contact and she surrendered herself to the gentle caress of his lips pressing against hers. His heart pounded against her breast, heating her blood with its incessant beat. She wrapped her arms around his shoulders, drawing him closer, delighting in the feel of strength and power ingrained in the essence of him.

He pulled back slightly, his teeth nipping her lips, then he returned. She opened her mouth, welcoming the taste of him, the warmth of his breath. Never in her life could she recall the heady sensation caused by his embrace.

Suddenly, he moved away. She opened her eyes to see the terror on his face as he stared at her in disbelief.

His breathing labored, he raked a hand through his hair and turned away from her. "Leave!" he growled.

Arina opened her mouth to protest, but before a word could escape her, he turned around and grabbed her by the arms.

All the anger and primal violence of nature burned in his glare. She trembled in sudden fear.

"Woman, as you value your life, take yourself from my presence."

He released her. The bitter taste of terror stung her throat. Horrified by his actions and her own, Arina fled from the courtyard and back into the safety of the hall.

Daemon watched her flee, guilt gnawing at his innards. Why he had kissed her, he couldn't imagine. He knew better than to lower his defenses and yield to the wants of his body. And yet she made it so simple to forget all he'd been taught, all he'd suffered.

"Arina," he whispered to the wind, the name rolling from his lips like the sweetness of wine.

If only he could claim her, but he knew better than that. She reminded him of sunshine and love, of all the things he had yearned for as a child, all the things he knew as an adult he couldn't have.

Long-forgotten memories surged through him, and he remembered the numerous times in his life he had dreamed of a peaceful existence, of a home with someone who cared for him, someone who saw more than just his physical deformity. Daemon clenched his teeth, angry over the uselessness of his wants.

He must return to the battlefield. There, he knew himself, his place. There, no reminders existed of his childhood, or the nights he had lain beaten and forgotten. On the battlefield, no one dared whisper behind his back.

Aye, he would send another messenger to William in the morning, and this time he would demand that his brother release him from his duties.

Belial drifted out of the courtyard, joy pounding in his chest. It almost seemed a sin for his plot to go so easily. He muffled his laugh and traveled through the yard, past the men who couldn't see him, and out the gates into the dark forest.

Following the guttural chant of the crone, he

made his way through the trees to the small fire she had started in the middle of a clearing. How he loved accomplices. They eased his job considerably, and what's more, he always got two souls for the price of one—or in this particular, blessed case, three of them.

In order not to frighten her, and in spite of the fact it greatly diminished his powers, he returned to the form of man and approached the crone, who stirred a thick, pungent liquid inside her black cauldron. "What is that?" he asked, wrinkling his nose in distaste.

She looked up at him with a malevolent smile. " 'Tis vengeance. I would have thought you of all things would know its sweet scent."

"Sweet?" he asked, coughing as a breeze blew a whiff in his direction. "Smells worse than the bowels of Lucifer's lowest pit."

She shook her head, her eyes glowing from the light of the fire, and from the inner light of madness. "Were they together?"

Belial backed a goodly distance from the pot. "Aye. He wants her. But Daemon is a man of fierce control. We'll have to weaken him."

The crone pulled the ladle from the pot and tapped it twice against the side. "What do you think this"—she gestured to the pot—"is for."

Belial frowned. "What are you going to do, wave it under their noses until they faint?"

She gave him the nastiest glare he'd ever received, and Belial wondered about her sanity to insult him so. "This is my part of the bargain. Yours is to supply the heat to their loins."

"Lust is my specialty." Belial floated to a low-hanging tree limb where he could watch the crone and her concoction. "Indeed, you should witness the dreams I've imparted to Daemon for this night. I'd hate to be in the physical pain he'll experience come morning."

Belial started to laugh, but another thought struck him. "Come to think of it, I know just a way to make the angel herself a little less resistant." A slow joyous smile spread across his face. He faded back to shadow. "Aye, she'll succumb, all right."

Gentle music floated through Arina's dream. Images accompanied the song and she jolted upright from the bed. For a moment, she thought her dream had left her, but with each frantic beat of her heart she recalled more and more of her dream, her life, until she thought she'd burst with happiness.

She remembered herself!

With a happy laugh, she threw her blanket off, scooped up her kirtle, and ran to seek Lord Daemon. She couldn't wait to tell him of her newfound self.

Pausing briefly in the hall, she looked about but he wasn't there. She had to find him. On trembling legs, she ran out the door in search of his pallet.

Sherrilyn Kenyon

So intent on her quest, she failed to notice the horse and rider rushing from the stable until it was too late to do anything more than scream.

Chapter Three

Suddenly, strong arms wrapped around Arina and pulled her back. Her body shook in fright as the horse and rider sped past. One instant more and she would have been crushed beneath the hooves of the rushing horse.

"Dammit, woman, what are you trying to do?"

Arina collapsed against Daemon, her heart pounding in her breast. She laughed nervously in relief. "I'm sorry," she whispered, placing her hand over the arm he had encircled her with. Taut muscles flexed beneath her palm in a sensuous rhythm that only added to her fright and discomfort, and brought a strange new fluttering to her heart.

"You should be more careful," he said, his voice strangely gentle.

He leaned his cheek against her head, then moved away so quickly, she almost stumbled.

"I trust you weren't hurt?" he asked.

Arina stared at the handsome lines of his face, and she realized she'd gladly hurl herself under a hundred horses to have him hold her again. "Nay, thanks to you."

He looked away from her as if her gratitude made him uncomfortable. When he looked back at her, she caught a brief flash of concern.

"Tell me, milady, what was of such great importance that you near rushed into death?"

All her fear and uncertainty vanished beneath the heady intoxication of happiness as she recalled the reason for her search. She stepped forward and touched the long blond braid he had draped over his left shoulder. "I wanted to tell you that I remember myself, my past!"

He pulled the braid out of her reach and tossed it over his shoulder, his eyes dull and somehow sorrowful. " 'Tis glad news, indeed."

"Nay," Arina said breathlessly, too relieved and giddy to allow him to dampen her joy. She spun in a small circle, arms outstretched. " 'Tis incredible!" Leaning her head back, she watched the sky spiral in blue and white. Her laughter bubbled up through her and she felt as free as the gentle breeze rustling through the bailey.

"Milady, please," Daemon said, reaching out to stop her dance. "All who watch will think you mad."

She surrendered herself once more to his arms. With one last laugh, she looked up at him, delighting in the feel of his chest against hers. "I care not what they think. I am too happy to worry over others."

A dark shadow leapt into his oddly colored eyes.

"Why does that make you sad?" she asked, her laughter dying under the weight of her concern.

" 'Tis naught but an old memory," he said, stepping away from her.

Frowning, Arina ached to ease the pain she'd glimpsed, but she knew she'd been forward enough. She opened her mouth to apologize, only to withhold her words as another rider stormed through the bailey.

"Milord!" the knight shouted, skidding to a halt just before them. "There's been an accident where the men are working on the castle fortifications."

"Were any hurt?" Daemon asked the knight.

"Aye, milord. I know not how many; they were still digging men out of the rubble as I left."

A fierce curse left Daemon's lips. Arina stared at him, amazed at the hostility in his voice, but he betrayed no other sign of emotion. How could anyone keep himself so controlled?

Daemon turned around and called to a young groom. "Saddle my horse."

When Daemon started past her, Arina grabbed his arm. "Let me come with you. I can help."

His taut muscles relaxed beneath her grip, then quickly grew even more rigid and unyielding. She held her breath, certain he'd deny her request.

"Very well," he said at last. "Ask one of the women for herbs."

"Thank you," she said before running off toward the manor.

At the steps of the manor, Arina met the old crone who had frightened her on her arrival. Uncertainty fluttered in her breast, breaking her stride.

"Here, *hlafdie*," the crone said as she extended a faded brown bag to her. "Everything you need is in this."

Why couldn't she place the woman? Arina remembered much of her past, but suddenly she realized great, forbidding holes existed. Holes that left her uneasy. This woman belonged to one of those holes and for her sanity, she couldn't place it.

Her hands cold and trembling, Arina reached for the bag. "My thanks," she said, her voice tight with suspicion.

"Arina!"

She turned at Daemon's insistent call, her

heart thumping heavily against her breast, and all her doubts disappeared. Her name on his lips sounded more beauteous than the very choir of Canterbury. Something warm and invigorating rushed through her body and stole her very breath. He looked magnificent astride his horse, the sunlight glinting against the short-sleeved mail hauberk that accentuated every bulge and curve of his well-muscled body. Desire claimed her fully and she knew she'd do anything to be his lady.

Lifting the hem of her kirtle, Arina ran back to him.

Unsure if her breathlessness came from her short run or his presence, she quickly mounted her palfrey.

Daemon barely gave her time enough to situate herself before he kicked his horse into a run. Arina followed behind, wrestling with her mount. Her mind told her she'd ridden thousands of times before, but for her life, her body denied it. The reins felt strange in her hands, and she couldn't recall much about controlling the beast. She struggled to remain astride. With each step of the horse, she was most certain she'd find herself sprawling in the dust.

By the time they reached the top of the hill less than a league from the manor, she was more than ready to dismount, and more than a little grateful she'd made the journey intact. But the sight that greeted her quickly stole her relief.

Bile stung her throat and her legs quaked. All around them men lay on the ground moaning and praying. Panic kept her feet rooted to the spot where she stood.

Daemon rushed toward one of the fallen men and knelt on the ground beside him. "Master Dennis, what happened?"

Arina couldn't see that man's face, but his weak voice drifted back to her. "Mortar, for the ramparts . . . The rope broke."

She looked at the section of wall that had collapsed. Large chunks of stone lay around the field like the broken hearth of a giant.

"Help me."

The frail voice took her attention from the wall. Arina scanned the men until she saw a youth of no more than 13 summers holding his side. She went to him, sensing somehow his need as more urgent.

She knelt beside him, her body quaking from dread. Blood soaked his head from a gash just behind his left ear and a large metal spike protruded from his side.

So much pain. Arina felt a wave of empathy tear through her.

"Have you come for me?" he asked.

A chill stole up her spine at the haunting familiarity of the words. Forcing herself to fight against her panic, she took his hand and comforted him. "I've come to help you," she said.

He smiled, his eyes lighting for just a flicker of a heartbeat. Then all the glow of life drained slowly from them until she stared into the dullness of death.

Gasping, Arina dropped his hand. Her breath caught in her throat. Strange images tore through her head—images of people clinging to her in fear and gratitude, the treetops far below her as she . . . as she—

"Arina?"

She blinked at Daemon's soft call. Tears gathered in her eyes. Fierce pain ripped through her body, twining itself around her heart as if it would devour the organ and leave her every bit as dead as the child before her.

Daemon reached out and wiped away the one tear that had escaped her control and fled down her cheek. "Be strong, milady," he said gently. "These men need you."

Men need you. The words drifted through her head. She'd heard them before.

When? It was important that she remember.

"Milady?"

Daemon's voice broke through her haze. He was right; she must help these men now. Pushing herself up from the cold ground, Arina made her way toward the next man who needed urgent care.

With the help of Daemon and several others, Arina sewed wounds, set bones and applied poultices until she feared she'd go mad from the stench of blood, the sight of mortal injuries. Her stomach churned in painful knots that contracted with each beat of her heart.

"Here," Daemon said as she reached to stitch yet another gaping wound. "I'll finish this one. You should take a moment and rest yourself."

In spite of her need to stay and help as many as she could, Arina nodded her head and dutifully handed him the needle.

Daemon watched her leave, a strange lump blocking his throat. All through the afternoon, he'd been amazed by her fortitude and control. She'd comforted the men, easing them the same effortless way she eased the pain lurking in the blackness of his heart.

Clenching his teeth against the burning ache that spread through his gut, Daemon started sewing the wound of the unconscious man. He didn't need the softness of woman. He was a warrior, fierce and hard. No one had ever comforted him and he had no wish to change his life.

Ye lie.

Daemon paused at the voice in his head, so crisp and loud it seemed to come from another source than his own mind. Nay, it wasn't a lie, he decided. He would never allow himself to fall victim to a woman. The risk was far too great.

With three quick stitches, he finished the wound and knotted the thread. He scanned the area around him, stopping when he saw Arina sitting on a piece of fallen stone, her face pensive and pained.

Why did he yearn for her, dream of her, when he knew she could never be his? His past and his deformity would never allow him the solace of a wife. He'd accepted that fact long ago. Arina deserved so much more than he could offer. He who had no understanding of love, of kindness. What could he give her? Naught save the scorn of people who feared him and called him monster.

Mayhap they were right after all. Aye, demons dreamed of corrupting young innocents, and ever since the moment he'd cast his first glance at Arina he'd had few thoughts save peeling her kirtle from her body and sampling the delicate flavor of pure, alabaster skin.

His body throbbed with the pulse of his desire. If he had one moral or decent part left inside him, he'd order both her and her brother from his sight. Daemon scoffed at the thought. If there had ever been any part of him decent, Brother Jerome had beat it from him long ago.

A clap of thunder rent the air, ushering in a sudden, brutal wind. Daemon stared at the sky, amazed at the swiftness of the storm.

He hurried to help load the last of the wounded onto wagons to carry them back to their families.

As the last wagon rumbled away, he turned

back to the vision who haunted him waking and sleeping.

Arina now stood at the edge of the hill looking out onto the valley far below. The wind whipped her dress against her body, outlining each and every curve of her slim form.

Daemon willed his body into submission. He must get her back to the manor before the storm drowned them both. "Arina," he called.

She ignored him.

Frowning, Daemon made his way to her. So much of her manner puzzled him. The way she moved as if all things were new to her, almost as if she were childlike, though there was nothing childish about her.

He started to touch her, but stopped himself just before he did. She stared out into nothing, and yet her eyes were focused, not dazed.

"Do you smell it?" she asked, her voice faint.

"Smell what?"

" 'Tis sweet like a summer garden, yet the bitterness of death and fear contaminate the very vial of life."

His frown deepened at her words. He knew not of what she spoke. "How does milady mean?"

She didn't move. "You think me mad."

Daemon stared at her. She'd voiced the very thought that had just played across his mind. "Not mad, milady, just confused," he said, wishing he could know for truth whether or not she was sane.

She looked at him, and the torment in her eyes took the very breath from his body. "Aye, I am confused. My mind tells me one thing, yet my body says it lies. It's as if the two are enemies waging war against each other and 'tis my soul that serves as prize. Or mayhap my sanity itself."

Daemon wanted to touch her, nay, needed to touch her, but he knew the consequences of such. Indeed, his body already burned just from the memory of her softness. "I know of what milady speaks."

Frustration darkened her brow and she turned back to scan the scenery below. "Nay, I don't speak of desire," she said. "I know the effects of that emotion, and it's not as though I don't feel it. I have only to look at you and I tremble from the core of my heart."

Daemon swallowed in shock. No one had ever said such a thing to him before and he found it difficult to believe.

"Please," she said without looking at him. "What troubles me is more than that. Deeper than that. Images haunt my mind. They tell me I know things, have done things, and yet I can't remember having truly experienced any of them. I know it makes no sense. And I . . ."

She rubbed her hands over her face, her features tortured. "Dearest saints, have I truly lost my sanity?"

And despite every argument inside him to keep his distance, Daemon could not deny the agony of her plea. He stepped forward and pulled her against him. Her soft curves molded against his body, inflaming him, tormenting him. She was all he had ever wanted, and more. If only he could give her what she longed for, but he knew better.

All he could offer was temporary comfort. Something no one had ever given him, something he barely understood. "I doubt any of us are truly sane, milady." And even as the words left his lips, he knew the truth of that statement.

Rain burst from the clouds. Huge drops fell, pelting their bodies. Arina shivered in his arms. He must return her before they both caught a fever.

"Come, milady. Fear no more for your mind. Everything will come to you given time."

She looked up at him, her eyes trusting and large. No one had ever given him such a warm, welcoming look. Before he could stop himself, Daemon pulled her against him. He lowered his head to take her lips. Without hesitation, she leaned her head back in sweet, intoxicating welcome.

Just as he brushed her lips, a bright flash of lightning struck a section of the wall. Daemon pulled back in shock, his gaze drawn to the scorched stone. He didn't know which frightened him more, the strike of the lightning or the folly of their kiss. But one thing stood certain. He must get Arina to safety before the storm turned even more violent.

Releasing her, he pulled her by the arm toward their horses.

He swung her up into the saddle. They rode toward the manor as quickly as they could given the fierceness of the storm.

Halfway there, a shriek tore his attention from the journey. Daemon reined his horse, his heart pounding. Arina lay on the ground just behind him. Panic ripped through him, numbing him to the cold rain.

He jumped from his horse and pulled her toward him. Her pale hair hung in her face, and he brushed the wet strands from her cold cheeks. "Milady!" he shouted, his fear making him unreasonable.

She coughed and opened her eyes. Her entire body shook, though whether from fear or cold, he could only guess. "I can't stay on my horse," she said, so low her voice barely reached him through the whipping winds. " 'Tis too slippery."

Daemon almost smiled in relief. Aye, she was well. Grateful for that fact, he lifted her in his arms and carried her to his horse. Within a heartbeat, they were headed back to the manor, Arina settled before him on the saddle.

She clutched at him, her warmth chasing away all the chills from the weather. Not even his imaginings of having her hold him could compete with the actual feel of her slender arms wrapped tightly about his waist. His heartbeat slowed to a deep, echoing thump. He would sell his soul for this woman—if he believed in such things. But he knew better. If a God existed, He had turned His back on the world long ago. And Daemon had no use for such a callous entity.

Yet a part of him still wanted to believe, and that same part taunted him with thoughts of Arina as his own. Daemon clenched his teeth. Why was his mind torturing him so?

An image of Willna flashed across his eyes. Hatred and violence sizzled through him so quickly, he almost jerked his horse to a stop. He had only been ten and seven that summer. Knighted several months before, he had been on a mission for his brother when his horse had thrown a shoe and he had gone to a small town to have a blacksmith repair it.

Willna had shown up with a cup of ale for her father. No older than himself, she, like Arina, had had a face that could make the very angels envious. While he waited for his horse, he had tried his best to ignore her, but his gaze had continually betrayed him.

Just as her father had finished with his horse, she had left her home, her arms laden with wash. Unable to see, she had stumbled. Without thought, Daemon had rushed to her side to help her up, and she had rewarded him with a quick kiss on his cheek.

Before either of them could move, her father had grabbed her by the arm and begun beating her. Daemon had done his best to stop it, but his size at the time was too small compared to the blacksmith.

The blacksmith had ordered him to leave, and reluctantly he had done so. But as he passed the house, he had seen Willna's face battered and bruised and had heard her mother's scornful words, "Would you be whore to the devil's bastard?"

Daemon closed his eyes against the wave of pain that ripped through his soul. Even whores shied away from him, only reluctantly offering him their services. No woman, other than Willna, had ever shown him kindness.

Until now.

For his life, he couldn't understand Arina and why she alone looked past his deformity and treated him as human, as a normal man.

Coughs shook her body. Daemon looked down at her. "Are you all right?"

She nodded her head. " 'Tis the cold," she said through her chattering teeth.

Daemon tightened his arms around her, drawing her closer to his warmth. His body throbbed with heated desire from the outline of her tender form pressed so close to him. Never had anything felt better, or more right, and he damned the part of himself that longed for nights spent with her by his side. Nay, he could never hold such thoughts. He kicked his horse faster as they reached the gates of Brunneswald.

Dismounting, he helped her down and quickly carried her into the manor.

Servants bustled through the hall, preparing the coming meal. "Bring milady a tray in her room," he ordered one without breaking stride.

He pushed open the door. Arina continued to cough and sneeze. Daemon set her on her feet, grabbed the fur cover from the bed, and wrapped her in it.

"You need to get out of your kirtle," he said, moving to the small chest beside the bed. He lifted the lid and stepped back. "The former lady left several of her kirtles."

Arina offered him the sweetest smile he'd ever beheld. "Milord's kindness is too great."

Daemon's heart pounded against his chest. Longing burst through him with such a fierce need, he feared he might explode. He took a step forward.

The door opened. Fighting the need to curse, Daemon eyed the old crone.

She handed a goblet to Arina, then one to him. "Forgive my interruption, *m'hlaford*. But the drink shall do you both good." She cast a hooded look to Arina. "I shall return shortly with *m'hlafdie's* food."

Arina followed the woman with her gaze.

"She still frightens you?" Daemon asked after the woman had left.

"Aye."

Daemon sighed, wanting to alleviate her fears, knowing he couldn't. He stared at the goblet of spiced wine. Steam drifted from the warm, dark liquid. Well, it might not chase away all his chills, but it should distract him from the gentle form sitting on his bed.

With one gulp, he downed the contents and placed the goblet on the table.

Arina followed suit, but at a somewhat slower rate. He moved toward the door.

"Daemon?"

He paused at his name on her lips, the sound cutting through him sharper than a dagger. "Aye, milady?"

She moved from the bed with a soundless grace. "Thank you for listening to my ravings. And for your patience."

She stood so close to him, he could smell the sweet rose scent that clung to her hair. He ached to touch her. He wanted to say something, but for his life he couldn't think of any response, at least not a verbal one.

She gave him a knowing smile.

Suddenly, her eyes clouded and the smile

faded. She looked up at him with a frown. "I feel so strange."

Daemon returned her frown. He moved to open the door to call for help, but before he could reach it, she crumpled. Grabbing her to him, he carried her back to the bed.

"Arina?" he asked, rubbing her icy hand, trying to warm her. Her face turned a horrid pale. He had to get help.

Daemon rose from the bed, but before he could make it halfway across the floor, his stomach erupted into fire. His vision dimmed. A loud buzzing started in his ears like a hive of bees gone mad.

He reached out to steady himself, but his knees buckled. Daemon tried to force himself to rise, but couldn't. Cecile ran out from under the bed to sniff at his cheeks. His throat dried to a burning thirst and felt as if it would ignite.

He must get help for Arina.

Cecile hissed at him, her back arching. Daemon rolled over, but before he could push himself up, blackness invaded his head, easing the throbbing pains in his body.

Belial materialized out of his corner shadow. The silly cat continued to hiss at him until he was tempted to drown the beast.

Just as he reached for it, the door opened to reveal the crone with her platter of food.

Her eyes widened as she noted his outstretched hands and the defiant cat. "Here now," she said in a chastising voice like a fool wishing for death. "Don't frighten that poor thing." Before he could react, she had the cat in her hands and set it outside the room.

Belial straightened. He'd pay the crone back for this, but it could wait. First he had more important beings to tend to.

"How long will they sleep?" he asked.

The crone moved to check on them. "Through the night."

Belial nodded, a happy smile on his face. Ah, how he loved mischief. And there would be plenty on the morrow.

Laughter bubbling inside, he moved to undress Daemon.

Before long, they had both Arina and Daemon stripped and lying entwined on the bed. Belial looked across the bed at the crone. "It won't be long now," he said with a laugh. "Between waking to this and the memories I've given them, they will consummate their lust in little time."

The crone frowned. "But what if he marries her?"

Belial snorted. "What if he does? She's a primary angel. Marriage is a human device, not heavenly." He said the word with a shudder. "Once she samples the fruits of lust, her fate is sealed."

Laughing at the thought of his presentation of her soul to his master, Belial started out of the room. "Come, wench, we've got other plans to make."

"Wait," the crone said. "You've forgotten something."

Anger scorched Belial at her audacity. "I forget nothing!" he snarled.

The smugness of the crone inflamed his anger more. "Then what of the virgin's blood? What will Lord Daemon think when he awakens to find no stained sheets?"

Belial faltered. He hadn't thought of that. As much as he despised admitting it, the crone was right.

She pulled the cover back from the bed and produced a vial from her bag of herbs. Sprinkling the blood between the two, she looked up at him with a smile.

"And for good measure," she said, then rubbed more blood on Arina's thighs.

Well, between the two of them, they'd thought of everything. Belial threw his head back and laughed. Aye, come morning there'd be true hell to pay! And he intended to be the tax collector.

Chapter Four

Daemon awakened with a start, his throat every bit as tight as it had been when chains bound him securely to a church altar. The Latin words of the priest rang in his ears as if even now the priest tried to exorcise the devil from him.

In reflex, he ran his hand through his hair, searching for the cross that had been branded into the back of his head. Only when he found the smooth scar hidden by the long locks of his hair did he realize he had been dreaming a vague memory of days long ago. Sharp anger washed over him and he had a difficult time remembering he had ever been so young, so vulnerable.

He took a deep breath to steady the erratic

beating of his heart. Brother Jerome had died years ago. The nightmares should have faded, and yet they lurked in the farthest reaches of his mind, waiting for sleep before they made their presence known. Nightmares were like memories, both of them cowards who always struck when a man was least expecting. He could battle them easily enough while awake, but at night, under the cover of darkness and sleep, they attacked and left him sorely battered.

A soft moan intruded on his thoughts. Frowning, Daemon turned to see the gentle form beside him. His gut contracted violently at the sight of Arina peacefully resting, with bloodstained sheets wrapped around her pale, bare hips.

Sudden memories blasted at his conscience and he damned himself for his weakness. How could he have done it? How could he have tainted someone so pure, so giving?

His mind whirled with images of her soft caresses, her body molding to his. Even now, his loins burned for her and his insides raged like an inferno. Why couldn't he end his damnable lust forever? Daemon rubbed at his temples, wishing he could turn back the morning and erase his actions of the night before.

For one moment of release he had condemned her to a lifetime of mockery and shame. His very soul screaming against his actions, Daemon rose from the bed and pulled on his breeches. Pouring water into a small basin beside the bed, he cursed his foul life. She had given him more than anyone and he had damaged her eternally.

As he splashed his face with water, a new, sudden terror struck him in the center of his chest, knocking his breath from his lungs. What if his seed had taken root? What if, even now, she carried his child?

Would you be whore to the devil's bastard?

Daemon clutched at the basin, the edges cutting sharply into his palms. Why had he not left her? Clenching his teeth, he knew he had only one course of action, and that was even more reprehensible than what he'd already done.

Which would cause her more ridicule? Their actions the night before? Or marriage to God's abomination? Even now he could hear Brother Jerome's voice ringing in his head. *The very angels wept at your birth. In the name of God, we must save your black soul.*

How cruel to realize now that Brother Jerome had been right all along. He *was* a monster who traipsed the earth seeking innocent blood. Arina's blood.

Growling with outrage, he knocked the basin from the table. Water hit the wall and splashed against his face and chest, and still his wrath against himself grew.

Arina awoke with a small shriek.

Daemon stared at her, the knot in his gullet tightening ever more while all his fury died.

Why couldn't her eyes condemn him as all the others did? Why was there no accusation in the crystal-clear depths? He could deal with her anger, he could deal with her hatred, but the shy tenderness that shone so brightly was more than he deserved, more than he could stand.

"You startled me, milord," she said softly, lowering her gaze to the floor. Her cheeks darkened and once again he damned himself for the wave of desire that coiled through him, devouring his will until he could not move for fear of tainting her further.

"Milady, I . . ." Daemon hesitated.

What could he say? He was cursed and bastard born, while she was the noblest of all creatures. No words would rectify what he had so callously taken, nor would they remove the seed he might have planted. He of all men knew the wounds given by people's hostile tongues. The thought of so gentle a woman bearing those scars tore through him.

How could he have allowed himself a moment of weakness? Surely he had learned the fallacy of such by now, and yet he couldn't control himself. Not with her.

She wrapped the sheet around herself and moved from the bed like a blessed angel coming to soothe his torment. Daemon stood immobile, needing her comfort and terrified of what receiving it would do. The morning light played against her skin like a mystical halo, lighting her hair, stealing his breath. For a moment, he could almost believe in angels, in love, in the very goodness of men.

Her face awash in beauty, her gaze tender, she reached up to touch his cheek. Daemon closed his eyes, forcing himself to stand before her and not flee. Just one more touch, one more caress. Would that be too much to ask?

But before he could feel her softness, the door burst open.

Daemon looked at the intruder and met the murderous gaze of Belial.

"Do my eyes deceive me?" Belial snarled, crossing the room to take Arina by the arm. "What villainous game be this? The benefactor demanding his tribute?"

Bitter, scalding anger swelled inside Daemon. His vision dimming, he could barely control the desire to forever silence Belial's overloud voice before it carried out into the hall where people were no doubt waking.

Belial raked Arina with a sneer. "How could you?"

Despite the quiver of fright inside her, Arina lifted her chin against her brother's scathing glare. " 'Tis of no concern to you," she said, her heart pounding. What she had done was wrong, she knew that, and yet she felt no shame, no dismay at her actions. Indeed, she would gladly repeat what they had done, and still, in fact, yearned for Daemon in a way she had never yearned for any other.

Once more it was as if her mind and body warred with one another. Nay, she decided, 'twas her heart that warred against her mind. Her heart that told her not to feel remorse.

Belial curled his lip. "Unrepentant whore!" He drew back his arm. Arina tensed, expecting the blow, but refusing to cower.

Before she could blink, Daemon came between them. He forced Belial's grip from her arm and shoved her brother against the wall, his face tense, his jaw like finely polished steel. "You will lower your voice," he said, his tone menacing. "And you will never lay hand to her, lest I tear the offending member from your body."

Belial narrowed his gaze and Arina feared for all their safety. "I demand restitution," Belial said. "You have made a whore of her and I will not stand for her to be mocked."

A shadow darkened Daemon's eyes and he released her brother. He looked at her and she saw all the sadness that burned inside him. Pain twined through her heart as she touched his arm, offering him comfort. She wanted to say something, yet no words would come.

Suddenly, Daemon's gaze turned dull. He pulled his arm free from her grasp. "I shall have a marriage contract drawn up."

Shock poured over her as she looked from Daemon's stoic face to Belial's smug satisfaction.

"No one is to know of our transgression," Daemon continued. "I will not have her shamed for my actions."

A strange glow appeared deep in Belial's eyes, striking a familiar cord in Arina's memory. The image of a white wolf came to her mind, but for her life she couldn't understand why.

"I will not have this marriage made in secrecy. For my sister's sake, I want all to know of it."

Daemon's jaw tensed, and Arina held her breath in expectation of his rejection. "I would have it no other way," he said.

She released her breath in relief.

An evil smile curled Belial's lips. Arina trembled as if a winter frost brushed against her spine. "Then her future is now your concern," Belial said. "I charge you to take care lest you harm her more than you already have."

His strange words drifted through her mind. She knew he meant something other than their coming union, but she couldn't think of what it might be.

Why couldn't she remember? All this would no doubt make sense if she could just recall her fleeting, translucent memories.

Belial cast them each one last, parting smile, then turned about and left.

Daemon raked his hand through his unbound hair, and she could swear it shook. He faced her with the most agonized gaze she had ever seen. "I did not ask you before, milady, but I do so now. Do you wish for marriage . . . with me?"

Though his voice was steady, she sensed an underlying tremor and she responded to it. Joy filled her heart. "Aye, Lord Daemon. There is no other I would rather have."

Heated fire sparked in his gaze, sending another chill over her. "Then you, milady, are a fool."

His sudden anger surprised her. What about her words had caused his rage? "I don't understand," she said.

He pulled his tunic over his head. Clenching his jaw, he stared at her until she feared he'd never answer.

Finally, he sighed. "I will send a messenger to my brother. The manor and lands shall be yours to control so long as you maintain the castle. I have a few lands in Normandy that will also be yours."

His voice sounded so distant, so cold. Her stomach cramped with fear. "You speak as if you're planning a will," she told him.

His back to her, he retrieved his armor from the floor. Arina ached to reach out and touch him, but the rigidness of his body warned her against such an action. "I won't be staying here much longer," he said. "I have other matters that need attention."

"You're leaving?" she asked, a painful knot closing her throat.

"I can't stay."

And before she could argue, he left her standing in the center of the chamber.

Arina glanced about the hall, her heart hanging heavy. Never had she seen so many dour faces. True to his promise to Belial, Daemon had drawn up the marriage contract and they had all signed it.

Wace had planned their wedding feast, but the people were far from festive. Even the poor musicians kept starting songs, only to stop when no one would respond or dance.

"Milord?" she asked, trying yet again to draw Daemon into conversation so that he would have something to focus on other than his people's obvious rejection of their marriage.

For the last hour, he had scarcely even picked at his food. Now he looked up from his trencher, his gaze as empty as the half-hearted cheers they had received when first they entered the hall. "Aye, milady?"

She opened her mouth to speak, only to close it as Belial leaned forward with his goblet. "'Twould seem our people have found common ground," Belial said. "Neither Norman nor Saxon has found a cause for celebrating."

A bitter taste filled her mouth and if she didn't know better, she'd call it hatred.

Belial stood and motioned for the befuddled musicians to stop. "Good friends, I wish to bless our happy couple with a toast."

"I'll not drink to them," a belligerent voice rang out. Belial cocked a finely arched brow and slowly lowered his goblet to the table.

Arina scanned the crowd until she saw the Saxon man who struggled against his companions.

"Nay, I'll not be silent," he said, shoving himself to his wobbly feet.

She glanced at Daemon, who sat silently watching. His grip tightened on the knife he held, and only by that could she tell how much the man's words disturbed him.

"This is an evil deed. How can I give my blessing when one of our fairest Saxon maids is sacrificed to the Norman dogs. Nay," the man sneered, stumbling against the corner of the table. "Not even a Norman dog, but worse. He won't even send for a priest to bless our dead!"

Tears gathered in Arina's throat and pain choked her breath. How could anyone be so blind to Daemon's goodness?

"He is the devil's own—"

"Enough!" Arina shouted, rising from her seat. " 'Tis my husband you address, and the only evil I see here this night is that brought by foul rumors and ignorance."

The drunkard looked at her as if she'd slapped him, but she didn't care. She refused to sit by and allow a decent man to be slandered.

Slowly, Daemon moved his chair back and stood. He scanned the hall, and his bland acceptance of the man's words tore at her soul. "Whoever calls this man friend should take him home."

When no one stood to offer aid, Daemon shook his head. He looked at her, his gaze awash with emotions she couldn't define. Arina ached to remove the man's words from his memory, but that would not take away all such whispers Daemon had heard. From what Wace had told her, Daemon had spent his entire life subjected to such. The pain brought by that knowledge invaded her heart and set it pounding.

Daemon looked back at the crowd. "Have no fear of me. I will not hold his words against him, nor will I punish those who help him to his bed. Go in peace." That said, Daemon tucked his knife into his belt and left.

Arina ran after him, wanting to comfort him, afraid nothing ever could. She stopped him just outside in the yard. "Daemon?"

Daemon shivered at the gentleness of her hand on his arm. No one had ever before defended him and he wasn't sure how to respond. "Go inside," he said.

She shook her head and he ached to pull her

into his arms and feel her supple curves against him, to once again sample the taste of her flesh, the comfort of her body.

But that was only a dream, a dream that could never be. No one would accept their marriage. Ever. His people's reaction had proven that. The best he could offer was to leave the lands in her possession and give her freedom to seek a more suitable husband.

Arina tightened her hand on his arm, and he allowed her to turn him until he faced her. "He was drunk," she said. "He knew not what—"

"He knew, milady."

The torment in her eyes surprised him. By now he should be used to her strange feelings where he was concerned, but too many years of no one caring whether he lived or died had left him easily stunned by any show of concern.

Thunder clapped over their heads. Though the rain had been a steady drizzle most of the day, the night threatened a volatile storm. Daemon glanced up at the dark, eerie clouds. "Go inside where 'tis safe."

Arina reluctantly released him. She searched her mind and heart for words that would heal some of the damage wrought by such callous insults, yet nothing came. "I belong with you now," she said, her throat tight.

A bitterness filled his eyes that tightened her throat even more. "Nay, milady. There is no place in a warrior's life for a noble maid."

"But what of his heart?"

Shock replaced the bitterness in his eyes for the short span of a heartbeat, then fled beneath a black scowl of anger. "Have you not heard? No heart exists inside me. 'Tis said Lucifer himself stole my heart and tried to give it to my human brother, whose goodness rejected the organ, thereby causing his death."

"Daemon—"

"No more words, milady," he interrupted, moving away from her. "I beg you return inside before I taint you further."

She wanted to argue with him more than she had ever wanted anything, yet she knew he was past listening. Only time could alleviate the pain and only time could help her reach the part of him she longed to claim.

Arina watched him step around the puddles, his spine more unyielding than a distant mountain range. Sighing, she lowered her gaze to the ground.

The shimmering depths of the puddles called to her, and she moved to stand next to the one just outside the manor's door. A rushlight rippled, its flame distorted by the light rain falling against the black water. From the deepest recesses of her mind, a memory rushed forward; a memory of screams and fire and the pungent odor of sulphur.

"Nay, angel, nay. I repent!"

She recoiled at the sharp shriek inside her

head. Images tore through her: demons surging forward, a wrinkled old man clinging to her in mortal terror as she . . . as she . . .

"Please!" she cried out, placing her clenched fists over her temples in an effort to recapture the vague memory. "What are you trying to tell me?"

" 'Tis late and you should be inside."

Arina whirled around at the sudden voice, her heart hammering in panic. Belial stood a few feet away, his face masked by shadows. For an instant, his eyes appeared red, but as soon as she blinked, they faded into the darkness.

"Who are you?" she whispered.

Pressing his lips into a tight line, he walked a small circle around her, his hands clasped behind his back. "You know me. We are kin, you and I. Created from the same flesh, we exist one for the other."

He stopped before her and tilted her chin to look up into his face. The coldness of his eyes made her flinch. "We *are* brother and sister."

Though her mind was filled with images of them together as children and adults, her heart denied it all. There was something wrong, something she couldn't quite reason. Deep inside her, she knew there was much more to their relationship than just kinship.

"Now come inside before you face another storm," he said. "One you are not prepared to deal with."

Despite the part of her that begged her not to trust him, not to follow, she allowed Belial to take her hand and lead her back inside.

Hours later, she sat inside her chambers, listening to the storm that raged, sipping a cup of cool, spiced wine. Each hour that passed, she was certain Daemon would return. Yet each one came and went while she waited, until she knew he had no intention of joining her.

Cecile stretched beneath her touch. Arina smiled at the small kitten and continued to stroke Cecile's soft underbelly. "Where is your lord?" she asked with a small sigh.

Over and over her mind replayed haunting images of the night before. Daemon taking her in his arms, his hard body sliding against hers, his hands seeking out the most intimate parts of her body. Yet something inside didn't quite accept the reality she remembered. Instead of crystal clarity, the images were as blurry as the rushlight in the puddle. Only her burning desire came to her in sharp, pulsing reality.

But with that desire came a tiny voice that warned against seeking Daemon out and fulfilling the ache that beat inside her heart. Why? What could be wrong about seeking one's husband? She belonged to him and he to her.

Still the voice persisted.

Arina shook her head in an effort to clear it. Mayhap she was indeed mad.

Go to him.

Startled, she glanced at Cecile as if the strange voice could have come from the tiny animal. "Methinks I have finally lost all wit."

Placing her goblet on the table, she snuggled down into the fur-lined covers. She closed her eyes, determined to think no more on the matter. It was late and past time for her to sleep.

No sooner had she dozed off, than she sat straight up. This time, there was no mistaking the voice she'd heard.

"Save him," she whispered, repeating the words.

For the first time since she'd awakened and seen Daemon standing over her, Arina knew what she had to do. Aye, she couldn't leave Daemon out in this storm any more than she could allow him to continue on his lonely, solitary way. She must save him from the destructive path he walked, show him that he belonged in the world of the living. The two of them had been joined and so long as breath filled her lungs, she must not give up on him.

Her heart hammering in uncertain fear of his reaction, she left the bed and dressed, her hands trembling and fumbling with the material. Would Daemon ever welcome her, or would he forever pull away, out of her reach?

Either way, she had no choice other than to try.

She ran through her mind all the possible places he could be, and settled on the stable.

With the ferocity of the storm, she doubted he would seek his pallet in the garden. Nay, he would be sheltered this night.

After closing the door to her chamber, she crept through the sleeping bodies in the hall.

Daemon came awake with a start. He glanced about the stable, looking for the cause of his dream, but only his horse met his eager gaze.

Sighing, he realized Arina was in her bed and he in his. Rain pelted against the sides of the stable and a few of the horses nickered and bucked nervously, fighting against the ropes that held them inside.

The stench of damp hay and oats filled his head, causing his stomach to twitch in disgust. How he hated stables and the memories they brought. Daemon draped his arm over his eyes in an effort to forget where he was, what he was, and listened to the sounds of the distant thunder.

But still his thoughts churned on against his will to silence them. How many nights had he spent alone and longing for things he could never possess? A hundred? A thousand? Yet this time he did possess the very object he craved.

If only he could claim his true rights. If only he could find the courage to rise from his pallet now and seek out his wife and feel her warm, soft body welcoming his. His own body inflamed, he could still feel the cool tickling of her breath against his neck as he claimed her, hear her gentle voice whispering his name.

He closed his eyes to savor the memory, and wished for a time and place where he could live with her as her husband.

Yet over and over he saw the dour, unaccepting faces of his people and knew the impossibility of such a wish. They would forever ridicule his union, and eventually that ridicule would spill onto his precious wife. And he'd be damned before he would cause her that type of pain. Nay, he'd never be that selfish again.

"Well, what a strange place to find a bridal groom."

Immediately alert, Daemon sat up.

With a sneer on his face, Belial stood at the entrance of the stall, leaning against one post. He set the lantern in his hand down before him. "I would have thought after the eagerness with which you took Arina's virginity that you would be on her this night like a wolf on a deer."

"Do not be crude," Daemon said, his lips twisting in disgust over the way Arina's so-called brother spoke of her. "She is a lady and I'll not have her name bandied about as if she were a common whore."

Belial laughed a bitter sound that shivered down the length of his spine. Not a coward by any standard, Daemon couldn't believe the involuntary reaction of his body.

" 'Tis a pity you don't defend yourself with the

same vigor," Belial said.

Daemon rose. "I can fend for myself well enough."

"Can you now?"

For just the tiny beat of a heart, Daemon could swear 'twas Brother Jerome's voice he'd heard.

"I don't see a fierce knight before me, but rather a scared little boy who allows a drunken fool to mock him before the whole of his people. A little boy who cowers from his own wife. What, do you fear she will mock you as well? Or are you just incapable of pleasuring her?"

Growling with rage, Daemon sprang at his tormentor, catching Belial about the waist. They stumbled back against the stable wall.

"So the cat does have claws," Belial said with another bitter laugh. "Come, Daemon Fierce-Blood, son of Lucifer, kill me and claim your true right. Even now your wife awaits, her loins hungry for your body. Would you deny her your seed?"

Daemon reached for Belial's throat, determined to squeeze the life out of his repugnant body. But as his hands closed around his opponent's neck, Belial's eyes darkened to a deep vibrant red. Shocked into hesitating, Daemon slackened his hold and Belial's eyes immediately turned blue.

Belial broke his grip and moved away. "Nay, you're no coward. You have fought long and hard to get what you want. Or have you?"

Rubbing his neck, he turned to face Daemon. "Tell me, Daemon Fierce-Blood, what do you truly seek?"

Still shaken by what he'd seen, Daemon stared at him, giving him due space.

Surely it had been the flame of the lantern that reflected the red light he'd seen in Belial's eyes, or mayhap some trick of his own mind. Daemon didn't know what caused it, but one thing was certain: He'd be damned long before he confided in the man before him. "What do you care?"

A sinister smile curved Belial's lips. "Since you married my sister, I have a vested interest in your future."

He picked the braid off Daemon's shoulder and dropped it to trail down his back. "I saw the careful instructions written in the marriage contract. How you left all your property to her in the event of your death." Belial leaned closer to whisper in his ear. "Is that what you seek? Is death the dream that haunts your sleep?"

Daemon tensed at hearing his fondest desire put into words. Aye, he longed for death, had done so for years. Every time he went into battle, he did so hoping someone's blade would at last end his pain.

Belial pulled a dagger from his belt and held it beneath Daemon's chin. Without flinching, Daemon studied the shining blade, the golden dragon head that protruded above Belial's fist. Raising his gaze, he noted the hollowness of Belial's eyes.

One corner of Belial's mouth turned up in a bitter, regretful smile. "Nay, I cannot kill you, but you could kill yourself. Tell me why a man who wants nothing more than death has never heeded its call?"

Daemon refused to answer this question. He refused to admit aloud that he had never given up hope that one day his life might change, that mayhap he would one day find a place where he belonged. For that reason, he would never end his own life. He would trust in the same cruel fate that had delivered him into such a brutal life to alleviate him of its burden one way or another.

"Do you fear damnation more?"

Daemon's gaze narrowed. "I fear nothing."

"Then here, take my dagger and end all you have suffered."

Knocking Belial's arm aside, Daemon faced him with a snarl. "You think little of your own life to seek me out with your simpkin wit. Be gone now before I yield to the desire to end *your* life."

The mocking smile did little to ease his anger. Nor did the curt bow. "As you wish, milord."

Then as quickly as Belial had appeared, he left.

* * *

Outside, Belial smiled at the rain that didn't drench him. Nay, the rain, unlike mortal fools, knew better than to evoke his wrath. He smiled again. How he enjoyed toying with them. 'Twas indeed a shame he couldn't end their pitiful lives. Oh, to have the heady power of life and death. But the actual giving and taking of life belonged solely to God. All Belial could do was tempt.

A hand touched his shoulder. He whirled about to face the crone.

"Why did you tempt him to die?" she asked in her screechy voice that sent painful stabs all the length of his humanlike body. "She must fall in love with him first, and then she must watch as his life drains away. If Daemon kills himself before she falls to her desire, you cannot claim her soul and we might have to wait years before she finds another man to love."

Putrid, hot anger suffused his mouth. He had never liked being questioned. It reminded him of too many nights spent in Lucifer's pit. "I know what I'm doing."

"Then explain it to my human wit."

Why could he never once find an intelligent accomplice? One who could understand the nuances of subtle manipulation?

Belial took a deep breath, his head throbbing from the strain of his anger and maintaining his human form. Soon he would have to leave and restore his strength. And Lucifer knew he needed every ounce of strength to deal with imbecilic humans.

Facing her, he allowed his full venom to enter his voice, turning it into its true echoing, demonic form. "I knew Daemon would never kill himself. I was merely reminding *him* of that fact." He smiled, cruelly relishing her fear and his coming triumph. "All these years past, he has lived solely on hope, and now that hope has a name. And *her* name is Arina."

Chapter Five

Daemon blew out the lantern, his thoughts drifting between Arina's innate goodness and her brother's evil. How could they have come from common origins?

He frowned as a familiar tightness settled in his gullet. Would he have been so different from his twin brother had his brother lived?

He leaned his head against the coarse wood of the stall, and allowed his pain to flow freely through him. All his life, he had wondered how things might have been had either his mother, father or brother survived. Would they have abandoned him too?

Nay, he preferred to think they would have been like William. Reserved and respectful, but not cruel, fearful or scornful.

Closing his eyes, he could still remember the first time he had seen William. His brother had ridden three weeks to visit the small monastery where Daemon's maternal grandfather had abandoned him. Brother Jerome had often described the fear in his grandfather's eyes when he gave Daemon to the church in the hope that the brothers could save his soul.

Ignorant old man. How could he have believed in such things?

Yet Daemon could never truly fault his grandfather for his fear, any more than he could fault all the poor religious fools who clung to their beliefs. Had he been born normal, he had little doubt that he would be every bit as pious as they and hold as many superstitions about people like him.

Not that William, for all his piety, had ever listened to those evil tales. And after all these years, Daemon still didn't understand why his brother had been different, why his brother alone had seen past the lies.

William had never told him why he came that day, nor did Daemon know how his brother had recognized him on sight. William had always attributed it to Divine Providence.

Well whatever it had been, it had changed his life. From that day forward, he'd ceased being the poor possessed child the brothers struggled to exorcise, and had become a hard-edged squire. He'd trained harder than the other boys, knowing he must be the fiercest if he was to ever silence their mockery and scorn. Aye, he'd cracked a few skulls, but in the end he had achieved his long-sought peace. No one dared taunt him to his face.

Until now.

"Daemon?"

He jumped at the gentle voice behind him. How had she come upon him without his hearing? "I am here, milady."

She walked forward into the stable, and he felt more than saw her. The horses immediately quieted, as if her presence soothed them as much as it did him. She held her arms outstretched, tentatively searching the area around her, and walked slowly into the darkness where he stood, the darkness where he lived.

Chiding himself for his foolishness in seeking her out, he closed the distance between them and took her outstretched hands. Her cold fingers trembled in his and the softness of her skin reminded him of everything he'd ever wanted, ever cried out for on long solitary nights. "Why have you come?"

"I was worried over you, milord. I kept thinking you would return and when you didn't . . . I just had a feeling inside that told me to find you."

Arina wished for enough light in the stable so that she could see what emotions played in his eyes. But the shadows of the night hid his face from her searching gaze. She shivered from the cold, her wet dress hanging heavy against her chilled flesh.

"You're soaked through," Daemon growled, his hands tightening on hers an instant before he released her.

Arina reached for where he'd been, but found nothing other than blackness. For a moment she feared he'd left her alone. In the space of a few heartbeats, he returned with a blanket and draped it over her shoulders. She smiled at his kindness, a strange warmth filling her and driving away her chills.

" 'Twould seem I'm forever drying milady off," he said.

She laughed and adjusted the blanket, her cheeks warming as she remembered what had happened after the last time he had chased away the cold. And at this moment she would gratefully welcome his touch. Aye, she burned for him in a way she never had before, and nothing would give her greater pleasure than to seal the bond they had made earlier this night.

"For your kind attention, Lord Gallant, I'd gladly hurl myself into a lake."

He moved away, and she sensed her words upset him.

"Oh please," she said, walking forward. "I didn't mean to—" She gasped as her foot caught against something and she stumbled.

Suddenly, strong arms surrounded her and lifted her against him. Her entire body shook from stunned surprise. Once more she remembered the night before, his tender passion, his bold caresses. Fire danced in her stomach, bringing a fierce demanding throb that only he could appease.

Would he ever again seek her out or would she forever be forced to go to him?

"Thank you," she whispered, reaching up to touch his face.

"Here," he said, his voice gruff as he lowered her to the straw-lined floor and took her hand away from his cheek.

When he started to move away, Arina grabbed his arm and pulled him to sit beside her. "Nay, Lord Daemon. I would have you speak with me, not flee into the darkness like a demon afraid of light."

"And what if I were just that?"

Again she wished she could see his face, but mayhap the darkness helped him to confide in her. Aye, since he couldn't see her, mayhap he would open the doors to the treasure he kept so heavily guarded. "We both know what you are, milord."

He snorted. "I know what you think me to be and I know truthfully what I am. You, milady, delude yourself with a fanciful image of a kind and noble man who will rescue you from the clutches of your foul brother."

She frowned in confusion. "Is that not what you did?"

"Aye," he said, his voice full of bitterness. "But in my haste I worsened your situation. Before, you were a treasure any lord would gladly take. Now that you've bound yourself to me, you'll know scorn the likes of which you cannot imagine."

"Like the Saxon in the hall this night?"

He released his breath in a rush, and for a moment she thought he'd leave. Then he spoke. "His words were mild, milady. Your people are defeated and they fear us now. Even drunk, he didn't say all that he could."

Biting her lip against a sudden swell of sympathetic pain, she thought about the Saxon man and his remarks. If only she could have prevented them from ever being spoken. If only she could take away all the years Daemon had been subjected to such.

A painful knot closed her throat and she drew a deep breath. Would she ever find a way to touch the heart inside him? Would she even be able to make him realize that he did possess a heart, a kind, noble heart that all men should have?

"Come," he said, taking her arm. "I must return you to the manor."

"Nay. I would rather stay with you."

His grip stiffened. "You cannot, milady. You don't belong in my world. It would destroy you."

Arina started to argue, but was too weary. Daemon was a stubborn man and it would take more than mere words to change his mind. Perhaps in time she might find a way to reach him, but would he give her that time?

She allowed him to lead her back through the stable with only the sound of crunching straw and falling rain breaking the tense silence between them.

He pushed open the door and paused. Loud thunder clapped and a new burst of rain broke. Wind howled in her ears.

Cursing, Daemon closed the doors with a loud wooden clatter and moved her back. "We'll have to wait a while for the rain to slacken."

She smiled, grateful for the weather's intervention.

His silence almost tangible, Daemon led her back to the stall. "Rest yourself. I'll awaken you when 'tis time." He moved away and her heart cried out for his presence.

"Will you sit with me?"

She felt his reluctance as he took a seat beside her. Arina placed her head on his shoulder. He tensed for a moment as if he fought with himself. Then he relaxed and draped an arm over her.

Savoring the rich scent of him, the warmth of his body so close to hers, she closed her eyes and wished for the courage it would take to strip his tunic from him and relive her memories of the night before. But should she try, he would push her away and leave her longing.

Nay, despite the demanding need inside her, she made herself wait. She promised herself she would find some way to reach him. Before it was too late.

"Milady?"

Arina came awake with a slow stretch. She opened her eyes to see Wace standing over her. Frowning in confusion, she pushed back the blanket that covered her and scanned her chambers. How had she gotten here?

"Where is Lord Daemon?"

"He left early this morn with several men. He said to tell you he would return this even."

Wace's smile beamed and he raised an annoying little brow, the implication of which she knew full well. "He carried you in at first light and warned me to make certain you were left undisturbed."

She returned his smile, but it went no further than her face. Why had Daemon not awakened her as he'd promised?

Wace shuffled his feet and looked past his shoulder, into the hall. "I wouldn't disturb you now, milady, but a friar has come and he seeks the lord or lady of the hall."

Arina looked up, her mind dazed by his words. "A friar, you say?"

"Aye, milady."

A sudden thought brought a new, heartfelt smile to her lips. This just might be the chance to ease everyone's fear of Daemon. Throwing her hair over her shoulder, she rose from the bed.

Arina hesitated as she noted Daemon had left her fully clothed. Why?

"Milady, he waits."

Removing her thoughts from her enigmatic husband, Arina followed Wace into the hall. The short, rotund friar immediately stood; his face aghast.

Wondering at his strange reaction, she moved closer to him. "Greetings, Brother . . . ?"

"Edred," he supplied, nervously brushing his hand over his tonsure. Even while she watched, redness spread over his cheeks and up to the small shaven circle on his head. He cleared his throat and settled a steely gray gaze upon her. "I received a message from Lord Daemon two days ago asking for someone to come bless graves and administer Last Rites. I understand some sort of accident took place?"

Daemon had asked for a friar? Arina frowned at the disclosure. Why had he not spoken up when the Saxon criticized him before all?

"I apologize for my delay," the friar continued. "But there was a poor possessed child who needed my aid."

"And how was she possessed, good brother?"

Arina looked up at Belial's mocking voice. He

leaned in the doorway, a menacing smile on his lips.

"She was . . ." The friar paused, then frowned. "How did milord know 'twas a woman?"

Belial shook his head. " 'Tis the look about you, good brother." He joined them in the hall and wound his arm about her waist. "And the look in your eyes when you address my fair sister."

The friar's jaw began to flop like a fish out of water. His eyes widened, and a wave of anger crashed through Arina.

"Apologize to the friar," she said through clenched teeth. " 'Tis no need for you to insult him so."

Belial's look of warning sent a frigid shiver of fear over her. Arina blinked, her mind faltering. *Be nice and sacrifice yourself for me.* The words spun through her head, repeating themselves over and over. Aye, 'twas Belial's voice.

She must remember. . . .

"Milady?" Brother Edred stepped forward and took her arm.

Arina glanced from him to Belial, whose brow was lined with . . . with . . . fear? Yet she couldn't make herself believe Belial would fear anything.

"My sister has had an accident herself," Belial said, and there was no mistaking the caution of his tone. "For days now, she cannot recall herself and is given to spells of dizziness."

"Is milady poss—"

"Nay, friar, do not say that," Belial warned.

Arina stared at him. What was going through Belial's mind? Strange, indiscernible whispers stole through her head, and a part of her told her if she listened carefully enough, those whispers would answer her question.

Belial brushed the hair from her cheek and her thoughts stilled. A strange glow hovered in Belial's eyes and one corner of his mouth turned up. He looked at the friar. "Don't treat her for possession until you meet her lord. I fear he will not take lightly your attentions to his wife."

Brother Edred frowned. "How mean you?"

The slow smile that spread across Belial's face appeared sinister and cold. A shiver sped up Arina's spine and into her stomach. "In due time, Brother. But come. I shall show you to the graves and families of the people who need your ministrations."

Arina watched the two of them leave, and the hazy images in her mind cleared.

Her brother's alliance with the friar didn't bode well. Belial was a wicked man, wicked and cold. Every time he placed a hand upon her, she could feel it in his touch, in the frigidness of his flesh.

Over the last few days, he'd made no attempt to speak with anyone other than herself or Daemon, and she knew he must have something evil planned to seek out the friar now. But who was his evil meant for? Her, Daemon, or the brother?

Part of her urged her to go after them and speak with the friar alone, but another part warned her to stay clear until Daemon's return. Listening to the warning, she returned to her chambers, where she could finish her morning toilette.

Daemon reined his horse to a stop. By the looks of his men, he could tell they were ready to return, yet each held his tongue. In fact, as he studied them, he realized not one man among them would even dare meet his gaze. As soon as he cast a glance at any of them, his subject would avert his eyes.

Bitter amusement filled him. There were some advantages to being well feared. No one dared voice a complaint, but then no one ever approached him for any other purpose either.

He'd never noticed that before. Not until Arina made him realize just how isolated he'd become; how many nights he'd spent alone, without friend, without comfort.

He shook his head at the thought. Three days. Just three short days since he'd first seen her, and already she had ingrained herself into his life, his soul. He knew better than to hold tender thoughts for another, especially a woman. Why, then, couldn't he block her from his mind?

Daemon winced at the pain in his chest. Never before had the prospect of taking lands appealed to him. So why this sudden devotion to a maid he scarce knew? A maid who had become his wife?

Perhaps it came from his need to protect her. With his lands and blood alliance to William, she would never again be homeless, never again know the fear of hunger or cold. Once he fell in battle, she would have her choice of any lord who met her fancy. Aye, that would be the best for all of them.

Ignoring the part of him that denied his claim, Daemon wheeled his horse about. "If there were bandits stealing from the crofters, 'twould appear they have fled."

As expected, none of his men replied.

"Let us return."

Daemon kicked his horse toward the manor. Foreboding rushed through his body, tightening his gullet. He would rather face the whole of the Saxon army than spend another moment with Arina. She posed a far greater threat to his sanity and life than all the Englishmen ever born.

He shook his head at the irony. He had stood in battle against the best England had to offer and no scratch had marred him. Now a simple Saxon maid had brought him to his knees, made him long for things he had always scorned.

Nay, he would never be a lord, any more than he would allow himself to grow fat and slovenly.

Men only respected warriors, and only as a feared warrior could he keep tongues still. And with his absence, Arina's goodness would win over the people. In time, they would forget and forgive her ill-begotten marriage.

No matter what, he must leave Brunneswald and her behind. Though his soul argued against it, he knew it was the only choice he had.

By the time he'd returned, Daemon had convinced himself he'd be far better off without Arina. Setting his mind on the actions he must take, he rode into the bailey.

Children danced about in frenzied haste, kicking up their feet and more dust than a herd of uncontrolled stallions. Laughter rang out as well as cheers and songs.

Daemon pulled his horse to a stop. Amazed by the sight, he stared at them in disbelief. Not since they'd landed in England had he heard the merriment of children.

Suddenly, the group of dancers broke apart and out of their center Arina rose to her feet with one child held against her bosom. His heart stopped. Never in all his life had he beheld a woman more beautiful, more stunning. The sunlight shone in her hair like finely woven gold. Pink circles darkened her cheeks, and she smiled the very smile that must make every angel in heaven tremble in envy.

Pain ripped through his chest as if daggers pierced his heart and fire coursed through his veins to awaken a part of him he despised. He struggled to breathe against the sensation. Once more he reminded himself why a life with her could never be. Why he must never go to her for comfort or release.

She set the child aside and they both joined hands with the others and circled around in a dance. Her voice rang out above the others, more enchanting than any he'd heard before. "If ever a man deserves salvation, because of a grievous separation, thee shall rightly be that man. For never a turtle in the loss of her companion was at any time more cast down than thee."

Arina smiled at the child to her right and drew a deep breath before continuing her song. "Everyone mourns for his land and country when he parts from friends of his heart, but there is no farewell, whatever anyone may say, so miserable as that of a lover and his sweetheart."

Her sweet melody and words echoed around him, taunting him, consoling him, whispering to his soul, to his craven heart. Savoring each fragile tone, he closed his eyes. Aye, she was a woman to make any man proud. So why must he, her husband, turn her away?

Because she could never truly be his. The people who surrounded them would forever call him monster, deformed.

"Fate, you cruel bastard!" he snarled under his breath, and dismounted. His belly roiling with anger, he tossed his reins to a waiting groom.

Pulling off his gloves and helm, he started toward the manor.

"Daemon!"

He closed his eyes in an effort to banish the joy her voice brought. He didn't want to hear his name on her sweet lips. It served no other purpose than to weaken his resolve.

She ran and grabbed him by the arm, her eyes shining with merriment. Daemon stared at her, his heart pounding, his body leaping to life. At this moment, nothing would please him more than escorting her to their chambers and sampling her glowing flesh.

"Come, milord, you must join us!"

He frowned. "Join you?"

"Aye!" she said with a laugh, pulling him by the arm toward the children.

Daemon shook his head, horror filling him. "Nay, milady. I cannot. I'll frighten them."

She hesitated for only a moment before taking his gloves and placing them inside his helm, which she set on the ground. "Pash! Frighten them indeed."

Leading him by the hand, she laughed and stopped before the children. "We have another dancer," she declared.

Daemon glanced around at the faces and noted their immediate fear and reservation. "Milady, please," he said.

A sharp frown drew her brows together as she noted their reactions as well. She released him and put her hands on her hips. She cast each of the others a chiding gaze. "Don't tell me *all* of you are afraid?"

No one spoke, but he could tell by the terror in their eyes that each and every one of them would rather face Lucifer himself than touch him. Daemon started to move away, but a small girl stepped forward.

"I'm not afraid," she said, her high-pitched voice sweeter than the first warm breeze of spring. "If milady says not to be afraid, then I have no fear."

Before he could move, she reached out and grasped his thumb with her tiny hand. Her touch was as light as a breath of air, yet it sent a wave of pain crashing through him that nearly toppled him. Daemon stared at her elfin face and the shining dark locks that surrounded her rose-hued cheeks. She smiled up at him, and he almost stumbled to his knees.

"Come, Lord Doubt," Arina said, taking his other hand. "We have a dance!"

Still unsure of himself, Daemon allowed them to start the dance. He felt like the greatest of all fools as he stumbled through the steps. Never in his life had he danced, and the intricate moves escaped his clumsy feet.

Arina laughed, then broke from the circle. Taking him by the hands, she leaned back and twirled about with him. Daemon stared in awe as the rest of the world spiraled in a dizzying blur around them. Only her face with its joyous smile and pleasing beauty could be seen clearly. And something in that suited him more than he cared to admit.

Held by her smile and enchanted, he struggled to breathe. He wanted her more than he'd ever wanted anything. Nay, he needed her, he corrected himself. He needed her more than the very air that nourished his starving lungs. She was his life, his soul.

Instinctively, he pulled her toward him. She stumbled in her dance steps and lurched forward with a gasp. Daemon grabbed her before she fell, but his effort to save her unbalanced him as well. Entwined, they tumbled to the ground.

Her laughter, joined by the children's, rang in his ears. Arina lay upon his chest, her hair spilling across his face in the most tender of embraces. He inhaled the warm, sweet scent and his body erupted into fire. Closing his eyes, he allowed himself for a moment to pretend that they could have a life together. That he could look forward to years of such enjoyment and laughter.

She squirmed on top of him until she sat by

his side, looking down. Her eyes sparkled like the finest sapphires to ever grace the earth. His body throbbed with a demand he knew he could never again satisfy. He'd shamed her once with his hated carnal desires; he refused to do so again.

She brushed back her hair and smiled the very smile that melted his wretched heart. "My thanks, milord. The ground appears far too solid, and I am most grateful not to learn for myself what bruises it yields!"

And before he could move, she leaned forward and kissed his lips. Though it was chaste and brief, it set a thousand flames flickering in his belly, his loins. His desire trampling his reason, Daemon pushed himself up and captured her in his arms, then pulled her back for another, more satisfying kiss.

She gasped, then surrendered herself to him. Daemon drank of her warm, sweet lips, which tasted finer than all the wines of Normandy. She opened her mouth in welcome and his heart pounded in his chest. Nothing would give him greater pleasure than to spend eternity in her arms.

"Milord, milady, the friar comes," the little girl cried, before erupting into giggles.

Arina pulled away, her cheeks a delectable shade of pink. She touched her lips with her hand and Daemon fought to win the war inside him. A shy smile spread across her lips as she stared at him, her eyes filled with warmth and love.

He'd never thought to receive such a look. He reached out and took her hand from her lips. Her soft skin reminded him of the finest silk.

"Lord Daemon?"

The unfamiliar voice pulled him away from his desire to seize her up in his arms and quench the lust of his body. Blinking in an effort to divert his thoughts, Daemon pushed himself to his feet. He held a hand out for Arina, and assisted her before he turned and faced the friar.

Daemon forced his lip not to curl, but could do nothing to staunch the flood of hatred that drowned his heart. He'd spent too many years with so-called Brothers of God who used their title to further their own corrupt ends. Even though he tried, he just couldn't muster any kindness toward one who wore their robes. If not for his people and their beliefs, he'd banish all such creatures from Brunneswald lands.

"Brother Edred?" he asked, uncertain if this was the same friar he had contacted, the same cowardly friar who, upon the arrival of Daemon's army, had run from his home and the people who depended upon him.

The little man smiled as he drew closer. "Aye," he said, his fat jowls flapping. "I've come as you . . ." His voice broke off as he looked up and met Daemon's gaze.

The look of terror was one Daemon had become more than accustomed to.

"Holy Mother of God!" Edred gasped, clutching at the wooden cross about his neck. " 'Tis true, Normans are the sons of Lucifer."

Daemon retrieved his helm and gloves from the ground, then approached the little friar. He narrowed his eyes. "If we are the devil's own, then I wager the Saxons are his mistresses. After all, 'twas your good King Harold who took holy vows to support my brother. And no sooner had Edward died than your King Harold seized the throne with lies and treachery." He raked the friar with a glare. "We are here under papal authority. So 'twould seem we represent your God, not your Satan."

Ignoring the man's gaping, indignant stare, Daemon headed for the hall. So much for his useless dreams. He could never remain here with Arina. The people of Brunneswald would always demand the presence of clergy and as long as clergy remained, so too would rumors of his birth.

Daemon swung open the door with such force that it bounced off the far wall. His fury simmered deep in his gullet.

Even now, he could feel the sting of the brand as it sizzled against his skull, hear the words of Brother Jerome echoing around him. A child no older than five, he had screamed and cried for them to stop. He had fought against the chains holding him until he had permanently scarred his wrists. Over and over he had stated his innocence and over and over they had condemned him.

So be it. He'd much rather be associated with the devil than with a God who could allow such abominations to be acted out in His name. At least the devil was honest about his treachery. He didn't hide behind so-called works of charity that masked horrors far worse than any hell.

And yet all he had to do was look at Arina and he could almost believe in God himself. Her goodness and beauty had to come from some truly divine source.

Daemon gripped his helm in his hand and struggled against the urge to throw it into the wall. He must calm himself. The past was just that, the past. He must concentrate on the future.

What future? his mind railed.

Daemon paused, all his fury wilting beneath a bitter, stinging wave of regret and despair. He knew he couldn't stay and pretend the past had never happened, that people would leave him and Arina in peace.

His only alternative would be to take her away and live in isolation. He closed his eyes, trying to imagine her on a farm, her back bowed by years of hard work, her gentle hands scarred and chafed. Nay, he could no more subject her to that than he could end his own misery. She was a noble lady and she deserved all the privileges and wealth her title granted her.

Sighing in regret, he knew what must be done. Once William released him from his vows, he would seek another war.

Chapter Six

Daemon splashed icy water on his face and scrubbed at the grime plastered there by his hard ride. And no doubt the dance had added even more dirt, not to mention his rather pleasant fall with Arina. He clenched his teeth as a warm rush of desire coursed through his body. Even now he could feel Arina's soft curves pressed against him, hear her melodic laughter, feel her lips welcoming his.

Anger curled his lip and pierced his heart. Why had the friar chosen that moment to show himself? It had been the first time in his life he'd truly enjoyed himself, had truly forgotten who and what he was. By hell, he never should have paid the Saxon peasant to find the odious brother and return him.

As if sensing his ill-tempered mood, Cecile yowled and jumped for the washstand. Miscalculating the distance, she hit the edge and fell back against the floor.

"Here now," he said, scooping her up and placing her where she had attempted to land. "Did you hurt yourself?"

She purred under his hand and gently nuzzled his fingers, her pink tongue roughly stroking his scarred knuckles. Until Arina, Cecile had been the only creature to show him love.

Nay, love could never be his. He was a harsh man who knew naught of comfort or gentle words. That was his lot and he had long ago accepted that fate.

All of his anger fled and he found the part of himself that accepted the life he'd been given. There was no need for his anger, not really. He had people's respect and fear; what man could ask for more than that?

A soft knock startled him from his thoughts. Pulling his hand away from Cecile's soft fur, he reached for his tunic and donned it. "Enter."

To his utter amazement, Arina walked in behind five of the children from the yard. He frowned at them, wondering what could bring them to his room.

"Edith has something she would like to say to you," Arina said, mischief glowing deep in her eyes.

The little girl who'd taken his hand stepped forward, her arms held behind her back. She bit her lip as if trying to keep her face straight, but the corners turned up until she was forced to smile brightly.

"Say it, Edith," one of the boys urged.

Her face turned pensive and she looked as if something greatly distressed her. A pain coiled in his stomach. Why was Arina forcing this poor, frightened child to confront *him*, a man who obviously terrified her?

"I don't remember what I'm supposed to say," she whispered.

Daemon stared at her in disbelief. Could it be she truly wasn't afraid of him?

The boy rolled his eyes and huffed. "The dance, silly!"

She looked back at the boy, her worry vanishing. "Oh, that's right!" She raised herself up on her tiptoes, her smile returning. "We wanted to thank milord for joining us. And we . . . we . . ."

"Would like him to join us again," the boy supplied for her in a highly vexed voice.

She nodded her head. "That's it! We want milord to join us again." Her chest swelling in obvious pride, she ran back to the boy, and Daemon noted the flower garland she clutched behind her back.

"Edith! You forgot something." The boy pushed her back toward him.

Her mouth formed a small O. Turning

around, she ran back to Daemon, holding the garland in front of her. "We made this for you, milord, so you'll have one next time you dance," she said, handing him the garland.

Daemon took it, his hand trembling slightly from the weight of some emotion he couldn't name. The carefully plucked flowers and greenery chafed the calluses on his palm, and soothed the calluses of his heart. His chest tightened. Nothing had ever touched him so deeply. The thought and time they had spent on the gift, a gift designed solely for him, made the garland the most precious item he'd ever owned.

The little girl leaned forward, cupped one hand beside her mouth, and whispered in a loud voice. "Creswyn said he wouldn't be afraid of you next time. He said if I—"

"Edith!" the boy barked. " 'Tis late; we must get home."

"All right," she said with a huff. Facing Daemon once more, she tugged on his tunic until he bent down to her level. To Daemon's utter astonishment, she gave him a light kiss on his cheek.

Shock jolted him and he nearly fell from it. Never in his life had anyone so young even spoken to him, let alone dared to touch his monstrous form. And here in this day, this one brave child had twice reached out to him.

In spite of everything he'd ever learned, ever

been taught, Daemon smiled, his throat far too tight for him to speak. He swallowed against the painful lump in his throat, and tried to squelch the hope that flared inside him. Nay, he knew better than to trust others to follow the child's example. He'd learned long ago not to trust in such things.

With a cry of outrage, her brother rushed forward and took her by the arm. Instead of the usual caustic comments, her brother shook his head. "Edith, you're not supposed to kiss a lord!"

Daemon cleared his throat and ruffled her hair. " 'Tis fine; I take no offense."

Creswyn looked up at him, his youthful eyes relieved. "Thank you, milord. She's a wayward child. I know not what we shall do with her," he said in a wistful voice far too old for his years, a voice he must have heard countless times from his parents.

Daemon plucked a flower from his garland and handed it to Edith. "Treasure her."

She smiled, sniffed the flower, then skipped from the room.

Arina closed the door behind the children, her heart lighter than a fairy's feather. She turned back to face Daemon, who stared in awe at the garland in his hand. He reminded her of a child clutching its most precious toy.

Smiling at the image, she crossed the room and touched his arm. Hard muscles flexed beneath her palm, sending a wave of heat dancing over her body. "Milord has a most handsome smile. You should practice it more often."

He took her hand and studied her palm. His lean fingers stroked her flesh and chills spread up her arms all the way to her scalp. "I've never had a reason to smile. Not until you."

Giddiness rushed over her as Arina clasped his hand in hers and reached her left hand up to cup his prickly cheek. Loose tendrils of his hair slid between her fingers in a sensual way that added even more chills to her body.

He closed his eyes and held her hand against his cheek as if savoring her touch as much as she savored his. "Milady, why have you come?"

His familiar words shot through her. Arina recoiled from him, her mind whirling. She stared at the floor, where an image of a battlefield seemed painted against the stones. Screams echoed, men clutched at her.

She whirled around, trying to remove the clutching fingers that pulled at her hair, her dress. "Leave me!" she shouted, pushing at her kirtle where their grips held fast.

"Arina?"

Suddenly, the images vanished. Blinking, she looked up into the concerned frown of her husband. And in spite of the comfort his eyes offered, her heart continued to hammer against her breast. " 'Twas horrible," she whispered. "Why do they haunt me?"

"Who haunts you?"

"The people." Terrified, Arina threw herself into his arms and clutched at his shoulders, needing the comfort and solace of his warm touch. "I see them, hear them, feel them. Why won't they leave me alone?" Tears washed over her cheeks. " 'Tis as if they want to hurt me and I know not why."

His arms tightened around her, and she welcomed the solace he offered. "It's all right, milady. I am here. No one will harm you so long as you live. I shall see to that."

Arina pushed herself away, feeling a sudden burst of anger despite his tender words. "But you want to leave me. Who will protect me when you have gone?"

A shadow passed across his eyes, and she could see her words had struck him.

She crossed the floor to stand before the window. Still the images lurked in her mind like a violent whisper from the past. "I must be mad," she whispered, her anger fading. "There can be no other explanation for what I see."

He grabbed her by the shoulders and turned her to face him. Fury sparkled in his odd-colored eyes, making them cold, unreadable, and sending a shiver over her. "You are not mad, milady!" he said in a bitter, angry voice she didn't understand. "You must never say that to anyone. Do you hear me!"

"Why?" she asked, stiffening her spine to

stand against him. " 'Tis the truth."

" 'Tis a lie. I have spent many a day next to those who are mad. Believe in me when I say that you are far more sane than any person I have ever met."

Shock poured over her and foreboding filled her heart. "What do you mean you have known those who are mad?"

He backed away from her and clenched and unclenched his fists as if he struggled with an inner demon that matched the phantoms stalking her.

When he spoke, his low voice barely made the journey to her ears. "As a child, I lived in a small community of monks and friars. For Sunday mass, the local villeins would bring in those judged mad. The brothers would tie us to the altar where we could receive God's benediction."

He turned to face her, and the emptiness in his eyes chilled her. "Having known them, I am most certain milady is quite sane."

Pain sliced her heart at the thought of him being treated in such a manner. "They tied you with madmen?"

"Aye," he said, his body and voice void of any emotion. Even so, Arina knew the event must have left him haunted.

"Were you not afraid?"

"Aye. I was terrified."

Images of him as a defenseless child invaded

her heart and mind. How could anyone do such a thing to a small boy? She could barely comprehend the action. "Oh, Daemon, I am so sorry."

He shook his head and moved away from the soothing touch she offered. "Don't be. It was a long time ago."

Rubbing his left hand over his right shoulder, he turned away from her. "At times it no longer even seems like it was truly me, but rather that it happened to someone else. Someone I never really knew." When he looked back at her, anger and hatred fired his gaze. " 'Tis the past and the past is best left behind."

A knock sounded on the door a moment before Wace opened it. "Milord, milady, the steward bade me tell you all are awaiting your presence to sup."

Wishing she had more time to explore the matter while her husband seemed willing to talk, Arina nodded. "We'll be right out."

Wace shut the door. She turned back toward Daemon, and by his face she could tell he had no intention of joining his people, or furthering this conversation.

Save him, the voice repeated in her head.

"Daemon, you should join us."

He faced her with a dark scowl. "I'd rather not."

His stubbornness sparked her anger. How could she save him when he persisted in his isolated ways? "Do you intend to spend the whole of your life in exile?"

A strange light filled his eyes. "Aye, milady, I do indeed."

She closed her eyes and prayed for Divine aid. It would surely take a miracle to persuade Daemon to her argument. "If you don't give people a chance to know you, then they shall never see past the rumors."

His snort of disbelief made her long to toss something at his head. "Should I go out there, the rumors will only worsen."

"Why do you think that?"

"I know."

Arina let out a deep breath, her body trembling from rage. How could he be so blind, so stubborn?

She approached him, but he refused to look at her. "Fine, stay here as long as you wish. But if you truly had put your past to rest, then you wouldn't continue to isolate yourself from the world. Your past still haunts you, Daemon Fierce-Blood, and until you face it and conquer it, it will never cease tormenting you."

That said, she left the room.

Daemon stood in the center of the room, her words echoing in his ears. He wanted to deny them, but deep down, he knew she had spoken truly. Aye, his past dogged his steps like a hungry wolf waiting to devour any tender part of him it could touch.

Why couldn't she just leave him in peace? All he wanted was for the entire world to just forget him. In the past, that had seemed simple. No one ever sought him out. Wace did as he was told and left him to his own devices. Why couldn't Arina do the same?

Just because she had some peculiar notion that she could somehow make everyone forget who and what he was, didn't mean she could. If he'd learned anything in his life, it was that people rejected him. So he'd learned to reject them first.

All the years past had tutored him well on what would happen should he join in a common meal. Perhaps 'twas time his bride also learned what he'd known for the whole of his life.

Arina looked up as Daemon entered the room. A smile curved her lips. Aye, she had won this battle; with any luck she might take the war.

Daemon sat beside her, his face drawn and strained.

"You could at least appear to look forward to the meal," she whispered.

The look he gave her chilled her soul. "I would think after our wedding feast, milady would know only too well why I take my meals alone."

"Pash," she said, wrinkling her nose. "The man was drunk."

He shook his head at her, and she knew the words in his mind as if he'd spoken them aloud. He thought her every bit as stubborn as he was. She smiled at the thought. Mayhap she was, but it was for his own good.

Once the servers had finished bringing in the meal, the friar motioned for all to bow their heads for prayer. Out of the corner of her gaze, Arina noted that Daemon kept his head up, his stare focused on the far wall.

The friar's words rang out, faltering only when he noticed Daemon as well.

Brother Edred finished his prayer, then looked at Daemon. "*M'hlaford* doesn't join the prayer?"

Daemon's jaw tensed. "I do not force my beliefs on you, Brother. I pray you give me the same courtesy."

Arina kicked him beneath the table.

He gave her a hostile glare that stole her breath. She opened her mouth to speak, but before she could, the steward stepped forward.

"Milord, there are travelers at the gate who wish a night's lodgings and food."

"Bring them inside."

The steward hesitated as if he wanted to say something more. Finally, he leaned and whispered in Daemon's ear. Arina frowned, wishing she knew what passed between them.

"It matters not. Bring them in and seat them as noble guests."

A surprised look crossed the steward's face, but he said nothing more and hastened to do Daemon's bidding.

Despite her need to ask about the steward's strange behavior, Arina held her silence, knowing she'd find out soon enough. After a few minutes, the steward returned leading three men, the oldest of whom appeared no more than 30 years. Their long hair and beards told her they were Saxons and their proud bearing and clothes bespoke their nobility.

Stiffly, they approached the table. Their gazes narrowed almost in unison as they noted Daemon's eyes.

"We thank you for your hospitality," the eldest man said.

Arina held her breath at the obvious slight. 'Twas indeed rude to beg hospitality and not at least acknowledge Daemon's lordship.

No doubt Daemon had noticed as well, but he gave no indication of the Saxon's omission. Instead, he nodded slightly, and the steward seated them at the end of the raised table.

Belial leaned forward to rest his chin in his palm, and Arina wondered at the mischievous look in his eyes as he scanned the newcomers.

Brother Edred engaged the men in English. Arina returned to her food, noting Daemon's tenseness, which set her own hands trembling.

She managed a few bites before Belial's voice rang out. "Now that we have a friar in residence, 'twould seem fitting that we have my sister's union blessed by him." She choked on her food, aghast at her brother's audacity, especially after Daemon's earlier declaration. "What say you, Lord Daemon? Should we not have a wedding mass?"

Why was Belial deliberately provoking him?

Daemon took a drink of wine, then turned to face both Belial and Brother Edred, who had paused in his conversation with the Saxons and now sat poised expectantly. " 'Twas my understanding the Church thinks marriage too sinful to bother with. I believe the official writ says it is a secular matter best left for secular courts."

Brother Edred nodded. "That has long been held true, but the last council held that all unions should be blessed."

"Then bless my wife and leave me in peace."

Outrage hardened the friar's gaze and Arina held her breath, praying his words would not be too harsh. "Why does milord refuse blessing? Is there something about Our Heavenly Father that frightens you?"

Daemon's gaze darkened to a dangerous hue that sent a wave of fear down her spine. "Nothing about your God could ever frighten me. Save your comforts and words for those who believe. I have no use for such."

"Blasphemer!" Brother Edred shrieked, coming to his feet. "Heretic!"

Daemon stood up and towered over the

smaller man. Brother Edred stepped back, his eyes wide and filled with fear. Arina swallowed the knot in her throat, uncertain what to do.

Daemon's lip curled as he raked his eyes over the friar. "If your God is not offended by the unseemly cowards who represent Him, then I doubt my few words will incur His wrath."

"Milord, please," Arina said, taking Daemon's arm. Only one thing bothered her more than to have her husband attacked, and that was her husband's lack of faith. "I beseech you to hold your tongue. 'Tis my Lord you also deny. And I know your words displease Him."

She shrank from the heated look he sent her. Removing her hand from his arm, Arina trembled.

"Do not defend this lecherous oaf to me, milady," Daemon said. "I know his kith and kind far better than you. And I *beseech* you to avoid his presence lest you soon learn what true horrors lie beneath his robes."

Heat stung her cheeks, his double meaning more than clear. Before she could reply, he left the hall.

Arina gathered up her kirtle and ran after him. By heaven, he would hear her on this matter! 'Twas time he put his blindness aside and saw the truth.

"Daemon!" she snapped, catching up to him just outside the door. "I cannot believe the words you have uttered."

In spite of the dark shadows that obscured his face from her view, she detected his angry glare.

Even so, she refused to let the matter die, not until she had finished this discussion. "You speak of men rejecting you when 'twas you who provoked Brother Edred."

"I provoked Edred?" he asked, his voice heavy with sarcasm. "He was the one to hurl insults, not I."

She lifted her chin and narrowed her eyes. "You could have guessed his reaction when you refused to bow your head."

"Bow my head for what? In respect to a deity I have a difficult time believing in?"

Her hand itched to slap him. Anger and pain joined inside her breast. Why could he not see the truth? "The Lord is alive. How can you not feel Him?"

Daemon took her hand and flattened her palm against his chest, where his heart pounded against her cold fingertips. Chills ran the length of her arm and prickled her neck.

"I feel my heart beat," he said, his voice hoarse. "I feel the wind against my cheeks. For the whole of my life I have listened to creatures such as Edred tell me that I am not human. That I am an abomination against God."

His grip tightened on her wrist. "They have cursed me, beat me and called me monster all in your God's name. If I believe in your God, then I must believe the words they say about me. Why else would an omniscient, omnipotent God allow me to suffer in His name and at the hands of His servants?"

She closed her eyes, praying for some way to make him see. "The Lord moves in mysterious ways. He gives us free choice to serve His will or that of Lucifer. Not all who swear to His name follow His dictates."

Arina reached up and brushed a stray strand of hair off Daemon's forehead. "All of us tread different paths and I don't know why you have been given yours, but I do know that the Lord is real and that He is far from callous or uncaring."

Daemon took her by the arms, his touch strangely gentle. "Forgive me, milady, but I cannot believe in what you say. If I accept your belief, then I must accept what the priests have told me about myself, and I refuse to believe Lucifer is my father."

He released her and headed for the stable.

Arina watched him go, her heart thumping heavily against her breast. Not only had he isolated himself from everyone around him, but even from God himself. She could barely conceive the loneliness, pain and despair such isolation must cause.

'Twould seem for the whole of his life Daemon had walked alone. Completely alone. She shivered at the thought. The human soul had never been created for such a journey. 'Twas a

133

wonder Daemon had lasted so long.

"Milady?"

She turned to see Wace standing in the doorway. "Aye?"

"The people are anxious. The steward wishes for your return so that they may be soothed."

Arina stepped toward him. She studied the youth, his face pensive and drawn. "Tell me, Wace. How long have you traveled with Lord Daemon?"

A frown drew his brows together. "Almost four years now, milady. Why?"

She sighed and glanced back at the stable as Daemon left it astride his charger.

Without looking in their direction, he galloped through the bailey and out the gate. Longing for him swelled inside her heart and she ached to claim him as her own, to soothe the pain years of hardship and mockery had embedded in his soul. "Has he always been as he is now?"

His frown deepened. "I know not what milady means."

She sighed and looked back at Wace. "Has he always avoided being with people?"

"Aye, milady," he said, nodding his head. "Truth, this is one of the few times we have stayed in a manor house for more than a day or so. Normally we travel from battle to battle, seldom ever sleeping indoors."

Her throat closed at the anguish that

pounded inside her. Would she ever find a way to reach her warrior husband? "Has he spoken to you about why he chooses to live in such a manner?"

"Nay, milady. He seldom speaks to me other than to give me my duties."

Her heart ached. Arina moved to return inside, but Wace touched her arm, making her pause.

"Do not judge him harshly, milady. I know the types of things servants and men whisper about him, but I swear on my own soul that they are lies. Lord Daemon may not be godly, but he is far from a demon. In all the time I have served him, he has never once raised his voice, or beat me. But many times my former master led me to Mass while bruises darkened my flesh from the blows he had delivered me. Lord Daemon is a good man, undeserving of such criticism."

She patted his arm. " 'Tis honorable the way you stand by your lord, but have no fear. You need not defend him to me. Like you, I know he is not the monster others think. You may rest easy on that account."

Wace nodded and returned inside.

Holding the door, Arina stared in the direction Daemon had ridden. Could she ever penetrate the armor shielding his heart? What would it take for her to reach inside him and make him realize the destructiveness of his ways? To

135

make him realize that she would stand by his side and never judge him for his shortcomings, or hold him accountable for rumors not of his making?

Arina gripped the door, the wood biting fiercely into her palm. She must find the loose rivet and remove the armor before it was too late. And, something inside told her, her time had almost expired.

Chapter Seven

A chill wind stole up Arina's spine as she stood on the battlements, looking out over the dark valley. The sentry moved past her, but said nothing. She knew he must think her mad the way she had stood here since supper broke up. Yet that didn't concern her. It was her husband's absence that continued to plague her thoughts most.

Though she could scarcely see more than a few feet from the gate and her body shook from the cold, she couldn't leave her post. She needed to watch for him. Something inside kept her feet still, her gaze locked on the eerie forest below. If she listened carefully, the rustling wind would fade and she could almost swear she heard Daemon riding over the land, searching for the comfort he needed.

"M'hlafdie?"

Arina turned, expecting to see the sentry; instead, it was the eldest Saxon nobleman. A frown lined her brow. Whatever could he want with her?

"Greetings, *m'hlaford*. What brings you away from the fire?"

"Like you, I couldn't sleep. I thought a walk might calm my troubled thoughts." His gaze drifted to the sentry several feet away and he whispered, " 'Tis most difficult to rest in the home of my enemies."

Were it not for the humble look in his eyes, she would suspect him of mischief. But as she watched him, she saw a cautious man, not one out to make more trouble. "We are not your enemies."

A shadow darkened his gaze to a deep, almost unreadable hue. "Nay, *m'hlafdie*, you are not, but your husband most definitely is."

She opened her mouth to speak, but he raised his hand to silence her.

"Nay, *m'hlafdie*. I mean no offense. In truth, you remind me too much of my own sweet Wenda for me to offend you."

She detected the softness in his voice as he spoke the woman's name. "Wenda is your wife?" she asked.

"Was," he corrected, his voice strained and

his eyes as sad as if his grief still lay fresh within his heart. "She died two years past while birthing our first child."

Sympathetic pain coursed through Arina and she reached out to touch his arm. "My condolences."

He nodded, looking away from her. "It was hard at first, but I have long since come to terms with her departure."

Rubbing her arms against the chill, Arina noted the catch in his voice. It was identical to the one in Daemon's when he had spoken nearly the same words earlier that night.

Did all men speak denials against their souls?

Did the denial help them? Nay, she decided, not likely. Men seemed to forever state the opposite of what they needed, what they yearned for most.

The Saxon took her by the arm and led her further away from the sentry. "*M'hlafdie*, there is a personal matter of which I would like to speak."

Suspiciously, she looked at him. "You speak of a personal matter when I don't even know your name?"

He smiled, yet it did nothing to allay her fears. "Forgive my oversight, *m'hlafdie*. I am called Norbert."

"And I am Arina."

"Aye, *m'hlafdie*, I asked your name several hours ago."

139

She stiffened her spine in apprehension. What would cause him to ask after her? "Why?"

"I . . ." His voice trailed off and he looked away. After several minutes, he drew a deep breath. "At first I thought you Norman, what with the way you spoke their language, but a short while ago your brother explained what had happened. How the Norman took your hand."

She could well imagine what stories her brother might tell. "And what did my brother say?"

"That the Norman demanded you marry him. That he gave you no choice."

Fury blotted her thoughts. " 'Tis a lie!"

He furrowed his brow and stepped away from her, his gaze wary. "What?"

"Aye, you heard me," she said, her hands trembling from anger over Belial's falsity. "Lord Daemon, unlike my brother, asked me whether or not I agreed to the union. I accepted Daemon of my own free will."

Still skepticism shone in Norbert's eyes and he laughed bitterly. "Do any of us have a choice anymore where our lives are concerned? Since Harold fell, I doubt any of us can choose aught without Norman consent."

The hostile fury in his voice surprised her. "I hear rebellion in your tone."

He looked at her in startled alarm. "Nay, *m'hlafdie*. I have accepted my country's defeat."

140

"Then why have you left your home?"

He shrugged and braced his arms against the wooden battlement before him, his gaze turned into the dark distance. "We were traveling through, on our way to see if our sister had survived the invasion. Ill rumors have passed to us of her abasement and we wish to see for ourselves what has become of her."

Her anger failing, Arina nodded her head. "Then I shall pray for her safety."

"My thanks, and I shall pray for yours."

"My safety?" she asked with a small laugh. "Why? I am not in danger."

He shook his head, but didn't look at her. When he spoke, his tone was grave. "Methinks you are in far greater danger than you know."

Belial knocked the crone away from him, his anger burning deep inside. Brittle leaves rustled beneath his feet as he walked a circle around the clearing, his thoughts churning at her disclosure. "How could you have been so foolish!"

Rising from the heap where she'd landed, the crone wiped the blood from her lip and narrowed her eyes. " 'Twill work, I assure you."

"But why?" he insisted between clenched teeth, his hot, angry breath forming a cloud. "Why would you make the Saxon swoon for her when 'twill serve no purpose other than to turn Daemon away from her?"

"Nay, 'twill raise his jealousy!"

141

Belial seized her again and drew back his arm. Before he slapped her, he stopped himself. No need to abuse her further. The damage had been wrought. All he could do now was try to salvage as much as he could. He wiped his hand over his chin, trying desperately to think of something. But he was weary, too weary to think clearly.

Daemon refused to stay by Arina's side long enough to consummate their union. Dammit! How he hated self-control.

"Just you wait," the crone began again. "When Lord Daemon sees his beloved in the arms of another—"

"Arms of another?" Belial spat. "Arina will never allow such. And even should she, Daemon will no doubt leave. He will look upon the Saxon as a replacement for himself, a far better replacement."

Belial sighed, forcing himself to calm so that he could clear his thoughts. "Nay, 'twill take some thinking. I must show him that no other man will do for Arina. That he needs her too much to let her go."

Daemon paused at the castle's ramparts. Darkness lay across the stones and half-built walls, turning their shapes into ghastly, evil beasts that could frighten even the stoutest of hearts. Aye, that was what people thought when they glanced upon his own likeness, even in the full light of day.

Against his will, Arina's words drifted through his mind, and he flinched at the truth. Perhaps he did provoke some of those fears. But then it had always been easier to allow people their beliefs than to try and make them see past his deformity and into his human soul.

As a child, he had reached out to the brothers and they had recoiled in horror. As a squire, his lord had shied away from him, only reluctantly approaching him. Indeed, if not for William's determination, no lord would ever have accepted him as squire.

Even now he could hear his brother's men arguing over who would take him and William's voice ringing out in an order for Leon to accept his request. Leon had quickly made certain Daemon knew better than to approach him on any matter. And when Leon had bothered to train him in war, Daemon's lessons had been hard, even brutal.

Ever since Daemon's knighting, William had urged him to take lands and a wife. And each time he had turned William's offers aside. He could well imagine the happiness on William's face when he received news of his union, but Daemon knew he could never have the happy marriage William shared with Maude.

Nay, no matter how much his heart cried for him to stay, he must leave.

Once more hope filled him, just as it had all those years past when he was nothing more than a young, foolish child. Daemon cursed at himself and the yearning that went through his veins like a sickness.

Part of him longed to believe that Arina, William, Willna and the children could not be the only ones to accept him, the only ones who would reach out to him. Surely others would also look past his deformity.

Daemon shook his head, bitterness swirling in his gullet. Acceptance; it was only a dream. A vague, elusive phantom that stalked his heart and his thoughts; a phantom that would never survive one moment in the sun of reality.

A handful of kindness could not mend or prevent the lifetime of pain that came from constant rejection.

William was king and no one would dare mock him, but Arina and the children could easily meet Willna's fate. They would be abused and tormented for their kindness and he had no desire to see them hurt. Not when he could prevent it.

Despite the denial of his soul, Daemon knew what he must do. In a few hours, when dawn arose, he would summon Wace and make his way toward London. Once there, he would make certain William gave him his release. Then he would return to battle, to the one thing he knew, the one place where he could trust himself.

Wheeling his horse about, Daemon headed for the manor.

Out of nowhere, something streaked before his destrier. Ganille reared, kicking in fright and bucking as Daemon jerked the reins to avoid the unknown object. He struggled with his mount, but his horse refused his commands.

An unfamiliar stench filled Daemon's nostrils, choking him with its vile intensity. Ganille shot up the hill and again the streak appeared.

"Whoa!" Daemon shouted, pulling the reins.

Shrieking, the horse reared against the partially finished wall, pinning Daemon against the damp stone. He cursed as the rough masonry tore through his tunic. Pain engulfed him, but still he kept his seat.

Then suddenly, the reins broke from his hands and Daemon found himself on the ground beneath the thrashing hooves. Instinctively, he put his arm up to shield his face. Sharp hooves struck the bone of his forearm, numbing the full length of his arm until he could scarce lift it.

Lowering his head, Daemon tried to get away, but Ganille followed, kicking and bucking. A thousand pains racked his body from each and every strike of the hooves. Barely able to breathe, he finally succeeded in pulling himself away from the frightened horse. Daemon lay to the side of the wall, his body aching more than it ever had before.

Dampness covered his right temple and cheek. Without checking, he knew it for blood. Aye, the salty taste invaded his mouth, choking him with its thickness.

He must return to the manor before his consciousness left him. Attempting to rise, he stumbled and fell to his knees.

Daemon drew a ragged, pain-filled breath. He would never make it back in this condition.

Out of the hazy corner of his gaze, he saw a white wolf approach. His body burning with agony, he pushed himself up and stumbled toward his horse. Daemon tried to reach his sword, but Ganille bolted at his approach.

Too tired to resist, he fell to the ground and waited patiently for the wolf to end his useless life. At least Arina would be spared his presence and the mockery of his people. Mayhap it would be best for him to expire this way.

Belial snapped at his fallen victim. What luck to find Daemon out riding while he traveled in demon form!

"Thank you, Lucifer!" he said, but his voice came out as the feral snarl of a wolf.

Even so, he noted the lack of fear in Daemon's eyes, the bland acceptance of his fate. Belial approached him, snarling and snapping.

With a curse Daemon hurled a stone, but it

missed by a wide margin. The warrior collapsed against the wall, his breathing labored.

Belial approached him until he stood less than a full arm's length from Daemon, and still bravery shone deep in the man's eyes. Pulling back, Belial stared in amazement. What would it take to break this human's spirit?

Never before had he encountered such an opponent. Indeed, he almost felt guilty for pursuing so noble a man. But then, he'd never been one for guilt. Nay, the Norman was his price out of Hell. Once he gave Arina to his master, his soul would again be his own and nothing, especially not such a petty emotion as respect, would keep him from that one precious moment.

Come morning, sweet Arina would discover her husband, and for once, Daemon would have no escape. Now he would be forced to endure her attentions and the full force of his lust.

Belial howled in delight. Lucifer willing, his servitude would soon be over.

Arina came awake with a start. Her body trembled and shook until she could scarce draw a breath. A haunting howl echoed in her ears from some faraway beast that stalked the night. A beast she feared might somehow stalk her dreams. Her heart beat fiercely in her chest.

A sudden image pierced her mind and she recoiled in horror. Even now, she could sense

Daemon's pain, hear his short, raspy breaths as he struggled for consciousness. He was hurt, she knew it. She didn't know how, yet she couldn't deny the part of her that heard him call her name, the part of him that reached out like a desperate soul.

Throwing back the covers, she bolted from the bed. In seconds, she donned her clothes and rushed into the hall seeking Wace where he slept against the far wall.

"Wace," she whispered as she shook him gently awake.

He yawned widely before opening his eyes to stare at her in disbelief. "Milady?"

"Aye," she said, pulling his blanket from him. She glanced to the other people sleeping nearby and reminded herself to keep her tone low. "We must hurry."

"Hurry?"

"Aye," she repeated, trying to stifle the agitation in her voice. "Your lord needs you!"

He glanced about the hall like a drunkard seeking his ale. "Is he here?"

"Nay," she said, and handed him his tunic and breeches. Despite the part of her that wanted to shake him for his questions and delay, she forced herself to patience. "Come, you must help me go to him."

Frowning, he stifled another yawn as he shrugged on his tunic over his wrinkled linen under-tunic. "What do you mean, go to him?"

148

Angered over his reluctance, Arina gathered his shoes from the floor and urged him to take them. "He is injured and we must find him before more harm befalls him."

"He's injured?" Wace asked, immediately alert as he tied his breeches. He grabbed his boots and donned them. "Where is he?"

"The castle ramparts," she said instantly, then froze, her eyes widening. How did she know that? And yet she was most certain she would find him there.

Wace paused in jerking the leather boots on and stared up at her as if he doubted her sanity. "What do you mean he's—"

"Enough questions! We must hurry."

Though she could barely see his face in the dark shadows, Arina had the distinct feeling he wanted to argue further, but he held his tongue and soon they were headed across the yard, and into the stable. Without a word, he began saddling their horses.

Once he finished, Arina started to mount, but his hand on her arm stopped her. " 'Tis unsafe, milady. Many outlaws and rebels travel by night. I think I should awaken—"

"Nay, Wace. We shall be fine. I know it."

He bit his lip, and for a moment she feared he would gainsay her plea. "All right, milady, but if harm should befall you, Lord Daemon will feed my hide to the dogs," he said, helping her mount.

"Lord Daemon will be too grateful for your help to be overly harsh."

He shook his head and she saw the doubt on his face. Even so, he mounted his own horse, mumbling under his breath, and they were off.

Arina clung to her saddle and tried to ignore the cold wind that whipped against her cheeks and settled in her bones, where it chilled her very soul.

Daemon had to be all right; she couldn't stand the thought of finding him otherwise. Nay, he had to be fine. The images of wolves were just the devil's playthings of her mind. And yet she could feel a wolf's warm breath on her neck, smell its putrid scent as if it stood over her even now.

Her stomach knotted in fear. It must be an image created by her frightened mind, not the reality Daemon faced. He would be safe. He must be!

Eternity seemed to have passed before they topped the hill where the castle's half-finished walls stood. Anxious and frightened, Arina scanned the area for any trace of her husband, but only the vacant, isolated stones greeted her eager gaze.

"No one is here, milady," Wace said, urging his horse closer to her.

"Nay, I know. . . ." Arina paused, listening carefully.

Once more she heard the soft groan. "Over

there!" she said, leaping from her horse and running toward the sound. Rounding the stone wall, she hesitated.

Hot and cold battled each other for a place in her stomach as she saw her husband. Her head light from panic, she bit her lip to block the tears that threatened to fall. Then she ran to him.

Daemon lay on his side, facing the woods. Even in the darkness, she could see the blood that soaked his clothing, feel his pain as if it pounded through her own body. Arina choked on a sob.

"Daemon?" she cried, kneeling beside him. But he made no move, no further sound.

Was she too late? Her heart pounded in fear and she pulled him onto his back. His eyes were half-open and his chest was so very still. Terrified, she wiped the blood off his icy cheeks. "Milord, please!" she begged, her throat so tight she could scarce draw a breath.

"Arina?" he whispered in such a low tone she barely heard him.

Relief shot through her. She drew a deep breath and, grateful for his life, gave a small nervous laugh. "Aye, milord. I am here."

Wace knelt beside her, his face grim. "We shall need a litter or cart to move him."

Arina nodded, her stomach knotting over her worry. She had known Daemon would be hurt, but never once had she considered that *he*, her fierce, untouchable warrior, would need assistance to return. "I'll wait here while you go for help."

"But milady . . ."

"I shall be fine until your return," she insisted. As Wace opened his mouth, Arina shook her head to silence him. "Please, no more arguments. You must hurry. I know not how much longer he can last."

Reluctance shone deep in his eyes, but Wace said nothing more.

As he mounted and rode away, she tore strips of cloth from her smock, her hands trembling from fright and uncertainty.

Arina staunched the flow of blood as best she could, but she feared her efforts wouldn't be enough. With each frantic beating of her heart, it seemed his breath came shallower and shallower.

"You should have gone in his place," Daemon whispered.

Pain gripped her chest at his strained voice. "You shouldn't speak," she said, gently brushing his hair from his cheek. "You must save your strength."

He reached his hand up to take hers, his grip so weak it brought tears to her eyes. He placed her hand over his heart, and she felt the soft, feather-like beating beneath her fist.

Warm, sticky blood clung to her skin, but she refused to draw her hand away despite the panic inside her that urged her to run, to leave his pain and suffering, suffering that penetrated her body and made her feel it as if 'twere her own.

Nay, she must be strong for him. No matter how great her fear, she must give him her own strength.

He swallowed and jerked her hand as if a wave of pain shot through him. How he could sustain the number of injuries he had and not cry out, she couldn't fathom. Indeed, she wanted to cry for him, but she knew he wouldn't welcome her tears and that alone kept her eyes dry.

She wanted desperately to know what had happened, yet she knew better than to ask. He needed his rest far more than she needed her answers.

"Would you sing for me, milady?"

A painful lump closed her throat at his quiet request. Knowing she could never deny him, she searched her mind for a soothing song. At last a tune came to her, one whose origins she couldn't name but whose melody had seemed to haunt her much of late.

Drawing a deep breath, she squeezed his hand and began, "I feast off joy and youth, and joy and youth do sate me, for my love is most joyful and that is why I am pleasant and gay."

With her free hand, she stroked his pale, cool cheek and traced the stubble lining his jaw.

"And since I am sincere to him, it is right for him to be the same for me. For I have never renounced my love, and could not find it in me to leave him."

He stiffened at her words, but said nothing as she continued. "I am greatly pleased that he is most valiant. I most want him to have me as his own, and I pray to God for him to bring great joy to the one who first brought it to me, and that He would not believe anyone who speaks ill of him if it is something which I do not reproach him for. For very often people pick themselves the rods they hit themselves with."

"Milady?"

She looked down at his pained face. "Aye, milord?"

"Please, no more song."

Arina almost laughed at the underlying tone in his voice, but the pain in his gaze kept her from it. Daemon closed his eyes, and panic gripped her heart. "Milord?" she asked, her voice trembling.

He opened his eyes and looked at her.

Arina drew a deep breath. "I thought you—"

"I shall live through this, milady," he mumbled, giving her hand a tight, reassuring squeeze. "The injuries are not as bad as the blood makes it appear."

She returned his squeeze, praying he was right. "I shall hold you to that, milord, and if you speak falsely, I shall never forgive you."

154

The intense look in his eyes made her tremble.

You must watch him die!

Arina flinched at the raw, angry voice filling her head. Chills spread across her body and she tried to grasp the fleeting memory. Yet it vanished into the depths of her mind like an errant child fleeing at its parent's approach.

She must remember! But for her life, she could not.

"Arina?"

Her thoughts scattered at his weak call. "Aye?"

"I know not what . . ." His voice broke as he grimaced against his pain. He cleared his throat and gripped her hand. "I know not why you are here, but I am glad you came."

Holding him tightly, she smiled, her throat tight with joy and fear. As she started to respond, she heard Wace call out his approach.

A large cart rumbled up the hill, and several men jumped down. Though she recognized them as Normans and therefore Daemon's men, none appeared overly concerned about their lord's health. Indeed, their faces betrayed nothing but deep aggravation.

Reluctantly, Arina released Daemon to their hands, and watched with nervous anxiety as they lifted him onto the cart, where she quickly joined him. As soon as she was settled, the driver called to the horses, and the cart jerked in the direction of the manor.

She tried to cushion Daemon's injuries with the leftover hay that lined the cart's floor, and he rewarded her with a tight smile, a smile that meant more to her than any amount of gold. Yet even as relief settled in her heart and she realized he would live through this, a chill crept up her spine.

For the first time since she had met him, a part of her urged her away from his side. She didn't know where the foreboding came from, yet she couldn't seem to banish it.

Deep inside her heart, she heard a tiny voice instructing her to run as far away from Daemon as she possibly could.

"I must be mad," she whispered, grateful Daemon hadn't heard the words. "I belong with him."

But even as the words faded into the rumbling sound of the wheels, a part of her she couldn't name called her a liar.

Chapter Eight

Fog drifted over Daemon, stifling him with its damp, oppressive heat. He pushed against the thick fog, but cold hands took his, preventing him from escaping the cloying thickness. Voices whispered around him with words he couldn't understand.

"Sh, milord," a gentle voice echoed as someone lifted his head from his pillow and held a cool goblet to his lips. "Drink this."

His blurry vision scanned the murky shadow who spoke, but no matter how much he tried, he couldn't bring the person into focus. He drank the warm cider.

"Fetch me the broth."

His vision cleared enough for him to see Arina holding his head, her brow puckered into a frown. When she looked back at him, her face smoothed and she gave him a tender smile.

Suddenly, all went black and Daemon heard fierce voices that soon faded and left him in peace.

For days he lay in partial awareness, his mind drifting between brutal dreams of his past, dreams that vanished when he heard one soft voice that spoke or sang to him. Dreams that scattered as soon as Arina touched his flesh.

No matter when he awoke, he always found her nearby. Never in all his life had anyone so cared for him, nor stood by his side.

"Daemon?"

Gentle hands stroked his cheek with a warm softness he could scarcely comprehend. Opening his eyes, Daemon stared up into the tender blue gaze of his wife. He swallowed at the thought. His wife, his mind repeated, and for once the title didn't fill him with fear. Nay, it was more like a caress, a haven that he was longing to try.

A slow smile spread across her lips and her eyes softened even more, bringing a raging fire to his loins. Though a thousand aches pounded his body, not even they could detract from the need her nearness provoked.

"Good evening, milord," she whispered, rising from his bed with a gentle grace that intensified the ache in his loins.

Daemon reached for her arm. He didn't want her to leave. Not after the hellish nightmares that had tormented him. Nightmares he knew would continue should he choose to abandon the only person who truly cared for him. Emptiness consumed him, filling him with such pain that it nearly blinded him.

Without her, he had nothing, was indeed nothing. She alone gave him life, and in her touch he found a reason to look forward to the morrow. Arina was his, and everyone would be damned before he would put her aside.

A frown lined her brow as she covered his hand with her own. "Daemon, please, your grip is too tight."

Regretting that he had caused her pain, he released her arm. He opened his mouth to speak, but only a hoarse croak left the dryness of his throat.

She poured a cup of wine and brought it to him. He stared at her graceful movements and despite the agony pounding through his body, he wanted to claim full husbandly rights.

A brief image of people taunting her came to his mind, but he banished it. Never again would he let that fear govern his mind, his life. He'd crack the bones of the first person to ever bring the blush of shame to her cheeks. And if he must kill every person in Brunneswald valley to keep her safe, then by hell he'd gladly do it.

She helped him up and tilted the cup to his

lips. Daemon drank deeply of the warm, spicy wine, and though it sated his thirst, it did nothing to appease the hunger in his loins.

No sooner had she removed the cup from his lips, than he grabbed her and pulled her close. He tasted the sweet nectar of her lips, and breathed in the rich, heady scent of her rose bath oil. She stiffened for only a moment before she submitted to his embrace. Delight shot through him. She'd never deny him. Not his precious Arina.

After a moment, she pulled away and gave a short laugh. "Milord, you must be careful lest you pull the stitches from your side."

Daemon followed her gaze to his bare ribs and on his left side, he saw the neat even stitches that closed a wound. The thought of Eve being created from Adam's rib came to his mind, and he grimaced. Though he was every bit as cursed as Adam, he could only hope that his mate would never be forced to bear the brunt of his own sin.

Mayhap he should leave her after all. But as soon as he looked up at her, the thought scattered. Nay, never again. He was through entertaining such thoughts.

"How long have I slept?" he asked, his voice still far from its usual tone.

"A sennight."

He frowned. "A sennight?"

"Aye," she said, bringing a wooden platter of

food to him. "You have raged with a fever since we returned you."

And she had stayed with him the entire time. Of that he was certain. Indeed, her wrinkled kirtle, unkept hair, and the deep circles beneath her eyes told him much of how little she had left his side. Even so, she was the most beautiful woman he had ever seen; Her rumpled garments more regal to him than all the Queen's finery.

His heart warming at the thought, Daemon took a slice of cheese from the platter and carefully ate the sharp cheddar. His head pounded needles of pain that darkened his sight, and as he wiped at his damp forehead, he noted the healing wounds there as well.

"How are you feeling?" Arina asked, refilling his cup.

He took the cup from her grasp and glanced up at her, marveling at her beauty and the fact that she had come to him when he had needed her most. "Like my horse trampled upon me."

Her sweet laugh rang in his ears. "I do believe the correct way of riding is on the horse's back, not under his belly."

Her eyes twinkled as she sat next to him. Once more desire coiled through his stomach, demanding he heed another need that she alone could answer. But even as the thought emerged, his aching body refused to cooperate. For now just being with her was enough.

"Care to tell me what happened?" she asked.

Daemon swallowed his food, his mind focusing on the night before. He remembered the streak and the wolf, but everything else was jumbled. "Something frightened my steed and he threw me."

She cocked a finely arched brow. "Threw *you*, milord?"

Her teasing voice lightened his heart and he rubbed his hand over her arm, delighting in the feel of her soft dress, a dress that hid even softer skin that he longed to sample with his lips. "Aye, milady. And I'm most shamed to admit 'twas not the first time I have fallen from the saddle."

She tilted her head, her demure smile lighting coals in his belly. "But surely the first time since your childhood?"

Her light mood was infectious and he reached out to finger her cheek. "Most certainly."

She laughed and touched his hand, sending another wave of heat through him. Arina glanced to his forehead and her smile faded.

"Milady?" he asked, concerned over the sudden absence of her mirth.

A smile returned to her lips, but its hollowness did nothing to alleviate his worry. She shook her head and pulled his hand from her cheek. " 'Tis nothing, milord. Just a thought."

He set his food aside and took her cold, trembling hand in both of his. "And what is your thought?"

She moved away from him and wrung her hands at her waist. Standing before the open window, she looked out into the dark yard. The confusion and pain on her face brought an ache to his own chest. Daemon longed for a way to soothe her, but was uncertain what to do.

Her silence rang in his ears, stilling his heart until he was certain she wouldn't answer. Had she already been mocked by his people? Did she regret ever having signed the agreement for their union? A hundred such thoughts poured through him and he waited patiently for her response.

At last she drew a deep breath, but still refused to face him. "Before you awoke, you spoke of demons and . . ." She paused, her frown darkening. Shaking her head, she drew another deep breath. "Well, 'tis naught save foolishness."

"What is foolish?" he asked, his dream playing fresh in his own mind.

Arina turned to face him, her light eyes troubled and sad. She took a step forward and stood at the foot of his bed. "Last night when I found you, I heard a voice whisper that I must watch you die."

A chill crept along his spine, bringing a frown to his face. "Watch me die?" he asked, disbelief filling him.

Arina bit her lip and again wrung her hands. Her distress reached out to him and he longed to soothe her fear. "Well, maybe not you," she said, her voice barely more than a whisper. "But it said 'watch him die.' The voice sounded so evil, so cold, that I wondered if it might be the devil himself whispering it to me."

Daemon held his hand out to her, his chest tight. It warmed him that she fretted so for his safety, but he had a difficult time believing in her words. "Milady, come to me."

She walked forward and took his hand, her own like ice inside his palm. He held her shaking fingers and softened his gaze. " 'Twas nothing more than your fear speaking. There are no demons who stalk the earth seeking victims. Our greatest enemy is ourselves. You said it yourself while you sang your song. People often choose the rod that beats them."

Her gaze lightened and a smile curved her lips. "I told you 'twas foolish."

"There is nothing about you foolish," he said, pulling her into his arms and holding her against his chest. He stroked her hair and delighted in each silken strand caressing his palm. "You were worried. 'Tis more than understandable and more than appreciated."

Arina nodded, but inside, she found it hard to believe him. No matter how many times she had told herself the words meant nothing, a tiny voice in her heart kept reminding her of them and telling her to listen well. That same voice urged her to run, yet for her life, she couldn't.

She wanted to stay with her lord, bear his children and grow old by his side, letting him hold her on long cold nights such as this. His warm breath fell against her cheek, his muscled chest strong against her side. Aye, this was what she wanted, all she would ever want. And should she leave, she knew she'd never again feel safe or happy.

Even now, nothing would give her greater joy than to have him take her in his arms and claim her as his own. If he would just consummate their union, then her fears would ease. Or if he would just utter one word of promise that he intended to stay by her side and live with her as man and wife.

Was that so much to ask?

He leaned his head back into his pillows and tensed as if another wave of pain cut through him. Guilty that she clung to him when he needed his rest, Arina rose and retrieved his platter from the floor. Placing it on the table, she felt his gaze upon her like a tender touch that caressed her heart.

She turned around to see his gentle eyes and the adoration that shone brightly in his unique gaze. At this moment, she wondered how she could ever fear he might not want her, and yet his words about leaving echoed in her mind like a quiet thief sent to steal her safety, her happiness. She offered him a smile, but couldn't quite shake her fears.

"Arina?" he asked, his voice drawing her toward him against the voice inside her that warned her to keep a goodly distance between them.

But he was her husband and she could never deny him. And the pain in her chest that battled her incessant, warning whisper told her that she didn't want to deny him. Nay, she would always do whatever he asked of her.

Arina crossed the room to stand beside him. He pulled her down to the bed and back into his arms. The platter fell against the floor with a loud clatter. Ignoring it, she smiled, a wave of happiness rushing through her.

Daemon might not say he wanted her, but his actions spoke loudly enough. She lay her head on his chest, careful not to tug any of the stitches, and closed her eyes. His heart thumped beneath her cheek, delighting her with its healthy song.

As she lay there in soothing silence, it surprised her that he didn't try to leave and take his bed elsewhere as he had done since their marriage. Though his wounds must surely plague him, they were not so severe that he could not leave should he choose to do so. Indeed, his current wounds were slight compared to the deep, horrifying scars that lined his back and wrists. Scars that had stolen her breath when she had first seen them last night.

"Milord?" she whispered.

"Aye?" he asked, his stomach tightening under her jaw.

"Where did you go last evening?"

He stroked her hair, his hand pausing for a moment on her cheek as he played with stray strands that tingled against her face. "I needed time to think, time to plan."

She sensed his sadness almost as much as if it beat inside her own heart. "And what were you planning?"

When he didn't speak, she looked up at him. By the sadness hovering in his eyes, she knew exactly what he'd been planning. And that thought tore through her with waves of resounding pain that crashed against her heart until she feared they would tear her heart asunder.

Emptiness filled her and she tried to imagine living without him, but all she could see were years of misery stretching out before her. Years of longing for someone who refused to stay with her, his wife. "When are you leaving?"

He stiffened, and before he could answer, a knock sounded on the door. Her chest tight and limbs heavy with defeated sadness, Arina moved to answer it.

Wace held a small bowl of steaming water, his eyes lighting as he noted his lord's improved condition. But as he entered the room, foreboding replaced the happiness in his gaze. Arina offered him an encouraging smile, but still fear shone deep in his brown eyes.

"I brought you fresh water to tend milord's wounds," Wace said, placing the bowl next to the platter on the table before the fire.

He approached the bed with a reluctance that brought an ache to Arina's chest. She gave a quick squeeze on his right shoulder to offer him courage, and nodded her head for him to speak.

Even though Wace kept his spine straight, she could feel the tremors that shook him. Had she known last night the terror she would cause poor Wace, she would never have sought his aid.

The youth cleared his throat and bravely lifted his chin as if he faced the worst horror imaginable. "I didn't mean to leave milady unattended last eve, milord," he said quietly, his eyes downcast.

Though Daemon's face was stern, she saw the twinkle in his eyes. "Aye, she could have been harmed," Daemon said.

Wace gulped and nodded. "I know, milord."

Daemon met her gaze, and she took his chiding to heart. It was her fault, she knew. She only hoped Daemon would continue to hold gentle scolding in his gaze and not anything more sinister.

He looked back at his squire. "But then milady is rather impossible to argue against. I have a feeling had you not returned as she asked, the three asked, the three of us would still be up on that hill trying to decide who should go and who should stay."

A smile broke across Wace's lips. "Then you are not angry?"

Daemon shook his head. "Nay, I owe you my life. How could I fault such noble actions?"

The joy in Wace's eyes brought an ache to her chest.

"But," Daemon said, and immediately Wace's face sobered, "in the future I would have you seek others when dealing with milady's requests. Though you should always obey her, I would not have her harmed, no matter what argument she may broach. I trust her safety to you, and I would be much sorrowed to have that bond of trust broken."

"Aye, milord," Wace whispered, and guilt gnawed at Arina that she had caused his chastisement.

She wanted to say something to ease the sting of Daemon's words, but any argument she gave would undermine his authority. Pressing her lips together, she forced herself to silence.

"May I take my leave, milord?" Wace asked.

Daemon nodded.

Bowing to them, Wace made his exit, and as he left, she noticed the lightness of his step. Arina shook her head and smiled. Well, maybe the chastisement hadn't been so terribly bad after all. Indeed, often the dread of an encounter was far worse than the actual experience.

She turned back to face Daemon, and saw the paleness of his cheeks. A moment of fear whispered through her body, but she squelched it. He was merely tired and needed his rest. The voice she'd heard last night meant nothing. His wounds would not cause his death. He was safe, and in little time he would heal.

Aye, he would heal, she repeated, pain tightening her chest. And once healed he would be on his way.

Desperately, Arina longed to repeat her question of when he intended to leave, but she didn't want to further tax his strength. Nay, he needed his sleep. Soon enough, she would learn when he intended to depart his lands and her presence.

For now she had her husband at home, and though she wished for an eternity spent with him, she would take the time they had and be grateful for it.

As she moved to retrieve the platter from the floor, he looked up, his gaze burning deeply into her soul. "I would have you join me," he said, his voice as ragged as the wound in her heart that feared their limited time.

Arina nodded, her throat too tight for her to speak. Leaning the platter against the wall, she doused the candle, removed her kirtle and joined him in the bed.

He wrapped his strong arms about her, drawing her closer to his warm, fevered body. She trembled at the foreign sensation of his heat against her bare flesh. Not since the night he'd taken her innocence had he held her in such a manner, and she found the reality far better than her weak memory.

Indeed, she burned from the desire his touch wrought. She longed to roll over onto her back and bring his body back into hers, to ease the throbbing ache inside her. Her stomach pitched and tightened from the weight of her desire, but she reminded herself that she must remain still. His wounds were far too fresh for him to carry out her fondest desire.

That is if he even wanted to.

Her heart hung heavy at the thought. What if he didn't care for her? Could that be why he had ignored her these past days? Too often men fell to their desire only to regret their actions in the full light of day. And yet she couldn't quite believe that.

Daemon had been nothing save kind since the moment they had met, since the moment they had signed their marriage document that bound them together.

"Milady?"

She tensed at his voice that sliced through her thoughts. "Aye?"

"Why do you weep?"

Arina licked her lips, tasting the salt that stained her face. She wiped at her eyes, amazed by the wetness. When had her tears started?

The moment she'd realized Daemon intended to leave. The moment she'd realized that all her dreams were nothing more than fantasies that could never be hers.

"I am merely happy that milord is well," she whispered, unwilling to tell him the truth. Nay, she would not beg him to stay. His life had been hard enough without her adding any more guilt or pain to it.

He rolled her onto her back and kissed away the dampness. "I would never have milady shed a single tear on my behalf," he whispered, his voice bringing a flood of bittersweet joy to her breast. "I would never cause you pain."

His lips covered hers and she reveled at the taste of warrior, the taste of wine on his tongue. Chills shot the length of her body and she prayed for a piece of him before he left. If she could have one wish it would be to take his seed inside her and carry his child. To give that one precious child all the love he had been denied.

He slid his body against hers and she moaned from the pleasure. It seemed like an eternity since he had held her. She ran her hand through his unbound hair, the silken strands lacing through her fingers in a wicked rhythm.

He nipped at her throat with his teeth and pulled back with a groan. "Would that my body belonged to me this night," he said with a wistful sigh.

She smiled at his words, but still the ache pounded inside her heart. "There is always the morrow, milord," she said, hoping for her own sake that she was indeed right.

Chapter Nine

A fortnight passed and Arina marveled at the quick recovery Daemon made. But each day was mixed joy and sadness, for every day he recovered brought him one day closer to leaving her. And though she knew his absence would tear her apart, a part of her rejoiced.

If he were gone, then mayhap the voice inside her heart that forewarned her of his death would cease.

Belial had also been strangely silent and absent. Pleading illness, he had seldom come near her. Now she sat outside in the small garden, mending a tear in one of Daemon's tunics.

Even though she would much prefer being with her husband and listening to his rich voice rather than the rustling leaves that surrounded her, she took a measure of happiness from the fact that he had healed so quickly. And after all, he had given her several days to coddle him. It was only two days ago that he had started pleading with her to allow him to be about, and at last she had judged him well enough. Provided he didn't stress himself overmuch.

"Aye, it sounds like an omen."

Arina frowned at Brother Edred's voice drifting through the shrubbery. She started to call out and let him know of her presence when his next words froze her voice.

"The Norman is the devil's own without a doubt. Since first I saw him, I have wondered at his strangely colored, long hair. Never before have I witnessed a Norman wearing his hair long. I wonder at what marks he seeks to conceal."

"The beast's mark, I'd wager," Norbert sneered with a hostile venom that sent a wave of anger through her.

Their voices faded for a moment; then the friar spoke once more. "I too have seen visions of hell where the very demons bowed down before him."

"But what of the lady?"

She stiffened at Norbert's question.

"Like blessed Mary Magdalene, her heart is pure, but she follows the corrupt path of the flesh. I fear his good looks have blinded her to his true form, or mayhap he has enchanted her pure soul. She will not see her husband's evilness."

Evilness, indeed! Arina threw the tunic aside, rage burning raw in her throat. What could be more evil than a gossiping tongue, especially when that tongue belonged to one who should heed the Lord's words about bearing false witness? Clenching her fists, she intended to give Brother Edred a sermon he would not soon forget.

"Arina!"

Before she could take another step, Daemon rounded the corner of the pathway and headed toward her. Her anger melted at the joy in his eyes. A blush stained his cheeks and he was still breathing heavy from his ride.

"Milord," she said, trying to sound stern, but failing. No matter how much she might want to castigate him, his obvious happiness prevented her from saying anything that might dampen his mood. "You should not tax your strength."

He came to rest by her side and seized her hands in his, bringing them to his lips where he kissed first her right, then her left. Chills spread over her body at the gesture and the warmth of his touch against her flesh.

He offered her a hesitant smile and all thoughts of chastisement vanished. "Aye, I know I promised, but I couldn't wait to return."

She cocked a playful brow, but couldn't prevent one corner of her mouth from lifting in humor. "Well, you seemed eager enough to leave me this morn."

His gaze turned serious and he tightened his grip on her hands. "I apologize for that, but I had business most pressing."

Her humor faded beneath the sudden turn of his own mood and trepidation flooded her breast. What business had pressed him to leave her side so early? Did he plan to leave so soon? Her heart stilled at the thought. Had he been making final plans with the masons before he took his leave?

She swallowed against the stinging lump in her throat. Was this the good-bye she had dreaded, nay feared, for so long? "Business most pressing?" she asked, her voice cracking from the weight of her fear and pain.

"Aye," he said, his eyes once more bright and gay. "While you were tending me yestereve, I realized I had forgotten to take care of something."

She frowned in confusion. Had his fever and delusions returned? "Which is?"

Out of the pouch dangling from his girdle, he pulled a small wooden box and handed it to her. Arina stared in amazement at the silver inlaid box. He must have traveled as far as the town, eight leagues away, to purchase it. But why would he make such a journey?

"Open it," he urged.

She flipped the catch with her thumbnail and opened the box. A startled gasp left her lips and joy beat deep inside her. Nestled in a bed of fine linen lay a gold ring encrusted with tiny, sparkling emeralds.

Tears filled her eyes as she looked from her small treasure, to her much larger one. "A pledge ring?" she asked, her voice tight and hoarse.

He nodded, his gaze warm and loving. "I realized last eve that you were without one and I would not have anyone doubt you are mine."

Arina pressed her trembling lips together and pulled the ring from its container. The jewels winked at her as if they knew some jest that had escaped her notice. Never had she expected such a gift, and she shook from the weight of her excited anticipation.

Could it be that she and Daemon might have a life together after all? Dare she even hope for it? Yet why else would he give her such a present?

Daemon took the ring from her shaking fingers, kissed it, then placed the ring on her right thumb. He looked up at her, a small, timid smile on his lips. "Like your presence in my life, it fits."

She closed her eyes, savoring his words that brought a smile to her lips and joy to her heart. But still the doubt lingered beneath her happiness, quelling it until she could stand no more.

Despite the part of her that begged for her silence, she opened her eyes and spoke the question she most needed answered. "Does this mean you intend to stay?"

He looked away from her and she tensed, afraid to hear his response. For several terrifying minutes he stared at the small postern gate surrounded by vines. Emotions crossed his features and she struggled to name them, but they passed so quickly she dared not try.

His grip tightened on her arms and he sighed. "Aye, milady. I intend to stay."

Crying out in relief, she threw her arms about his shoulders and held him tightly. The strength of his chest against hers stole her breath and caused her heart to pound. He wrapped his arms around her, holding her close, and she gave a small prayer of thanks that at last she had won her war.

Suddenly, his lips claimed hers.

Arina opened her mouth, drawing him into her so that she could taste him fully. His rich, masculine scent filled her head and she trembled. Aye, this was what she wanted. All she would ever want.

Her body burned for his touch and she ran her hands over his back, delighting in the dips and curves of his muscles. He entwined his hand in her hair and cupped the nape of her neck, tingling her scalp. Moaning against his lips, she throbbed for him.

180

The very next thing she knew, Daemon swung her up in his arms and carried her into the manor and to their chambers. With a gentleness she could barely fathom, he laid her against the bed. Arina trembled at the force of her desire. At last she would have her fondest wish.

Daemon stared at her like a starving man eyeing a king's feast. The raw hunger in his eyes sent waves of throbbing heat through her. She wanted him to devour her and she longed to taste the rich, salty ripples of his muscles until she'd had her fill. But part of her heart told her that she would never be sated with him. Nay, she would always want him, always yearn for his touch.

Licking her lips, she offered him a hesitant smile. "Come, milord Norman," she whispered, pulling him back into her arms. "I have waited for you."

Daemon closed his eyes at her words, savoring each and every syllable. Mayhap he was damning both of them to an eternity of rumors and hostility, but for his life he couldn't stop himself from seizing this one moment, this one woman. He needed her, and the only way he could let her go would be to cut his own heart from his chest.

Nay, he couldn't leave. If there was a God above, then this must be His way of making amends for all he had suffered. And if this was his reward, Daemon decided it had been worth each and every torment ever delivered, and he would gladly relive all of it for this one instant in time.

She wrapped her arms about him and he shivered from the tenderness. Lying next to her, he tasted her silken lips, her neck where he inhaled her divine, rose scent. His lips tingled from the saltiness of her skin and he drank of it deeply. This was the only nourishment he needed, the nourishment for which he had starved for the whole of his life.

Heated fire replaced the coldness in his heart. Every color and scent seemed amplified and more vibrant to him, as if he'd opened his eyes for the very first time; as if he had been reborn.

Her hesitant touches echoed through his soul, crashing through every barrier he had ever erected, and he lay there scared and trembling like a naked babe on the edge of a cliff. And just like that child, he wanted to cry out in fear and desperation. Never had he felt so exposed, so very vulnerable, and indeed he knew one word of rejection from her would destroy him.

She pulled his tunic from him, her hands eagerly exploring each dip and curve of his flesh. Daemon closed his eyes, his body burning.

"Do your wounds still plague you?" she whispered, running her fingers over the stitches in his side.

Daemon shook his head, his throat tight. In truth all his wounds both past and present seemed completely healed, and for his life he couldn't fathom the peace that invaded his heart. "All I feel is you, milady, and you could never bring me pain."

Arina's breath faltered at his words. She smiled, her body afire with her need for him. No man would ever mean so much, ever be such a part of her.

Her head reeled with the masculine scent of him, the gentle pressure of his strong hands roaming over her flesh. Everywhere he touched, hot chills ran the length her. Arina brushed her lips over the hard stubble of his neck, delighting in the salty taste of his skin. His throaty moan reverberated under her lips and thrilled her more than all the glorious mornings of the world.

"I need you," he whispered against her cheek.

Arina pulled him closer. "I will always be here for you."

She shivered as he pulled her kirtle from her and heat stole up her cheeks. Even though she had already given herself to him, embarrassment filled her heart. Before it had been dark, but in the full light of the day, she lay completely exposed, completely vulnerable to his gaze, his touch.

His eyes burned with an intensity that stole her breath as he moved again and took her lips.

Daemon savored the rich taste of her skin, the welcome of her mouth. Nibbling a path to her throat, he nipped at her tender flesh. Sharp, pulsing fires burned inside him. It seemed as if he had waited the whole of his life for this moment, as if the first time with her had never been.

Not a callow, untried youth, he still found himself shaking from expectation; nervous almost beyond endurance.

Her lips brushed the flesh just below his ear and he shook from the boiling desire that pitched inside him. "Come to me, milord," she whispered, her husky voice urging him further.

He separated her thighs.

Arina shivered in expectation as she reveled in the feel of him lying against the length of her. She held her breath, afraid he would yet change his mind and send her away. Or worse, that he would decide to leave. Nay, she could never let him go. She mustn't.

Daemon was her life, her breath.

His body heat reached out to her and she raised her hips to him. With a groan, he buried his face in her neck and slid inside her.

All of a sudden, a horrible, body-wrenching pain tore through her insides. It seemed as if she were being halved in two. Her stomach lurched and burned and Arina gasped from the agony.

"Arina?" Daemon asked, his voice sounding so far away that she longed to ask him where he had gone.

Yet her head spun as if *she* had fallen into a well or some other deep hole. Strange lights and images spiraled around her, stealing her breath. A hundred foreign voices spoke simultaneously, some accusing, some in pity. From somewhere, she heard weeping and lamentations. Her chest tight, she tried to focus her thoughts, but like a falling person, she couldn't find anything solid to grasp.

Suddenly, the images stopped. Brutal pain exploded inside her body, jerking her limbs, stilling her heart. Out of nowhere, her memories returned with rich, sharp clarity.

"Dearest saints!" she cried, shoving against Daemon.

His gaze confused, he held her against him. "Milady, what is it?"

Milady. The word hovered in her mind like a nightmare, an unbelievable terror that paralyzed her with fear.

"Nay." She wept, moving away from him to cover herself with the fur-lined blankets. She cowered against the edge of the bed, too horrified to think. "What have I done?"

Daemon looked at her as if she'd struck him, and he slowly moved from the bed and retrieved his breeches. The pain in his eyes told her that he thought her rejection was of him.

Wiping away her tears, Arina swallowed the painful knot in her throat and stiffened her spine against the terrible, unbelievable truth she must deliver to him.

" 'Tis not you, milord," she whispered.

She glanced up, but couldn't bring herself to face the misery that burned in his eyes. Arina stared down at her blanket, tightening it over her breasts.

Why? she wanted to scream. Why had this happened?

But no answer came, only more pain, more regret, more guilt. "I—I have damned us both."

A frown lined his brow as he moved around the bed to touch her and though he appeared calm, she could sense the roiling anger inside him. "How so?"

Arina closed her eyes in an effort to banish the warmth of his hand against her bare shoulder, the comfort he offered. Comfort she must shun. And shunning Daemon was the last thing she wanted to do. Nay, she needed him and that need was what would cause his damnation!

How was she to tell him? He'd never believe her words. In truth, she found it impossible to believe and she knew it for reality.

Belial had played her well. Aye, the demon had surely earned his place in hell for his treachery.

"Milady, what has caused you such distress?"

Her heart pounding against her breast, Arina considered several ways to broach the matter with him, but nothing seemed right. How could she tell him the truth? That both of them had been nothing more than the devil's pawns in a game they had no part in beginning. "You will think me mad."

He brushed her hair away from her shoulder. "I will never think that of you."

She shook her head, refusing his reassurance. She must maintain distance between them.

Demon grabbed her by the shoulder and forced her to look at him. "Tell me."

Arina bit her lip. Fury sizzled in his gaze, scorching her with its intensity. She wanted to cower from him, to run away and never let him know the truth. But how could she? She owed him an explanation.

His jaw twitched. "What vexes you, milady?"

In his eyes she saw his fear that she had rejected him, and his anger no longer seemed important to her. The anger was merely his cover to keep her from knowing how much he had been wounded by her rejection. Pain coiled inside her and she knew she couldn't allow him to think that, allow him to believe that she had spurned him when he was her very life.

Before she could think, the truth tumbled from her lips. "I am an angel."

Daemon narrowed his eyes. Of all the dreaded horrors that had echoed through his thoughts, not one of them could compare with her declaration. Disbelief filled him. "You're an angel, milady?"

She sighed and reached for him, but her hand

187

stopped just inches from his cheek. She lowered her arm to her side and cast her gaze to the floor. "I know you don't believe me, but I swear 'tis the truth. I am heaven born and now hell bound."

Daemon looked away, his heart strangely blank. It was as if his body didn't know how to react to her words and so decided to feel nothing. She was mad. The truth of it rang in his soul. Of all the women alive, he had finally found one who warmed his life, one who filled the emptiness of his heart and one who was obviously insane.

"I am not mad," she declared. "I know you don't believe me, but you must!"

He just stared at her. Not even the urge to curse came to him. Mayhap he had already died. Surely that alone could explain the strange serene defeat that echoed through his body, whispered through his soul.

He could fight any demon, save this one. With her mind gone, there was naught he could do.

Arina licked her lips and glanced about the room. Cecile bounded out from under the bed, and Daemon moved his foot to allow her access to her food. Arina followed Cecile's erratic path with her eyes, then looked back at him. "I can prove my words."

"Prove them?" he asked, his throat raw and tight. "Will you sprout wings or a halo?"

Anger shone in her eyes, firing his own. What

could have caused her delusions?

Infuriated at fate, he lashed out against the only thing he could—her. "I thought angels never felt anger, milady. The brothers always swore angels possessed infinite patience."

She stiffened her spine and raised her chin as if she faced an army. "In my true form I do. However, I have lived too long in the guise of mortalness. 'Twould seem human emotions have corrupted me."

The fury wilted in her eyes and she rubbed her left shoulder with her right hand, her lips quivering.

"Not that it matters," she whispered, the pain in her voice reaching out to him, making him feel like the lowest of all forms. He longed to soothe her, but would she even be aware of his comfort in her deranged state?

"I am surely damned for what I have done," she whispered, her words searing him.

A bitter snarl curled his lips and all his pity shattered. There it was, his worst fear spoken aloud. The rumors and mockery had finally robbed him of the one thing he had foolishly thought would always be his—Arina's heart.

Rage blackened his sight and he longed to tear the tongues out of every head in Brunneswald valley.

So be it.

"Aye," he growled. "You are damned. You

have lain with the devil's bastard son. Is that not right, milady?"

Arina stared at him aghast. "Nay, I have lain with a man, no more, no less. And that alone is enough to jeopardize my soul."

He gave a bitter laugh, his anger and fury sizzling deep inside him. "Then I beg milady's forgiveness for corrupting her."

Innocence shone in her eyes, and for a moment he almost believed her incredulous claim. But he knew better. No God existed and without a God, there could be no angels.

"You did not corrupt me." Arina tried to pull Cecile to her, but the kitten refused her touch.

Daemon grabbed Arina's arm and hauled her upright until she faced him once more. He had to make her see reason. If he could force her to think through her claim, mayhap her mind would return. Aye, she was an intelligent woman. Surely she would see truth if he showed it to her. "And tell me of your brother, milady. Is he an angel as well?"

Shock poured over her face as if she'd forgotten her sibling. Her gaze widened and fear darkened her eyes. What caused that fear? The fact that he had found fault in her logic, or the possibility that in her madness she thought her brother every bit as heavenly born as she claimed to be.

"He is not my brother," she said at last, and Daemon found it hard not to shake her. He must maintain his patience.

"Then what is he?"

She opened her mouth to speak, then closed it.

"Tell me, milady," he insisted.

"You'll not believe me."

That he found easy to accept. But after her earlier words, how could she dare say that? "Could it be any more preposterous than your being an angel?"

She swallowed, her eyes fired by indignation. "Aye, to your understanding it is."

"To my understanding!" Now she dared question his powers of reasoning? At least he knew truth from fantasy.

Anger heated her gaze. "Aye, milord."

Daemon clenched his teeth, his entire body shaking from the weight of his anger. It had been a long, long time since anyone dared question his mind and he found her insult hard to take. "Most call me an intelligent man. Why don't you at least try my humble abilities? Who is your brother?"

She turned away from him, and once more he had to fight the urge to shake her. Why was she doing this? Was his touch so abhorrent that she must make up such tales to save herself from having to bear it?

Well, he certainly had no intention of staying with a woman who had no use for him. Nay, he had been denied before. Granted not quite so elaborately, but he knew when someone didn't want him and he refused to abase himself further.

"Very well, milady. You may stay here with your brother and have no more worries about my attentions. I in my earthly, bastard ways would never dare taint one as fair as you. You may rest in ease."

She gave him a sharp frown. "What do you mean?"

He narrowed his eyes and retrieved his tunic and shoes. With quick, angry jerks, he dressed himself. "I will not bother you further. You and your heavenly brother may take my lands. I don't give a damn what you do with them."

"You're leaving?" she asked, seizing his arm.

Her touch burned him even through the layer of rough material that separated his flesh from hers. The devil help him, he still wanted her, and he hated himself for that weakness. When would he learn not to lust after things that could never be his?

"You want me gone, is that not so, milady? Why else have you conceived your ludicrous tale?"

She shook her head and the pain in her eyes tore through him, but he steeled himself against it. He couldn't afford to fall victim to her, not again.

" 'Tis not ludicrous," she insisted. "I am an angel."

"And your brother?"

She swallowed, her grip tightening on his arm an instant before she spoke. "He is not a man, nor is he my brother. He is the demon, Belial."

Chapter Ten

Arina braced herself for his laughter. Even though he didn't so much as smile, she could tell Daemon struggled not to laugh at what he no doubt considered an absurd notion.

Trepidation filled her. Should she have even told him? Mayhap it would be best if he didn't believe. If Belial found out Daemon knew the truth, what would he do? Shivering at the myriad of possibilities, she reached for her kirtle and donned it.

Silence hung between them like a thick pall, choking the very breath from her lungs.

Daemon turned away from her and she slumped her shoulders in bitter defeat. To think she had been so worried about his leaving; as if physical and emotional distance were the worst things that could separate them.

Anguish squeezed her heart. What separated them was far more than just his brutal past, far more than what could be eased by a few tender words. They were two different beings from two different worlds. Nothing could ford the chasm between them.

Tears filled her eyes, but she refused to cry. Angels didn't cry. That was for humans.

Yet in spite of her divine status, she ached to touch Daemon and soothe some of the pain from him, but his rigid spine made him seem unreachable, formidable. For several minutes, he stared at the closed shutters and she felt so alone, so frightened of what was to become of both of them.

Too afraid to speak, Arina watched him.

Suddenly, he faced her, and once again anger darkened his gaze. "Then what am I, milady? Am I also a demon?"

She shook her head, her heart thumping heavily. "Nay, as I have already said, you are a man."

"Aye, a man," he whispered, drawing closer to her, so close she could smell his pain. Bitterness glowed deep in his eyes, forcing her to look away. "Just as you are woman and your brother is human."

For some reason, she needed him to believe her, to prove that he could believe in the illogical. If he could, maybe there was some way they could overcome their impossible situation. "Why do you refuse to believe my words?"

"Because they are those of a madwoman."

She reached for Cecile again, this time determined to make him believe. "Then allow me to show you."

"Aye," he said, taking her by the arm and pulling her away from the cat. "Let us find the truth. Surely your brother knows what he is. Let us ask him for the facts."

A tremor of fear went down Arina's spine. What would Belial say? As twisted as his mind was, she couldn't begin to contemplate what horrors he might brew.

Dare they give him even more power? If Daemon knew what Belial really was, then his fear would feed Belial's strength. Whatever she did, she must prevent that from happening.

Before she could protest his intent, Daemon pulled her out of their chambers and into the hall.

"Nay, milord!" she pleaded, but he refused her words. Instead, he hauled her through the yard and to the stable. She continued to struggle, yet he paid no heed.

They found Belial lying in a darkened corner atop a bale of hay. The horses had been turned out to roam the corral, but even so she could hear their displeasure at being so near the stench of hell. Wrinkling her nose in distaste, she wondered how humans could be immune to the pungent odor.

Belial rolled over, his features pale and pinched. Though uncertain how he had come to be in such a condition, Arina immediately realized he had overextended his powers. No sickness bothered him, but rather the demon's weakness.

He looked up at their approach, but made no move to rise.

Daemon pulled her to rest by his side and together they confronted the demon. "Greetings, Belial," he said, stressing the name.

Suddenly a cognitive light flickered in Belial's gaze and Arina knew he had deduced what had happened between her and Daemon. Her heart pounded in fear. Who knew what evil he would plot now.

Again she wished she had never confided in Daemon, and yet she couldn't banish the part of her that needed his belief, the tiny voice that gave her hope.

Some of the stress left Belial's face. "What brings my dear sister and brother-in-law seeking me this day?"

Daemon looked at her, his gaze strangely blank. "Do you wish me to ask?"

She clenched her teeth against a new surge of anger over Daemon's stubbornness. If only she could have kept him from seeking Belial. But it was too late. Now the demon knew the truth and she had no doubt that soon he would regain his strength. Heaven and the saints help them then.

"It matters not. He will only lie. Dishonesty is his nature, his nourishment."

"Arina," Belial chided. "Your words cut me deeply. I have never been dishonest with you."

"Nay," she said, her lip curling. The bitter taste of hatred scalded her throat and though she should never have felt it, she couldn't contain the evil emotion that contaminated her blood. "You made it clear what you wanted from the very beginning. And now having brought about my corruption, what do you intend to do?"

He frowned, a believable look of confusion on his face. "We have already taken care of that, have we not? I married you to your husband."

Daemon turned to face Belial, who watched them with an amused gleam in his eyes. "Milady has a notion that she is an angel and that *you* are a demon," Daemon said.

"A what?" Belial asked, then broke into laughter. "Do I look like a demon? Are my ears pointed? Have wings sprouted from my back?" Rising carefully from his bed, he turned around and presented his rear for their inspection. "Do you see a forked tail?"

He clucked his tongue and turned to face Daemon with a snide smile. "Only my worst enemies have called me demon. And as for her being an angel, can you not tell by her face that she could easily be one? Her beautiful face is such that any angel would weep in envy."

Daemon glanced at her. Arina tensed at the accusation and agony in his eyes. She started to contradict Belial, but held her tongue. The tiny voice in her mind warned her against speaking.

"Then you deny it?" Daemon asked Belial.

Belial shook his head as if scolding an errant child. "Dearest Arina, please tell me that you have not succumbed to madness. I thought your mind would be sound."

"There is naught amiss with my mind," she said in an angry whisper.

He shook his head and sighed, as if too weary to deal with her.

After a moment, he raked a cold finger down her cheek. One corner of his mouth turned up in an evil sneer that sent a shiver down her spine. "But surely you do not think yourself heavenly?"

Agony and rage reverberated through her. She lunged at Belial, but Daemon captured her about her waist and pulled her back. "Deceiver!" she shouted, struggling against Daemon's iron hold. "Nay, not heavenly anymore. You and your accomplice saw to that."

"I and my what?" he asked, his bewilderment feigned so well that even she almost believed it. "What evils are you accusing me of?"

"You know full well."

Daemon encircled her waist with his arms. "Rest easy," he said, his breath warming her cheek.

Arina's anger wilted and left her vulnerable to the feel of Daemon's body against her own. All the will to fight Belial vanished and she ceased her struggles before she reopened Daemon's wounds.

" 'Twould seem Belial knows naught of your claims, milady," he said, his arms tightening for an instant.

Belial sighed. "Aye, but I do."

Daemon released her, and Arina tensed in expectation of what lies or half-truths Belial would relate.

"Our mother suffered from such delusions. She once even claimed to be the Virgin Mother herself. Like Arina, she started simply at first. Her memories would fade, then she would make outrageous claims."

So he chose the path of lies. Arina frowned, wishing she could read Belial's mind, but that power belonged to neither angels nor demons. They could sense moods and at times see into the hearts of those around them, but the mind belonged to the individual until the individual sold that right.

Belial walked forward. He cupped her chin with his icy hand. He gave Daemon a sorrowful look. "I fear all we can do is confine her."

Daemon visibly tensed at his words. Rage

flickered deep in his eyes as he removed Belial's hand, and Arina gave a small prayer of gratitude that Daemon was still willing to defend her. "Nay, there shall be no confinement. Milady is no threat to anyone."

Belial feigned a look of shock that made Arina long to applaud his acting abilities. "But what of the dangers she may do to herself? Our mother killed herself during one of her fits."

Arina shook her head. "Should death befall me, 'twill be at your hands, not my own."

"Dearest," he cooed, his features patronizing. "You know I cannot harm you."

"Nay, you are forbidden to take life. But easily you can use your wiles and deceive another into following your commands."

He looked back at Daemon. "You see how she is. Soon she will turn against you and you shall be the demon who wants her dead."

"Nay!" Arina cried, afraid Daemon would believe the lies. She clutched at his tunic, his muscles contracting beneath her tight fists. "Do not listen to him. He is playing on your fears to turn you against me."

Daemon opened his mouth to speak, but a groom called to him from the stable's entrance. "Milord, there is a messenger come. He needs to speak with you."

Belial nodded toward the entrance. "Go on. I shall watch over my sister until your return."

Though she longed to keep Daemon close,

she released him. With a reluctant sigh, he left them alone.

Hesitantly, Arina turned to face Belial, her anger and fear pounding through her veins. "You are truly wicked."

He smiled an evil, mocking smile that would make Lucifer himself proud. "Of course I am. What else would you have me be?"

She shook her head and remembered a time when he had been something more. A time when Belial had been one of the most virtuous of all angels. Arina opened her mouth to appeal to that side of him, but she quickly stopped herself. Those days had long passed. He had aligned himself with the powers of darkness, and it would take much more than her or her arguments to convert him.

"Why not tell Daemon the truth?" she asked at last. If she were careful and clever, she might be able to discover a few of Belial's plans.

Though he was more intelligent than most, Belial loved to brag and play. Always looking for a new opportunity, he could often be led into traps that betrayed him. Indeed, it was that part of his personality that had led him to his downfall. "What good is it to continue this farce you have started?"

He laughed. "What good would come of the truth? You are mortal until your death. If he really found out what you are, he would cast you aside. Where would you go then?"

She cocked an eyebrow. What was he planning? "What do you care?"

He shrugged and if she didn't know better, she might believe his nonchalance. "Here or there, I still claim you, but why not enjoy yourself a little before you leave? After all, you are already damned."

Sudden realization dawned in her mind. Arina sucked her breath in sharply between her teeth. 'Twas more than Daemon's death Belial and his crone sought. "You plan to take his soul as well!"

He didn't speak, but the look in his eyes confirmed her suspicion.

"He has done nothing wrong."

Belial laughed, the evil sound scraping against her ears like the feral clawing of beasts against ravished bones. "He has done more to earn his damnation than I," he snarled, his voice echoing around her. "He has cursed God before all and before I am finished here, he will do far more than that."

"Nay!" she cried. Whatever she did, she must protect Daemon. Her own soul was trivial when compared to his. "I shall prevent it."

His eyes turned vibrant red. "Interfere with me and I will again steal your thoughts."

He stumbled against the stable wall. Some of her fear vanished and she stiffened her spine to confront him. "You are too weak. Indeed, your powers have faded to the point that I can wound your demon's flesh."

Anger heated his eyes. "Remember who shall be master over you when you leave this world, angel."

"You may claim my soul, but my heart shall always reside where you cannot touch it."

He pushed himself from the wall and approached her. He paused by her side, his stench overwhelming her.

"You may resist me, even in hell. But what of your *husband?* Remember, I shall have governance over him for eternity as well."

Daemon narrowed his gaze as he scanned the letter from William. His grip tight, he again read William's dispensation of Brunneswald lands and titles to him.

Why had he sent that last message to William, informing him of his desire to stay? What had he been thinking?

An image of Arina drifted through his mind, her arms open, her lips curled in a warm, welcoming smile. He had placed all his hopes at her feet, carelessly tossed his useless heart into her hands, and now he more than paid the price for such stupidity.

Aye, he had asked for the lands so that he could grow old by Arina's side. Daemon shook his head, disgusted by the mere thought. He should have known better than to even consider such a fantasy.

Cursing himself for his weakness, he crumpled the parchment in his fist. Why hadn't he listened to himself and left England? If he had any sense left, he'd leave at first light.

Your wife needs you.

Daemon flinched at the voice inside his head. Whatever was he to do? She was mad and he was a fool.

Mad. The word chased through his thoughts like a silent, fearsome phantom seeking blood. Terror reached deep inside him, making him pause. He'd had plenty of experience dealing with the deranged. The last thing he sought now was a return to his youth.

Arina's madness would only grow until she became a stranger. Not the lady who had won his heart, but someone he would never recognize, someone who could never ease his pain the way she did when her mind belonged to her.

And what would she be like once her reason fled? Would she be violent, or one of the poor souls who curled up like a tiny kitten afraid to move?

And what then? Would Belial give her to Edred for exorcism, or worse?

Daemon closed his eyes against the pain in his chest. He wanted to leave, and yet he couldn't make himself give up on her. Of all the things in his life, she alone was worth saving, worth protecting. Nay, he could never leave.

His throat tight, Daemon looked back to the stable in time to see Arina leaving.

"Milady?" he called.

She continued her way toward the manor.

Daemon started to walk away, but stopped after two steps. Had she finally lost all wit? Belial's words about their mother echoed in his head. Could she truly hurt herself?

Fear riding him fierce, he ran after her.

As he neared her, she turned her head toward him. Panic flickered in her gaze a moment before she lifted the hem of her gown and sped inside.

Daemon ran after her and caught her as she entered their chambers. "Did you not hear my call?"

She looked at him with a crystal gaze that spoke of intelligence and clarity, not the mad, vacant gaze he was used to when confronting insanity.

"Aye, milord, I heard you. But I needed to come in here before you stopped me."

"To what purpose?"

She pulled away and moved to retrieve Cecile from under the chest by the window.

"Nay," she said as he reached for her. "You stopped me before, but this time you will allow me to finish."

Before he could move, she covered Cecile's

207

eyes with her hand. The kitten squirmed and hissed.

Daemon tried to free the angry kitten, but Arina held fast. He stepped away, afraid to fight lest he hurt the kitten. All of a sudden, Arina's face changed, and she turned away from him.

Arina drew a deep breath to steady her nerves as guilt gnawed fiercely at her innards. She must make Daemon believe she had lied. So long as Daemon accepted her as human, then maybe she could help him. She should have realized that before she ever spoke of her true form. But Daemon had been so adamant she tell him why she had pulled away, and lies were not in her nature.

Yet Belial had taught her an important lesson in the stable. She mustn't allow Daemon to learn the truth. If she revealed either her or Belial's true form to Daemon, and Daemon truly believed, then the demon would be free of his human form and able to use his full powers all the time.

As long as Daemon believed Belial over her and thought them mortal, then Belial would continue his farce, a farce that would cost him dearly in strength and power.

No matter what, she must keep Belial in human form. At least until she could find some way to hold back his powers or regain her own.

She released Cecile and sighed. The cat shot across the floor, hitting the chest, then darting under the bed. "You were right, milord," she said, her shoulders slumping. "I am no angel."

Daemon stared at her, more confused now than he'd been when she first uttered her claim. "What game is this?"

"No game. I am merely agreeing with your wisdom."

Unsure if he could trust his hearing, Daemon shook his head. She must be mad. There could be no other explanation for her actions, for her vacillations. "And what of your brother?"

She swallowed and looked away. "As you have said, he is a man."

He noticed the trembling in her hands as she clasped them together. She was lying. He could tell by the way she refused to look at him, the way she fidgeted with her sleeves. For whatever reason, she did believe herself an angel and her brother a demon.

" 'Twas a momentary delusion," she said, glancing his way, her eyes betraying turmoil.

"A what?"

Arina turned away from him, unable to face him while she spoke falsely. "I was wrong about my identity," she whispered, the lie stinging her throat.

"Then why did you claim it, milady?" he asked, his voice ragged. "Was my touch so abhorrent that you made up this entire story just to keep me away?"

His pain reached out to her, pounding inside

her own heart in wave after wave of agony. "Nay!" she gasped, cupping his cheek with her hand, offering him what temporary comfort she could. "I would never see you harmed."

And as soon as those words left her lips, her mind replayed the crone's hostile declaration. *You must watch your mortal lover die. Hold him in your arms as his life seeps away.*

She dropped her hand from his face, her sight dimming in terror. How had she forgotten that part of the curse? Why had she not remembered that first?

Her fear of their damnation must have completely overshadowed that part of her memory. Arina staggered away from him, her body trembling.

Watch him die; the phrase echoed through her mind and tore at her soul.

Daemon was to die and all because of her. Arina closed her eyes against the nightmare. Her precious knight was to be sacrificed for one woman's vengeance, for an act she had made that she could not undo. "I must get away."

Daemon clenched his teeth at her whispered words. She moved from fire to ice as quickly as a kestrel pouncing upon a tiny hare. One moment she warmed him with her touch, the next she spoke of leaving him.

Could she truly be mad? And yet he couldn't quite accept that either. No matter how much his logic argued against her sanity, deep in his heart, he knew her sound.

Sighing, he ached for an answer. What was he to do with her? If he left Brunneswald, Belial would like as not give her over to the good brother to confine, or exorcise. Having seen that type of treatment firsthand, he refused to allow it. Nay, he had married her and he intended to protect her no matter what.

Besides, William had granted him the lands and he couldn't disappoint his brother. Nor did he trust any of his own men to see to his lands during his absence. Arina would have been the only person he would have trusted, but with her current moods, he didn't dare leave her in charge.

He was bound to the land and to his wife more firmly than he'd ever thought possible. More than he'd ever wanted.

"Here, milady," he said, placing his arm about her waist and moving her toward the bed. "Rest yourself."

She looked up at him with soulful eyes that cut him deeply. "You've a right to think me mad, milord. But I promise you that I am sane."

He nodded, a knot of uncertainty in his throat. "I know."

Arina stared at him, memorizing the odd colors of his eyes, the warmth of his touch on her waist. The thought of living out a mortal life without him sliced through her heart, leaving it empty. She could barely contemplate the thought. Indeed, she wondered how she had ever survived without him. How she had made it through the centuries without his gentle touch.

For the first time in her existence, she wanted to be human, wanted to experience the trials of their lives. What would it be like to hold a child in her arms, a child born from her body and created from Daemon's seed?

Arina closed her eyes, savoring the image.

But regret stirred in her breast. She would never know that pleasure, or that kind of love. She was cursed, brought to this world for the devil's twisted pleasure.

Whatever she did, she must keep Daemon away from her. Yet how? If she honestly convinced him of her status, would that frighten him away? Dare she chance it?

Arina sighed, her heart even heavier. What good would it do? He would never believe her again. Besides, knowledge of her true identity would place him in even greater danger. Belial no doubt waited for just such an opportunity.

Nay, she must think of another way to keep them apart. Glancing out the window, she remembered him mentioning his brother a few days past. "Did you not wish a journey to London?"

He started at her question as if his thoughts

were a thousand leagues away. "I know not what milady means."

"You spoke of it while you were fevered. You said you wanted to speak with your brother."

"I have no reason to at present."

Arina sighed, hearing his intent to stay as clearly as if the thought filled her own mind. Whatever was she to do?

Leave him. It seemed so easy, so simple, and yet the mere thought brought an ache to her chest that pounded through her veins.

But what choice did she have? If she stayed, he would die and she could never allow that. Nay, come the night she would leave this place before she caused him harm.

Chapter Eleven

Belial lay against the prickly, sweet hay, his body throbbing in twisting, heated agony. At this moment, he didn't even possess enough strength to change into his true form and leave this desolate world. But he didn't care.

His plan had cost him much, but it had been well worth the price. True he had expended much of his powers remaining in human form for so long, yet he would gladly do it all again.

A giddy rush surged through him and he laughed out loud. The Norman and the angel had finally fallen to their lust. Now all he had to do was plan Daemon's death. With the curse fulfilled, he could claim Arina.

His smile widened. How simple. Let them both roast in Lucifer's court. What would he care?

And yet a foreign flutter filled his heart and for an instant he almost regretted what he'd done.

"Cowardly fool," he snarled, disgusted by the mere thought of regret.

Why would such a petty emotion even occur to him? Pondering the answer, Belial frowned. Never since his damnation had a tremor of pity or regret shaken his resolve. And why should it? People were weak; there was nothing about human beings that could not be corrupted—given the right inducements.

As for heavenly angels, well, he had even less use for them. They held themselves far above him and everything else. He held no love in his heart for them, especially the ones who had stood together and passed judgment on his soul.

Surely it must be Arina's powers that gave him pause. Aye, that must be it! Narrowing his gaze, he vowed to take care in the future. He must not fall to the angel's wiles. Though her powers were no match for his, they were enough to affect his will. He must guard himself against her.

"There you are."

Belial looked up at Brother Edred, who stood at the stall's opening, leaning against a wooden post. Worry filled the old man's gray eyes and for an instant, Belial feared Edred might be able to detect his true identity. "Greetings, friar. What brings you to the stable?"

"I have a matter I would like to discuss with you."

Again fear surged through Belial. Had he betrayed himself? Or worse, were his powers so weak that even a corrupted friar could smell the sulphur that permeated his flesh, see the red tint of his pupils?

Sweat trickled down Belial's face, itching his cheek. "Brother Edred," he said quickly, stopping the friar before he came too close. "I beg you stand back before my illness taints you as well."

The friar returned to the opening of the stall, and darted his gaze over Belial's body. "Are you yet ill?"

"Aye," he answered, his voice quivering from strain. " 'Twould seem ill humors have tainted my blood."

The friar's gaze darkened, his face a mirror of earnestness. "Mayhap 'tis the evilness that resides in this hall that taints you."

"What's that?" Belial asked, his attention immediately riveted.

Edred stroked the wooden cross that dangled about his neck and cast his gaze about as if seeking something or someone. "Can you not feel it? 'Tis like a serpent crawling in the bowels of the earth beneath our feet, waiting for just the right moment before it burrows its way up and bites our ankles when we least expect it. Since first I came here, I have felt Lucifer's presence."

His heart thumping heavily in trepidation, Belial cocked a brow. "Lucifer's presence, you say?"

"Aye, and Lord Daemon is his servant."

Belial bit his tongue to stifle the laughter brought by his sudden relief. 'Twas too simple. Yet he couldn't resist so easy a victim, so easy a ruse. "Aye, Lord Daemon is surely damned and can no doubt benefit from your grace. What do you intend to do?"

"First I must make your lady sister understand the beast she has married. Mayhap I am not too late to save her precious soul."

If only he knew. The bald little man was too late to save even his own wretched soul. Belial fought his urge to smile. He must tread carefully lest the friar uncover who the true servant of Lucifer was. "Ah, but she will be a tough one to convince," Belial said. "She believes her husband innocent and pure."

The friar dropped his cross and moved a step closer to whisper, "Will you help me?"

"Help you how?"

"If I could expose the vileness inside him, then she would have no choice other than to believe us."

Belial cocked a brow. "And how would you expose him?"

The friar pulled forth a vial. His good humor fleeing, more sweat trickled down Belial's cheek as he recognized the pungent stench of Holy Water.

"A drop or two of this upon his skin and all will know his true origins."

Swallowing, Belial eyed the vial in terror. A drop or two of that on him and he would know more pain than even the fires of Lucifer's blackest hearth.

He resisted the need to push himself back against the wall, and planted one last seed of fear for the friar to reap. "But what if his powers are so strong that even God's water will not stain him?"

Edred's brows shot up in shock and he crossed himself. "Could he be so powerful?"

"Aye, he could."

The friar gulped, his heavy cheeks paling considerably as he tucked the water away. "Then what shall we do?"

At last Belial smiled the smile that tugged at the edges of his lips. "We shall find a way."

Arina stared out the window, her gaze following Daemon across the yard. She closed her eyes, savoring an image of his proud, handsome bearing, his hair loose and falling gently over his shoulders while a hesitant smile played at the edges of lips too little used to such. Her heart hammering and her body burning, she imagined him again standing on the edge of the cliff, reaching to comfort her.

She clenched her teeth and cursed her weak human body. Why had this happened to her? Even now her need for him beat inside her, echoing through her body with a steady rhythm that robbed her of all sense.

She wanted her husband, ached for a lifetime spent with him, and now she knew how impossible such a dream was.

Opening her eyes, she stared at the wooden rafters above her head. Never before had she needed shelter from weather or harshness. Such damaging agents were unknown in her world. And though she had always been happy, she had never known the type of joy that flooded her breast when she thought of Daemon.

Why could she not be human? If she could have one wish, it would be to have a human life, but it could never be.

One single tear slid down her cheek. Could she find some way to protect him, to keep him from Belial's grasp?

A knock sounded on the door.

Arina wiped the tear from her cheek and cleared her throat. "Enter," she called, expecting Wace. Instead the old crone walked in.

A brief flicker of hatred singed Arina's breast,

but as quickly as it appeared, it died. She couldn't hate the woman for what she'd done. Now, after being in their world and sampling the raw vitality of their emotions, especially that of true human love, she well understood the woman's motivations.

The crone moved forward with a tray laden with covered dishes. *"M'hlaford* bade me set a table for the two of you to sup here this even," she said, placing the tray on the small, round table before the fire.

Arina watched her slow, careful movements as she set the dishes on the table and prepared it for their meal.

The woman appeared serene and completely at ease with her treachery. For her soul, Arina couldn't understand her peace of mind. "How could you?" she asked, needing an answer as to why the woman had betrayed them.

The crone paused and looked up. "Bring you food, *m'hlafdie?"*

"Nay. How could you damn an innocent man?"

The lines around her old eyes wrinkling even more, she gave a malevolent laugh and continued pulling rounded covers off the food.

"Innocent man?" the crone finally spat, gesturing at her with a lid. "I dare you to convince the good Saxon people around you of his innocence. He and his kind have robbed us of our lands and stolen our dignity."

Arina shook her head in denial and took a step toward her, determined to make her see reason. "He has committed no more crimes than any other man in his position."

Snorting a denial, the crone lifted her empty tray before her like a shield and backed away. Her gaze heated by hatred, she raked a sneering glare over Arina. "One more Norman damned—what does it concern me? Damn them and all men."

A shiver rushed through her body. How could anyone be so cruel? "Even your son?"

Her eyes changed. Deep, dark sadness and grief swam in the crone's aged gaze and a wave of pity and empathy filled Arina's heart.

"Nay," the crone spoke, her voice cracking. "My son was the finest of any born. Unlike the other callous fools of this world, only goodness beat in his breast." The fire returned to her eyes. "And you took him!"

The accusation stung her. Arina hadn't understood the woman when first they met, but now she knew only too well what love felt like. Yet she couldn't forgive the woman for damning Daemon too.

"I merely did as I was told."

"Nay!" the crone said, the platter shaking in her furious grip. "He was healing. Just as I was about to cure him, you came in and stole him! You murdered him!"

Aghast, Arina stared at the woman. How

could the crone believe it? "I had no part in his death. 'Twas your cure that killed him."

The woman stiffened, her face mirroring shock. She drew her brows together into a fierce frown. "My cure?"

"Aye," Arina said, softening her voice to ease the sting of truth. " 'Twas the Devil's Bit that poisoned him."

"Nay!" she cried, dropping the platter and covering her ears. "You lie."

"You know me better than that." Arina reached out a comforting hand, but the crone scurried away. "I speak the truth. You have damned me for something I couldn't help. But it doesn't matter what killed him. 'Twas his time to leave and naught could have saved—"

"Nay. I," she said, pounding her breast with her fist to emphasize her words, "was his only hope. I could have saved him had you not stolen him away."

Arina shook her head. "God alone has the power of life and death. Neither of us could have done aught to save or kill him. Your son's time had ended, but I can assure you he is happy where he is."

Her ancient lips quivered and tears filled her hollow eyes. "He was happy here with me. If he'd had a choice, he would have stayed."

"But he didn't have a choice," Arina said, touching the old woman's arm. "Anymore than I do, or you, for that matter."

"Aye, but I do have a choice," she snarled, moving across the room where she eyed Arina like a feral beast. "I'll have your soul damned for what you did."

Arina lifted her chin and drew a deep breath, hoping for a way to make the woman see how wrong her actions were. Before 'twas too late. "Don't forget that your own soul was lost through this as well. You sold yours for a useless curse against two innocent beings. Was it worth it?"

The woman pursed her lips.

Arina moved closer, but the woman fled the room.

The door slammed shut and Arina sighed in heartfelt disgust. Why had she made that last statement? It had been petty and cruel. Never since her creation had she uttered anything so mean.

What was happening to her? Arina bit her lip. When she had first recovered her memory, she had possessed a number of her powers, but with every hour that passed, she steadily lost more and more of them.

No longer could she hear far away noises, read people with the same clarity. All that remained of her angelic form was her memories. Only they attested to the fact that she had ever been more than mortal, more than Daemon's wife.

But where did that leave her? Pain coiled

around her heart. Once a curse had been posed, nothing could remove it, except its fulfillment. But could she prevent it? If she left Daemon and isolated herself away from any other mortals, mayhap she could stop the curse.

Arina shook her head. How simple her life had been when she had never known human thoughts, human taints. Human love.

"Arina?"

She started at the voice behind her. Then she turned around, and her heart stilled. There before her stood her senior angel, Kaziel. Though he had always been handsome, he had never been more beautiful to her than he was at this instant, standing in a ray of sunlight, his alabaster wings glistening. His golden eyes glowed as he watched her, a sad smile hovering over his blessed lips. "Kaziel?"

"Aye, dearest sister. I felt your turmoil and realized you needed strength."

Arina crossed the room. Joy and relief coursed through her body and she gave a small laugh. "I didn't think any of you could sense me."

Kaziel squeezed her tight, then pulled back and stared into her eyes with an earnest look that stole her happiness. "We know your dilemma. But there is naught we can do. Even now I brave displeasure by coming to you."

"Displeasure?" she repeated, needing to understand what was expected of her.

"Aye." Sighing, he tucked his wings down and

shook his head, his face grim. "You know we cannot interfere with the course of human events, not without the Lord's approval."

"What am I to do?"

He looked away, and though she could no longer read his thoughts, she saw the grief that pinched his features into a frown. "You must fulfill your destiny."

Tears filled here eyes. "Is there no other way?"

He shook his head and her throat tightened. When he again met her gaze, she saw his concern for her. "Even though you were tricked, you have lain with a man. Gabriel and Peter know not what to do."

Arina crossed her arms over her chest and rubbed the chills that ran the length of her arms. Fear pounded in her heart and she dreaded the next question she must ask. "Am I damned for what I've done?"

"You know I cannot answer that. 'Tis for Peter to decide, not I."

Arina nodded. The knot in her throat tightened as she thought of her husband. "And what of Daemon?"

The sadness in Kaziel's eyes stole her breath. "Do you truly need my answer?"

Arina swallowed, her heart hanging heavy in her breast. She wanted to scream out a denial, to plead Daemon's cause, but it would be useless. Peter and the others already knew the circumstances of Daemon's life. Yet not even those events, in all their horror, would be enough to save his soul or his life. "Then there's no hope."

A light appeared in Kaziel's eyes. "My sister, there is always hope."

"But—"

The door opened and Kaziel scattered into a thousand shimmering fragments.

"Arina?"

She blinked, her heart thumping, her eyelids as heavy as if she awoke from a sound slumber. Staring into Daemon's confused eyes, she wondered if Kaziel's visit had been a dream.

Had Kaziel truly come to her?

Daemon looked at her with a sharp frown. "You are pale," he said, taking her by her arm. He moved her to sit on the bed. "Are you not well?"

"Aye," she whispered. " 'Twas a passing moment of dizziness."

Suspicion hovered in his eyes as if he doubted her answer. "Then I am glad I decided we should take our meal alone this night."

Arina smiled sadly. "I would like that very much," she said, grateful he had included her in his solitary meal, but dreading the time they would share. Time that could serve no purpose save to cause her greater pain.

Agony consumed her, but she knew there was no other way. Come the late night hours, she must leave him. 'Twas the only way she knew to save his life.

She would savor these last few hours and be grateful for them. Aye, mayhap they would be enough to ease the ache of a human lifetime spent alone.

A new, sudden terror settled in her heart at the thought. What if she wasn't mortal? What if she retained her angel's immortality and death never came for her? Would she spend eternity hidden away from the mortal world in fear of loving another?

But even as the thought appeared, she knew the foolishness of it. There would never be another man who would mean as much to her as Daemon. Nay, no man would ever be able to make her feel as he did.

She watched as he doffed his mail and set about washing the grime and sweat from his face and chest. A myriad of scars crossed his back, attesting to the brutality of his life. Looking away, she longed for a way to take each and every deep, brutal mark away and to erase the memories he no doubt carried from the moments he had received them.

Even now, she wanted nothing more than the courage to bridge the distance between them and touch the rippling muscles of his back, to slide her fingers over the ridged planes of his stomach. Her nerves danced with desire, and a heated throb pounded in her blood, demanding she yield to its call.

How could she leave him? He needed her and

though it pained her to admit it, she knew she needed his smile, his touch. It almost seemed worth the price of her soul to stay with him and make the most of the time they did have together.

But that time would bring an even higher price—his life.

She shivered. Nay, that price was far too high.

Rising from the bed, she retrieved a tunic for him from the chest near the window. He wiped his hands on a towel and his features softened as he took the tunic from her hands. "My thanks," he said.

Arina offered him a smile, hoping he could not read the thoughts in her mind. He shrugged his tunic on and she clenched her fingers into a fist to keep them from reaching out to him.

If she left him, he might have enough time left in his life to do penance for his sins. But if she stayed and he died, then she would be every bit as much to blame for his damnation as Belial. She could never do that.

Nay, she must leave him no matter how much it hurt her.

Daemon held out a chair for her. "Come, milady."

Arina took her seat, reveling in the close proximity of his body while he adjusted her chair. His warm, rich scent invaded her head and she breathed it deeply. She would miss that most.

That and the feel of his arms wrapped about her.

Daemon filled their cups, his fingers brushing against hers as he placed her goblet near her sliced trencher.

"Thank you, milord," she whispered, but the tightness of her throat made the words painful to utter.

Daemon took his seat and for the first time, she allowed herself to look fully at his face. Instead of the usual tenderness in his gaze, she noted a tenseness, a barrier that shielded his emotions from her.

She frowned in confusion and reached for her knife. "Does something vex you, milord?"

He sliced the roasted venison and placed a large portion on her trencher. Glancing up at her, he shook his head. "Nay, why should it?"

Her frown deepened at the faint sarcasm underlying his words. For a moment she wondered if she imagined it, but as he set about filling her trencher with lamprey and apricots, she saw the tightness of his grip, the tautness of his jaw.

Had she done something wrong? A new fear invaded her heart. "Have I or my brother done something to offend you?"

Cocking an eyebrow, he sat back in his chair and studied her with an unreadable stare that set her hands trembling. "Why would milady think that?"

She shook her head and looked back at her food. Something was amiss, but Daemon made it obvious that he had no wish to discuss it. Arina drew a trembling breath and concentrated on her supper.

They ate their meal in silence.

Daemon constantly downed his goblet of wine only to refill his cup. She frowned as he again filled the goblet to the brim with the rich, burgundy liquid.

He didn't act besotted, but heaven knew he had consumed more than enough wine to intoxicate three or four normal men.

Trying her best to pay his strange mood no heed, she ate slowly but didn't taste any of her food. Indeed, everything she tried tasted like unseasoned porridge.

At last he looked up at her with a grave frown that made her wish he would again ignore her presence. "Tell me, milady, why did you marry me?"

What an odd question. But the intense look in his eyes warned her of his seriousness. Arina swallowed her bite of food and considered why he had asked it.

Was he thinking of confining her as Belial had suggested? Or did he merely seek comfort; the knowledge that she cared for him and held no regrets over their marriage? She paused at that thought. Did she have regrets?

Arina wiped her mouth, her hands trembling

in fear and anxiety of how to best answer. The only regret resting in her heart came from their differences. If she were a mortal woman, would she have any remorse over their union?

And without hesitation the answer entered her mind. Nay. Had she been born human, she would have gladly taken him for husband.

Arina cut another piece of her venison and smiled at him. He deserved her honest answer. "I wanted to."

He swallowed his food and took another drink of wine. "Why? Why would you bind yourself to a hated stranger, a man not of your kind?"

His words startled her until she realized he meant that he was Norman and she supposedly Saxon. Lowering her knife, she leveled her gaze at his. "You are a noble man, milord. You follow your conscience."

Daemon snorted. "What conscience is that? The same one that took your virtue?"

He leaned forward against the table, his gaze piercing her with its probing intensity. "But then I didn't take your virtue that first night, did I, milady?"

Her heart stilled at his implication. A shiver of foreboding darted up her spine and she tightened her grip on her knife. "What do you mean?"

"I have given much thought to you this day. Things that had escaped my notice found their way to my mind and at last I know what to call you."

Arina tensed at the seriousness of his voice, the emptiness of his eyes. "And what is that, milord?"

"Angel."

Chapter Twelve

Shock poured through Arina at his unexpected declaration. "We have already explored this," she said, carefully directing her attention back to her roasted venison and away from Daemon's searing glare.

"Aye, and I wish to know why you lied about being human."

Setting her knife aside, Arina swallowed in fear and uncertainty. What could she say?

Uncomfortable with the turn in their conversation and terrified of any more difficult questions, Arina moved to leave the table, but he captured her arm. His grip tight about her forearm, Daemon pulled her back into her chair.

"I have asked you a question and I fully expect

an answer," he said between his clenched teeth.

The heat and anguish in his eyes, in his touch, scorched her. She ached for his pain, longed for the words or spell to undo the curse and to keep him safe for all eternity. If only there were some way . . .

"I didn't lie, milord."

"Which time? When you spoke of being an angel, or when you denied it?"

She swallowed and wished he was not so astute. A lesser man would have heard what pleased him and not realized her ambiguity. But what more could she say? How else could she avoid answering his question?

Arina clenched her fists, anguish flowing through her. Dearest saints, why had she ever spoken of her true form? Why had she not had the foresight to silence her prattling tongue? She tried to invent some tale to explain her earlier words, but nothing came.

Too used to honesty, she had little experience with deceit. That expertise belonged to Belial and his kind.

Suddenly an idea leapt into her mind. Aye, she'd use Daemon's own logic against him.

Arina tried to loosen his grip from her arm, but he held tight, as if afraid she would leave him. "What of my brother then, milord?" she asked. "If I am an angel, what would that make him?"

The confidence in his gaze faltered, then his

eyes sparked fire. "He *is* a demon, isn't he?"

Arina refused to answer. Why had he asked such a direct question? One she couldn't answer without lying?

"Isn't he?" Daemon demanded.

His grip bit into her arm and her stomach churned. Arina chewed her lip, trying to decide what to say. What should she tell him?

Tell him the truth. Arina flinched at the voice—it sounded much like Kaziel's. Dare she trust that voice? Did she have a choice?

"What if I said yea? What would be your reaction?"

He released her arm and the fire faded from his eyes. Pushing his chair back from the table, he slowly stood. "I want the truth."

A knot tightened her throat as she watched him pace the area between their table and bed. Each step echoed in her head, her heart, and she longed to draw him into her arms and comfort the pain in his eyes.

If only she could think of some believable tale, but she could not bring a lie to her lips. Nay, she was an angel and she must answer him honestly. "The truth is that I am an angel. Belial is a demon and he is here to claim both our souls."

She half expected another denial, but instead he merely nodded and looked away, as if disgusted. "Why did you try to make me believe otherwise?"

"Because," Arina said, "so long as he thinks you ignorant of the truth, he will remain in the guise of man. It takes a great deal of power and concentration to maintain his present form. If you admit to him that you know he is a demon, he will be free to draw strength from the bowels of hell."

She paused and dared a glance at him, but she couldn't read his mood. "Since I have taken human form, I have lost my powers," she continued. "I cannot restrain him."

He raked a trembling hand through his hair and released a long, weary breath. "And to think I was hoping I had been misled, that my conclusion was wrong. That you were indeed mad."

She stiffened at his odd tone. "Why?" Never before had she beheld such malice, such coldness. He came to rest by her side, his fury pinning her to her seat.

"Tell me, milady, did your God have no better distractions than to send you to further torment my wretched life?"

She gasped at his question, shock pouring through her that he would draw such a conclusion. "Nay, 'tis not like that."

"Then explain why you are here."

Before she could think, the truth tumbled from her lips. "I was cursed for escorting the soul of a child to heaven. His mother blamed me for his death and decided to punish me."

Anguish shadowed his eyes and he averted his gaze. "So what are you now? Are you human or angel?"

Arina opened her mouth to speak, then closed it. How could she answer, when she wasn't really certain what she was. Yet as she looked down at her body, felt her heart quicken, her insides quiver, she knew the truth. "I am human, milord," she whispered, her voice hoarse.

"But not human," he snarled.

He stepped toward her. Rage darkened his eyes and she had the distinct feeling he wanted to beat her. She swallowed in fear and pressed herself back against her chair.

With a curse that brought heat to her cheeks, he turned about and headed for the door.

"Daemon?"

Daemon stopped, but didn't turn around. Fury and anguish tore through him and all he wanted was an escape. He clenched his fists at his sides and tried to still the frantic beating of his heart as he accepted the undeniable truth.

The rumors that had followed him the whole of his life had all been true. God existed and He had cursed him. Even now He mocked him. "Tell me why, milady."

"Why what?"

"Why your God punished me," he said, turning once more to face *her*, the one creature he had wanted, the one creature he could never have. "Is it true that I am Lucifer's son?"

239

She shook her head, her eyes filling with tears. "What do you believe?"

Daemon swallowed, his mind too weary to think. "I know not what to believe."

"Then follow your heart," she whispered, her gentle tone caressing his ears. "It will never deceive you."

He opened his mouth to speak a denial, but her sweet, precious voice stopped him. "Nay, don't say that you have no heart, milord. I can see it even now in your eyes."

Daemon shook his head, denying her comfort even though he wanted nothing more than to pull her into his arms and again feel her heart beat against his chest. Somehow that would make her seem human, make him forget that there was no hope of the two of them ever sharing a life together.

He curled his lip in anger at the callous entity who had divided them. "If you see anything in my eyes, milady, it is because your mind placed it there, not because it truly exists," he snarled.

Turning around, Daemon left the room and slammed the door behind him.

Pain coiling in his stomach, he made his way out of the manor and across the yard. His head pounded and with each step he took, his fury increased.

How could fate be so cruel? Long ago he had accepted his destiny—to die unloved and untouched by kindness. Then out of nowhere Arina had stumbled into his life and shown him how wonderful life could be. What it would have been like had he been born normal. And just when he had learned to trust in that reality, fate had seized it in its cruel fist and snatched it away.

But now what? No matter how much he longed to leave, he knew he couldn't. Only he stood between Arina and Belial. Though his own soul meant nothing to him, he knew he couldn't allow her to suffer for something she couldn't avoid.

She had said that Belial was out to claim both their souls. No doubt his soul had been damned from the moment of birth, but not hers. Nay, her soul had been created from the purest of pure, and he refused to see her harmed for something she couldn't help.

Cursing, Daemon paused at the door of the stable and glanced up at the clouded sky above. It would be a long, hard winter. A winter with him caught between heaven and hell.

But he must tread carefully. If Arina was right about Belial, then he couldn't allow the demon to know he had guessed the truth.

Daemon paused at the door of the stable. His stomach lurched in disgust. Their first night together had been nothing more than an illusion. No wonder he had seemed ill-satisfied the next morning, why the memory of that night had been so vague.

Belial had played them well. But now that he knew the tune, he vowed to alter the melody to something that made the demon dance to *his* command.

Arina waited until she was sure everyone had fallen asleep. Creeping silently through the hall, she pressed her lips together, afraid that each trembling breath rattling in her chest might awaken a nearby sleeper.

This was her only chance to save Daemon. She must leave him behind, no matter how much her heart ached for him, no matter how much she yearned to remain by his side.

A man spoke in his sleep.

Arina froze, her heart hammering in her ears. He turned on his side and began a steady snore. Releasing a quiet sigh of relief, she returned to her careful steps.

How she wished Daemon had sought their chambers to sleep, but after hours of waiting, she'd given up hope of his return. All Arina could do now was pray he wasn't sleeping in the stable.

Her legs and hands quaking in trepidation, Arina pushed open the manor's door, flinching as a tiny squeak echoed, a squeak that sounded louder than thunder in her anxious ears. A nearby sleeper rolled over, but no one awoke enough to question her. Taking a deep breath for courage, she wedged herself out the door.

Frigid winds whipped against her cheeks, numbing them before she had taken more than a few steps. An early, light snow fell against her face and hair. Arina drew her fur-lined cloak tighter, trying to banish the cold from her body. With any luck, the snow would cover her tracks and Daemon would never find her.

Pain swelled inside her breast, but she forced herself not to think on it. She must do this. For the sake of both their souls.

Arina entered the stable, then paused. Daemon lay inside the first stall, his gentle snore reaching out to her and warming every part of her. In spite of the knowledge that she should take a horse and leave, she moved closer to him.

Through a crack in the planking, a rushlight shone, illuminating his face. Arina stared, fascinated by the way the flickering light played across his lean features.

Aye, he was a handsome man. Far more handsome than any she'd ever beheld. And in sleep he looked so very vulnerable, so very lovable.

Her body burned for him, for one last touch of his flesh against hers, but it could never be. She closed her eyes, savoring the memory of his kiss.

If only she could stay with him, be his wife, she'd gladly pay the price of her soul. But how long until the curse worked its treachery? A day, a week? Every moment she spent near him, she jeopardized his life.

Holding that thought inside her heart, she forced her feet away from him and moved to take a horse. A gentle mare called to her as she neared the last stall.

"You'll not harm me, will you?" she whispered.

The brown mare stared at her with gentle eyes.

Arina smiled before reaching for a bridle. "You'll have to help me," she said, holding the bit to the animal's teeth as she'd seen Wace and the groom do. "I'm not sure how this should be done."

The mare took it in her mouth.

Arina stroked the mare's nose, grateful she understood her, and worked the leather straps into their correct positions around the mare's head.

With a wishful sigh, Arina glanced to the saddles, but decided against it. She doubted she could lift one, and even if she could, she had no idea of how to fasten it.

She took a blanket from the wooden post, draped it over the mare's spine and led the animal out into the cold, lonely night. Though she ached to look back at Daemon, she knew better than to try. One more glance at the one person who quickened her heart and her will would be destroyed.

Mounting the horse, she kicked her into a gallop. Arina expected the sentries to stop her at the gate, but instead they waved her through.

For leagues afterwards, she frowned at their unwarranted approval until a familiar chill stole up her spine and she held her breath in expectation. The mare snorted, and Arina sensed the horse's desire to bolt. Soothing her with her touch, Arina waited for what was to come.

"Leaving so soon?"

Demon stench filled her head and she struggled not to gag. "Return to the hall," she said.

Belial laughed, then materialized behind her. "Why would I listen to you?" he asked.

"Because you're too weak to be out here."

"Aye, but this is my strongest hour of night. You should know that."

She lifted her chin and laughed with a lightness she didn't feel. "But it doesn't give you all your powers."

He touched her cheek, his fingers colder than even the winter winds. "What did you tell the mortal?"

"That I was mad."

"Did he believe you?"

Arina braced herself for the lie and uttered it without hesitation. "Of course he did. You know humans are blind to our true natures."

"Aye, but he is not as the others."

Arina swallowed, knowing she must tread

carefully if she was to keep Daemon safe from Belial. She only prayed her next words didn't falter in her throat and that Belial in his arrogance would accept Daemon's logic without question. "Nay, he is worse. He denies God. If he believes in us, then he must believe in God. And if he accepted that, then he would deduce God had forsaken him. You surely know he will never accept or believe that."

Belial laughed. "That is what I'm counting on. So long as he dies blaspheming the name of God, I will have two souls." His breath scorched her cheek. "Which means you cannot leave!"

No sooner had the words left his lips, than the mare bolted.

Arina struggled with her terrified mount, holding tightly to the reins. Keeping her head low, she prayed. Limbs and shrubs tore at her hair, her body, beating her until she throbbed with pain.

Night animals scattered beneath the rushing hooves. They traveled on through the darkness and Arina tried to see what obstacles lay before them, but the mare continued her furious run at a pace that prevented her from seeing aught. Arina tightened her grip.

Out of nowhere, a large shadow appeared, its demon's teeth snarling.

The mare shrieked, then reared.

Arina fell from the marc's back and landed in

the snow. A fierce pain filled her head, then all went black.

Rough hands shook Daemon awake. Cursing, he reached for the culprit's throat, angered that anyone would awaken him in such a manner.

"Release me!" Belial snarled.

A cold shiver ran the length of Daemon's body. But even in the blackness, he saw Belial's human form and he relaxed a trifle. "What brings you here?" he demanded, fully aware.

"Arina is gone."

His anger evaporated under a fierce wave of fear, and Daemon immediately suspected Belial of treachery. "What do you mean she is gone?"

Belial's face appeared innocent, but Daemon knew better. The demon had had some part in this, he had no doubt, and if she were hurt because of Belial, then the demon would know what true hell was.

"I went to check on my sister," Belial said quietly, lighting a small lantern.

Daemon shielded his eyes against the sudden glare.

Belial hung it from a peg and handed Daemon his mail hauberk. "Since her newest outbreak of madness, I have been worried over her. I wanted to see if she still believed herself an angel, and when I entered her room, she was gone."

Panic tore through Daemon and he shrugged

his hauberk on, his gullet tightening in apprehension. Where could she have gone and why?

Scrambling to his feet, he glanced about the stable. Though the horses were a bit unsettled, he had little trouble locating the one that was missing.

"Dammit!" he snarled. Why had she left him and the safety of the manor?

Because you are too repugnant for her to bother with. Daemon flinched at the words in his head. Could it be true? Could that be the reason she would venture out and brave a world she barely understood?

"We must find her!" Belial insisted.

Daemon curled his lip, his heart pounding in bitter betrayal and rage. "Why, 'twould appear she left of her own accord."

Belial shook his head, and once again Daemon had a distinct impression the demon was somehow responsible for her absence. "But what if her mind has fled her again? Even now she could be lying in the storm close to death."

"Storm? What storm?" Daemon asked, a new terror burgeoning.

Belial threw open the stable door.

Daemon swallowed at the swirling snowflakes that cascaded so thickly around that the air appeared solid. Howling winds whipped the large snowflakes into a brutal dance until he could scarce see three inches before him. Unbridled horror rushed through his body and into his heart.

Arina would never be able to survive such a storm. She was heavenly, and unused to the harshness of his world. No matter what she thought of him, he must find her before she succumbed to the dangers that lay in the night, waiting for one such as she.

Chapter Thirteen

While Daemon saddled his horse, Belial gathered food and supplies. "I shall wake the others," Belial promised, but even as the words left his lips, Daemon doubted them.

Not that it mattered. His men wouldn't search thoroughly in this storm. And he'd rather seek Arina himself than be held back by reluctant men.

He mounted his destrier, his saddle tilting slightly as he adjusted himself. Drawing his cowl over his head, he looked down at Belial, who watched him like a trainer observing a squire carry out a command. Even from a distance, he couldn't miss the evil gleam in the demon's eyes. What had placed that gleam there?

Chills spread through him. If the demon had harmed Arina because of him, Daemon vowed to rip his insidious form to pieces. By hell, he'd better find Arina whole and hearty!

Kicking Ganille into a run, he sped across the bailey and out of the gate. Daemon cursed the weather that forced him to slow Ganille's gait. The stallion's hooves slid on the frozen soil until he feared both of them would fall. Worse than the ice, swirling flakes continued to obscure his vision.

His cheeks burning from the cold, Daemon gnashed his teeth in aggravation. How far could Arina have gone?

Belial had offered him a direction, south. Though he doubted the demon would ever be honest, he decided this time Belial told the truth. He didn't know why he believed that, but he did.

Hours sped by and with each one, Daemon grew more frantic. Could she survive in the cold? Did she wear adequate clothing? He didn't know how much angels knew about his world. He only hoped Arina knew enough not to jeopardize her safety.

Few humans possessed enough skills to live through a night like this. Would she even think to find shelter?

But of all the questions tormenting him, one stayed foremost in his thoughts. Why had she left?

Over and over images played through his mind: Arina laughing with the children, Arina reaching for him with desire glowing deep in her eyes. His body erupted in heat at the memory.

No other woman had ever wanted him, had ever welcomed him the way she had. She'd seemed so happy with him. Why then had she run away on a night like this?

Please, he begged silently, *let me find her alive*.

Daemon couldn't imagine a life without her, a life of returning to the empty isolation he had known since his birth. And yet did he have a choice? What kind of life could they share when they were two separate kinds of being?

Or were they?

Grinding his teeth in rage, he swore he'd not give up so easily. Arina was human for now, and that was enough for him. So long as she retained her human body, she was his wife and he had no intention of losing her.

At last, he saw the brown palfrey. Her reins had caught in a bramble bush and the small horse shrieked and tugged at the lines. A chill rocked his body and he wondered if the sensation came from the whipping winds, or the dreadful misgiving in his gullet.

After dismounting, Daemon approached the mare with caution. Cold wind bit into his flesh and his joints were stiff from riding.

"Easy now," he said, his breath forming a

small circle of frost around his head. He touched her neck, gently stroking her nose until she quieted.

Moving slowly so as not to alarm the mare again, he untangled her reins. Scratches marred her flesh and he rubbed his gloved hand over her damp flanks. Arina must have ridden hard.

"Arina!" he called, hoping she was somewhere nearby.

Only the howling winds answered his call.

Tying the mare's reins to his destrier, Daemon searched the area on foot, calling for his wife, his heart lodged painfully in his hoarse, sore throat.

Where could she be? Had the palfrey thrown her? His own body throbbed in memory of Ganille's attack on him, and he again mounted his horse and searched the forest.

Could Arina survive such an ordeal? Daemon closed his eyes, hoping she was all right, too afraid to think of her as otherwise.

Just as he was about to turn around and seek help searching for her, he found her lying near a large tree.

"Arina?" he gasped, dismounting from his horse and running to her side. He knelt beside her and pulled her over. Her face was a ghostly white and a large bruise swelled against her right cheek. Terror assaulted him.

She lay too quiet, too still.

"My lady?" he asked, his voice shaking with the weight of his emotions as he gingerly pulled the strands of hair free from her cheek.

Her eyes fluttered open. "Daemon?"

Relief washed over him. His heart hammering in gratitude, he lifted her in his arms and cradled her close to his chest. "Don't speak; I must find us shelter."

Nodding, she draped a finely shaped arm over his shoulders and snuggled her head against his neck. Desire and tenderness crashed through him. Nay, he could never let her leave him, not as long as breath filled his lungs.

Daemon pulled her cloak tighter around her and stumbled back to their horses, but with every step he took, he felt her wince from pain. Swallowing the lump of fright in his throat, he knew he must find somewhere close by to check her injuries.

He held her gently in his lap as he rode back the way he'd come. Another blast of wind and snow struck them, causing his horse to rear. Ganille snorted, pawing at the air.

"Whoa, boy!" he ordered, but the horse barely settled. More wind howled and Ganille panicked, running through the forest.

Daemon struggled for control of his horse and to maintain his tenuous hold on Arina. For several minutes, he could do nothing more than remain in his saddle as they crashed through the snow and foliage.

Suddenly, the snow thinned and there before them stood a small croft. Ganille shook his head and quieted, pawing softly at the snow.

Daemon blinked at the dark, little hut. Unsure if he should believe his sight, he turned Ganille toward it and reined to a stop in front of the door.

Throwing his leg over the saddle's pommel, he held Arina tightly and slid to the ground. Cautiously he approached the croft, waiting for an angry Saxon to rush out and attack him. When no light or sound appeared, he wondered if the hut was deserted.

Supporting Arina against his chest with one arm, he knocked on the door. It swung open, its leather hinges squeaking as a gust of wind caught it and sent it slamming into the interior wall.

Daemon entered, then paused to peer inside. Whoever had owned the small cottage must have left it years before. Cobwebs hung like palls over a few meager pieces of rough, wooden furniture, and a musty stench filled the air. Curling his lip, he made his way to the small cot that sat against the far wall.

With the toe of his boot, he tested the leather straps that crisscrossed the ancient frame. It appeared sound enough, but he couldn't quite banish his misgivings. Still not fully convinced it would hold even her light weight, he carefully lowered Arina to the cot.

When it didn't collapse beneath her, he sighed in relief and touched her cheek.

She looked up at him, her gaze betraying her pain, fear and exhaustion.

"Rest here while I tend the horses."

Nodding, she closed her eyes and placed her bare hand over his glove. "Thank you for coming for me."

His chest tightened. Did she think he could ever leave her in such danger? "Did you doubt me?"

"Nay," she whispered. "But a part of me hoped you wouldn't find me."

Misery raked his heart. Why would she hope such a thing? Daemon opened his mouth to question her further, but she tensed as if a wave of pain shot through her. Deciding to wait until she had time to rest, he doffed his heavy cloak and laid it over her.

She lay still, her damp hair fanning out around her. He longed to run his hand through the silken mass, but her words hung in his heart like an anchor stone. He ached for her explanation, but this was no time to press the issue.

Clenching his teeth, he turned away.

Daemon returned to the horses and unsaddled Ganille. Though the barn had seen better days, it still remained intact enough to offer shelter for the horses. He draped his saddlebags over his shoulder and retrieved an old, rusty ax from the barn's wall.

It took a while to find wood dry enough to use, and to locate the small piece of flint still laying in the aged coals of the last fire the dilapidated hut had seen. As he set about making a fire in the center of the room, he sensed Arina's gaze upon him. Glancing over his shoulder, he saw her blue eyes following his movements.

Unable to discern the emotions flickering in her gaze, he continued striking the flint until he had a decent fire started. Winds howled outside, striking the hut with a force that made him wonder how it continued to stand the abuse without collapsing.

Rising from his task, he turned to face her. "How do you feel, milady?"

"Cold," she said, her teeth chattering.

Daemon crossed the room to stand above her. In spite of the sympathy inside him, his anger mounted over her foolishness. "As well you should. What did you mean by leaving on a night such as this?"

She stiffened her jaw and averted her gaze.

Sighing in frustration, Daemon picked her up and carried her closer to the fire. Though she said nothing, he noted the rigidness of her body, as if she wanted him far away from her. Careful to keep the cloaks between her and the filthy floor, he set her beside the saddlebags.

When he reached to lift the hem of her kirtle, she grabbed his hand. "What are you doing?"

The panic in her voice sliced through him,

and he knew why she had left. The last thing an angel would want was the touch of the devil's bastard.

His throat tight, Daemon sat back and removed his gloves from his hands. Ignoring her question, he touched her left thigh. She gasped in pain and her entire body jerked.

"I need to check your injuries, milady. I felt you wincing as I carried you, and every time your hip touched against my body you trembled."

"Oh," she said quietly. She looked up at him, and he saw the battle she waged within herself.

Disgust burned his throat. She would rather sit in pain than suffer a few moments of his touch.

Why did he even bother with her? He ought to leave her in this croft and let her Lord take care of her.

"Daemon? What is it?"

He flinched at his name on her lips. Did she use it just to deepen the wound she'd already delivered? " 'Tis nothing," he said, moving to rise.

She took his arm and pulled him back. "Are you not going to check my leg?"

He stared at her in disbelief. "From the look of your face, I assumed milady would rather not have me tend her."

A smile curved her lips, and he frowned at her ill-placed humor. " 'Twas not your touch that

259

gave me pause, but rather the cold draft."

She tightened her cloak around her shoulders. "You, milord, should stop judging people's actions so readily. More times than not, you apply the wrong reasons to them."

He snorted. Who was she to chastise him? "I merely trust in my experiences, which have tutored me well on why people flinch at my approach."

"Have I ever flinched?"

Daemon swallowed the bitter lump in his throat. "Nay, milady. But you did brave this weather to leave me. Would you care to tell me why?"

She looked away, her eyes strangely void. She ran her hands over her arms as if to banish chills. "The weather was not so bad when I started my journey."

"You are avoiding my question."

Arina twisted her hand in the hem of her woolen cloak, trying to think of some answer he would accept. How weary she'd grown of making up tales for Belial and for Daemon, trying to keep both of them from the truth. Her head pounded and she longed for peace.

"Will you not answer?"

Arina drew a deep breath and met his gaze. "I had no choice."

"No choice?" he asked with a sharp frown. "You always have choices, milady. You fled this night as though someone drove you away. Was it Belial?"

"Nay, milord. I drove myself away."

His frown deepened and pain flickered in his unique gaze. "Why?"

Her soul cried out for her to remain silent. If she told him the truth, he'd never allow her to protect him. He was a warrior, used to protecting himself. He would never allow a mere woman to shield him.

But he didn't understand the powers that confronted them, the true hopelessness of their situation.

"Why must you continue to keep secrets from me?" he asked, pacing the floor before her. "I thought angels always gave honest answers."

She lifted her chin, his implication stinging her pride. "I seek only to protect you."

"Protect me?" he asked, his face aghast. "From what?"

Once more, she averted her gaze, afraid that he might somehow read her thoughts.

He knelt beside her and cupped her chin in his warm hand. Against her will, he forced her to look up at him. "What have you not told me, milady? What secret beats within your breast that has you terrified, that drives you away from your home on a frightful winter's night?"

She licked her lips, his touch and soulful look weakening her resolve. Part of her longed to tell him the truth, to have help dealing with Belial and the curse. But dare she?

Would knowledge help him, or harm him more? Closing her eyes, she prayed for a solution.

Daemon released her and moved away. "Very well, milady, keep your secret."

She looked up to see the suffering mirrored in his eyes. No doubt he thought she rejected him.

Her stomach knotted. Nay, she couldn't allow him to believe that. Too many people had turned him away, and she would rather die than have him think that she was no better than the others, that she held no love for him in her heart.

Drawing a deep, trembling breath, she spoke. "I left you, milord, because you are destined to die in my arms."

Shock reflected in his gaze a moment before amusement replaced it. "There is no other place I would rather die."

Her jaw fell slack and she sat still, stunned by his words until anger pounded through her veins. "How can you be glib? 'Tis no jest."

"I have never been more serious."

And though she longed to deny it, the sincerity of his gaze told her that he spoke the truth. "I do not take your life so lightly, and I wish that you were more heedful of my warning."

He shook his head and sat by her side. The light played in his hair, flickering shadows across the handsome planes of his face.

Arina longed to lift her hand and trace the dancing shadows, but she didn't dare. Nay, she had no time for that. She must make him heed her warning.

"I can't believe you fled because you fear I will die." One corner of his mouth lifted in a wry smile. "Milady, all men are destined to die sooner or later."

"Aye," she said, her heart heavy. "I know the mortality of men far better than you. I have spent eternity gathering souls and escorting them to Peter's Gate."

This time she yielded to her need to touch him. Reaching out, she brushed a strand of hair from his icy, red cheek. "But you, milord, should have an entire lifetime to live. You should not die so young just because of a curse that has nothing to do with you."

Fire burned in his eyes. It scorched her with its intensity, melting her will. "Curses have followed me the whole of my life. What do I care for one more?"

She buried her hand in the top of his braid at the nape of his neck and pulled him close. He wrapped his strong arms around her and she reveled in his precious touch. Trembling from the weight of her fear and love, she buried her face in his neck. "The other curses did not bring death," she said.

He stroked her back, his touch warming her

far more than the fire. "Aye, milady, those curses condemned me to eternal death. What do I care if I pass through this life as soon as possible?"

"I care."

He stopped stroking her back and his grip tightened around her waist. "As an angel or as my wife?"

"As your wife!" she cried, wondering how he could doubt her special feelings for him.

He scoffed and pulled away. "But can you be my wife? Can you take human vows?"

Could she? Doubt seized her heart, squeezing it until she wanted to cry out. "I know not, milord. But I feel as a human, care as a human."

His gaze darkened and the sudden suspicion in his eyes stung her. "How do you know you feel as a human?"

"Because I never felt this way before. In the past my senses were dull. 'Tis only now that I see true colors, smell true scents."

"And what do you feel?"

"I . . ." Arina paused. Nay, she couldn't say it aloud.

She cleared her throat of the painful lump. "What do *you* feel, milord?"

Daemon shook his head and rose. His emotions were so entangled he knew not how to answer so simple a question. Part of him would die for her, and another part wanted to curse her existence and all that she stood for.

"There is no ground for us to share in common, milady. You belong to light and God, and I am earthly and cursed."

She watched him with a tenderness that made him tremble. "You are not cursed. You are but a man."

"And I am cursed by men."

"But not by me."

Chapter Fourteen

Daemon stared at her in disbelief. "But you neither curse nor pass judgment on anyone. That is not your nature."

"I can no longer say what my true nature is," she said, lowering her head. He watched her trace the embroidery on his cloak, and chills went over his flesh as if she touched him. "I no longer know who or what I am."

She looked up, her features wistful and pained. "I remember flying, the air fluttering against my cheeks, but that air never felt as it does now."

Shaking her head, she gave a heartfelt sigh. "Am I angel or am I human? There are times

Sherrilyn Kenyon

when I feel myself going mad from the strain of trying to decide."

The firelight flickered against her flesh, and for a moment Daemon could swear he saw a gentle glow encompassing her body. She raised her right leg and encircled it with her arms. With one cheek pressed against her knee, she looked up at him with an innocent, needful look that tore through him.

Rubbing his jaw, he wanted to ease the ache in her eyes, but for his life, he could think of no way to answer her question. "But even if you are human for now, what of the morrow? Do you know when you will again take your heavenly form?"

"Nay," Arina breathed, wishing she did know. But the crone had never told her that part.

Would she be transformed as soon as he died, or would she live out a normal human life? "I know not how long I shall remain as I am."

"Then you are more human than you know."

She frowned, confused by his words. "How do you mean?"

Daemon returned to sit beside her, but he didn't look at her. Instead, he studied the fire. "None of us ever know how long or how short a time we have," he said. "We spend the whole of our brief lives afraid of death. It is the one true demon that stalks all men."

Sadness lined his face and she wished for a way to comfort him. He tossed a stray piece of wood into the fire and sighed. "At least you have one advantage over us; you know for certain what awaits you in death."

She shook her head. "Nay, like all mortals, I fear my human death more than anything. For I have no more certainty where I shall end than any other. I won't know until I face Peter and his book."

"So God is as unforgiving as I thought."

Arina stiffened her spine at his words and stared aghast at his conclusion. "Whatever do you mean?"

He turned toward her, his face lined with hatred. "What sin have you committed, milady? What could you ever do to cause your damnation? You are the purest of heart of any creature ever born. Only the most miserable, most callous being would condemn you."

"Nay, do not say such things," she said.

"Why? He has punished me for things I could not help and damned you for events you could not prevent."

"God has not damned me," she insisted. "Should I die damned, then I will have done it to myself. We cannot control the obstacles put before us, or what others think or may do. But we are all masters of our own end, of the choices we make."

Daemon snorted. "I seem to recall a story Brother Jerome used to tell of the pharaoh who was born to be damned. Do any of us truly have a choice?"

She nodded. "Had the pharaoh freed the Hebrews, even he would have been saved. 'Twas his stubbornness that damned him, his stubbornness that cost him his life."

A strange look crossed his face and she struggled to name it. "What?" she asked.

He looked away, his body more rigid than the sword strapped to his hip.

Arina reached out and touched his shoulder. The muscles beneath her fingertips were taut with strain. "Please tell me what haunts your eyes?" she said.

His jaw twitched. " 'Tis naught but an old memory that plagues me."

"Will you not share it?" she asked.

Daemon stared at her, and the pain on his face reached deep inside her and touched her heart. " 'Tis said my father, after seeing me for the first time, was stricken with a need to go pilgrimage and do penance for my birth," he whispered, his voice bitter and hard. "Though many tried to persuade him otherwise, he insisted, claiming that he owed it to God for helping bring such a foul child into this world."

Tears filled her eyes, and she bit her lip to keep from crying out at the injustice. How could anyone believe such a thing?

Daemon curled his lip, his gaze narrowing. "My father never returned, but was ambushed and slaughtered by the Saracens outside of Jerusalem. 'Twas rumored the Saracens carried out God's punishment. And while the brothers blamed me for my father's death, I blamed his stubbornness."

So much pain, so much sadness. Arina yearned for some way to soothe the torment that festered in his heart. "Then you believe we control our destiny?"

He shook his head. "How can I?"

Arina traced the line of his jaw, his whiskers prickling her fingertip, sending coils of pleasure through her. He sat so close she could feel his heat even stronger than that of the fire. "I wish I could make you believe," she whispered.

When he looked at her, her breath faltered at the tenderness in his eyes. "When I am near you, I can almost believe anything," he whispered, his words warming her breast.

Before she could move, he leaned forward and captured her lips. Arina moaned with pleasure, too little used to the sensation of his mouth claiming hers. She ran her hands over his back, desire besieging her heart, her blood.

Though she knew she should push him away, she couldn't bring herself to do so. Nay, this one time, she would stay with him.

Daemon nipped at her lips, drawing them between his teeth and gently scraping them. She shuddered, her body exploding with throbbing heat.

He laid her back against the floor and she went willingly, delighting in the feel of his weight pinning her down. Arina closed her eyes, savoring the raw, earthly vitality of his touch, his body.

Never had she imagined anything feeling so wonderful. Not even the freedom of flight could compare to the warm heady sensation of his kiss.

He left her mouth, and buried his lips in her neck. Arina arched against him, her body sizzling in response to his touch. She wanted him. Heaven help her for she could not find it within her to push him away. Though she did not truly belong in his world, she was his wife. And a wife belonged to her husband.

Nay, she would never hurt him, never deny him. Tonight she would lie with him as a human and try not to think of what might happen on the morrow. For now she needed his touch as much as he needed hers.

Daemon inhaled her rich scent, his head reeling as if intoxicated. He knew he should leave her. If he had any decency within him, he would rise from her body and sleep outside with the horses.

No one had ever accepted or welcomed him the way she did. And nothing had ever felt better than the luscious curves that molded against him, pressing against his chest, his hips. His body burned for her. Yet he couldn't bring himself to dishonor her further. Nay, he had corrupted her once, he would harm her no more.

Forcing his weary muscles to cooperate, he pushed himself away.

She encircled his shoulders with her arms. Daemon looked into her eyes and his breath faltered at the gentle need that hovered in their rich blue depths.

"Nay, milord," she whispered, her voice echoing through him. "For this night, I would have you as husband."

Arina watched the emotions play across his face—disbelief, longing and finally happiness. He returned to her lips, his breath sweeter than any wine. She pulled at his tunic, wanting to feel the strength of his chest against her palms.

The fire played across his face, displaying the raw hunger in his eyes. She trembled, unable to believe that he desired her so much. Reaching up, she took his braid and slowly undid it until his hair cascaded over her. Its ends tickled her neck and face. As she had longed to do so many times, she ran her hands through the silken strands.

Daemon closed his eyes and turned his face to gently nip at her arm. Arina sucked her breath in between her teeth, her breasts tingling. No man could compare to her warrior. He alone stood most honorable, most noble, and she vowed to let no harm befall him.

He reached for the hem of her kirtle. For the

briefest moment, she almost stopped him. But what did it matter? Either she was already damned for lying with him, or she wasn't. Would one more time make a difference? Nay, not to Peter. But to Daemon it might.

She shivered as cold air contacted her naked skin, her breasts tightening in response. Heat stole up her cheeks and she tried to cover herself from his gaze.

"Nay, milady," he whispered, running his finger down the center of her bare chest. "You have naught to be ashamed of."

Arina swallowed, still uncomfortable. But as he dipped his head to her breast and took it into his mouth, she forgot her nudity. All she could think of was the passion coiling in her stomach, the all-consuming pleasure running the length of her body. His hair spilled across her breasts, her stomach, tickling her, inflaming her senses.

She cradled his head as he suckled, his tongue sending a thousand quivers to her belly. His hands roamed over her flesh, but when he touched her left thigh, she gasped as pain slashed through her pleasure.

Daemon pulled back with a frown. How could he have forgotten her injuries? He ran his hand over her thigh and grimaced at her wound. The whole length of her thigh and hip was red and bruised.

As gently as he could, he probed the bruise. Finally he deduced no bones had been broken.

"You should have reminded me," he whispered, his voice hoarse with guilt that he had been so neglectful.

She touched his chin, turning his face until he met her gaze. "It didn't hurt until you touched it," she said, with a small smile.

He found her humor terribly misplaced. "And now?"

"The only ache I feel is the emptiness in my arms. Come, Lord Norman, I need you to banish that emptiness."

Daemon stared in disbelief of her words. Before he could stop himself, he pulled her against him. Her hands danced over his naked chest, exploring him. He closed his eyes, savoring each delectable touch.

Lying on his back, he pulled her atop him.

Arina gasped at her position. His leather breeches felt strange beneath her bare buttocks and a demanding throb pounded. He ran his hands up, over her chest, cupping her breasts. Her head swimming with pleasure, she arched against him.

Did all humans feel this way when they coupled? For some reason, she doubted it. Nay, what existed between them was something more than lust, something more special.

Daemon reached up and buried his hand in her hair, pulling her forward until her lips touched his. She gasped as her breasts brushed against his hard chest and she shook.

His warm strength surrounded her, chasing away all the chills brought by the drafts in the old hut.

Arina closed her eyes, wishing she could stay with him like this for all eternity. Oh, if only she could remain human and they could break the curse. She would never ask for more than Daemon's love, his touch.

Suddenly, Daemon rolled her over. Arina bit her lip as he fumbled with his breeches. Expectation flooded her heart and set it pounding even as heat crept up her face.

He pulled his breeches from him and she feasted on the sight of his bare body. Never had she seen anything so glorious, so beautiful.

Hesitant and somewhat afraid, she reached to touch him. She traced the trail of curls that tapered away from his belly. He drew in a sharp breath, and she smiled at her power over him.

Daemon closed his eyes, savoring her touch. Never before had a woman been so bold, so eager for him. What was it about his angel that made her reach out when others refused?

But would she leave him?

Fear tore through him and he vowed never to let her go. So what if he died on the morrow. At least he would die having known happiness, acceptance. And if he had to die, then nothing would please him more than to draw his last breath while staring into his angel's eyes.

Her hand cupped him and he gasped. Unable

to stand any more, he pulled her hand away. She looked up into his eyes and he shivered at the innocence, the love that shone so brightly. Would she still have that look when the sun broke them apart? Or would she weep in regret?

As if sensing his thoughts, she ran her hand under his hair and toyed with his scalp. She fingered his brand and a frown darted across her brow.

He tensed for her question.

" 'Tis a cross," he said before she had a chance to ask him.

Her frown deepened. "A cross?"

He leaned forward and parted his hair.

Arina gasped at the mark. She touched the scarred flesh, her heart pounding. Grimacing, she could barely imagine the pain such a wound must have caused. And without asking, she knew how and why he had received it.

She brushed his hair back over the mark and tilted his chin until he met her gaze. Misery swam in his green and brown eyes, but beneath that she saw his fear. "The ones who did that are surely damned for their actions."

He snorted and looked away. "Are they? I would have thought them rewarded for exorcising the devil from me."

She drew a deep breath and shook her head. "I can assure you the Lord doesn't hold with anyone giving such pain in his name."

Taking her hand, he brought it to his lips and

nibbled her fingertips. Fire danced in her belly. "For your gentle touch, milady, I would gladly suffer through it all again," he whispered, his voice ragged.

Warmth flooded her body and she pulled him against her chest. She held him tight, wishing she could have stopped the torture he had received. An image of a child screaming out drifted through her mind, and she wondered how anyone could be so cruel.

But as Daemon stroked her back, the image evaporated. He covered her with his body and her thoughts scattered. Arina trembled against the fire coursing through her veins.

Daemon kissed her deeply, separating her legs with his knees. Her head swam from the pressure of his lips, the taste of his mouth, and she reached up to hold him close. He braced his arms on either side of her, cradling her head in his hands. Warmth flooded her at the tenderness of his touch.

And then he slid inside her. Arina tensed at the sudden fullness. His hips resting against hers, Daemon began to nibble the flesh behind her ears.

Unbelievable pleasure spread through her, tightening her stomach, her loins. She threw her head back with a throaty moan. Never had she felt anything like the quivering pleasure pulsing through her. She gripped his shoulders, raising her hips to draw him deeper inside.

At her invitation, he began to slowly rock his hips. Arina bit her lip at the strange dance. With each gentle stroke, her body burned more.

Daemon closed his eyes against the elation bursting inside him. Not even his dreams could compare to the reality of what he experienced. Her swollen breasts rubbed against him, urging him faster. She ran her hands down his spine and over his buttocks, and he trembled from the magic of her touch.

Arina quivered as he buried his face in her neck. His breath echoed in her ears and his soft moans delighted her. This was her husband and she vowed to fight for him.

As he moved against her lips, a strange pulsing warmth grew. She arched her lips, pulling him in deeper, marveling at the bittersweet pleasure. He moved faster, and the throbbing grew until she feared she would die from it. Then, just as she could stand no more, her body burst.

Arina moaned, her entire body shaking. Never, never had she experienced anything similar. Her heart pounding, she wondered if she had died. Surely that alone could explain the falling sensation.

But then Daemon's arms tightened about her and he too convulsed. He groaned softly, then collapsed against her, holding her so tightly that she almost cried out in pain.

"Am I still alive?" she whispered.

His hold loosening, he leaned up and kissed her gently on her lips. "Aye, milady."

"Is it always like that?" she asked.

Daemon shook his head. "Nay, milady. 'Tis never so sweet as it was this night."

Warmth spread through her, and she swept his hair up over his shoulder. His arms braced on either side of her, he stared down at her with an intense look that stole her breath and left her even weaker. She traced the stubble on his jaw and she offered him a smile. "I am glad that I have given you what no other has."

And even as the words left her lips, she knew that she would gladly repeat her actions, no matter what fate and Belial brought their way.

Daemon lay in the still quietness, listening to the winds howl and the fire crackle. Arina's hair was spread out over his chest as she lay beside him. He'd give anything to stay like this for all eternity.

But what of the morrow? His own death didn't concern him, but hers did.

"Milord?"

He started at her gentle voice intruding on his thoughts. "I thought you were asleep."

"I had a wonderful dream," she whispered, turning in his arms until she stared up into his eyes. The brightness of her gaze warmed him. "You and I were drifting in a glorious ray of light so bright that we couldn't see one another, but I could feel you. Your breath was my breath, your lungs my lungs."

"My heart your heart?"

She smiled up at him. "Aye."

"But what happens when the night comes and ends the sunlight?"

She frowned and hit him in the shoulder. "Ever the doubter, aren't you?"

Daemon sighed, his heart heavy as he brushed her hair back from her face. "My life has taught me to be wary, milady."

She nodded, and sadness replaced the happy gleam in her eyes.

A twinge of guilt tweaked his conscience, but he couldn't share her optimism.

While she studied the flames, she gave a weary sigh to match his own. "How did you find me?" she asked.

Daemon wondered what had made her ask that question. "Belial sent me for you."

"Belial?" she asked, tensing in his arms.

"Aye."

She narrowed her eyes. " 'Tis his fault I fell from my horse. I wonder what mischief he plans."

Daemon stiffened, a chill of foreboding racing over him. The hairs on the back of his neck stood upright. How much power did the demon truly possess? "Is he with us?"

Arina shook her head and settled back in his arms. "Nay, I can tell when he approaches."

Daemon held her close, his heart thumping heavily. "Do you know his limitations?"

She ran her hand down his ribs, drawing small circles in a tender caress that seared him. Her breath fell across his chest, raising chills. "When he is in human form, he is very limited. He can only beguile and tempt. 'Tis his demon's form that is dangerous. Then he can infiltrate the mind or possess a body."

Again foreboding seized him. "Infiltrate the mind?"

"Aye. He can manipulate memories, or steal them as he did with me. He is also a master of dreams, using them to weaken his victim's resolve."

"As he did when I thought I had taken your innocence."

Arina sat back, her face stern. "I think he wants my soul more than he has ever wanted anything. There is no telling what he'll do to secure it. I pray you, milord, tread carefully. I would not have you sacrificed."

Daemon touched her cheek. He wasn't sure how things would end between them, but he had a great terror that he would lose her. She didn't belong to his world, and it would be only a matter of time before she left him. "I will not see you harmed. Belial will have to rid himself of me first."

Horror filled her gaze. "And that, milord, is my worst fear."

* * *

Morning came, but it brought no joy to Arina's heart. Though she was grateful Daemon had saved her and that they had shared the night, she feared what would follow.

The voice inside her heart urged her to flee, but where would she go?

Daemon entered the hut, his face pinkened by his exercise. "I've saddled Ganille," he said, removing his gloves. He stretched his hands out to the fire, and she admired the strength and beauty of them.

"Tell me, milady," he said, drawing her attention away from his hands, hands she remembered seeking out her most intimate parts and thrilling her. "Where is your saddle?"

Heat stole up her cheeks from both his question and her brazen thoughts. "I didn't take one."

He cocked an eyebrow. Lowering his hands, he turned toward her. "No saddlebags either?"

She shook her head.

"How did you plan to survive your journey?"

Arina rubbed the chills from her arms and sighed. "Forgive me, milord, but I've never had to plan such things before. 'Tis only recently that I have to worry over being hungry, needing shelter."

He crossed his arms over his chest and gave her a piercing glare. "Then I suggest you never again try and leave."

Though his words should have made her angry, they didn't. Instead her chest tightened, and her heart hung heavy at the thought of leaving him. Did she really have a choice?

If Daemon noted her sudden sadness, he gave no clue. "Come, milady, we should make our way back while the weather is pleasant."

Arina pushed herself up, but pain ripped down her leg and she was unable to rise.

Daemon rushed forward, a stern frown on his face. "Are you all right?"

"Nay," she said, her leg muscles throbbing. " 'Tis the bruise. I fear it won't allow me to walk."

He nodded, then scooped her up in his arms and carried her to the horses. Arina savored the feel of his arms around her, afraid of her joy, but unable to stop it. She damned the curse. Surely there must be some way she could undo or prevent it.

Daemon mounted his horse, settling himself behind her. He pulled her against his chest, and she wrapped her arms about his waist. Snuggling her head under his chin, she listened to the deep throb of his heart, grateful for its healthy, steady beat. He touched her cheek, his grip tense.

She expected him to say something, but instead he seized the reins and kicked his horse forward. Arina closed her eyes and tried to focus only on the moment, not on the future and what it might bring.

Around midday, they stopped for a brief meal. Daemon spread his cloak on the ground and set her upon it. He pulled the saddlebags from Ganille and set about preparing a light meal, but before he could finish, Belial and a group of Daemon's men joined them.

Arina met Belial's amused gaze. No doubt he had guessed what had transpired between them the night before—he had probably even planned it. So be it. As long as she remained in human form, she was Daemon's wife and she had no intention of denying her husband what comfort she could.

But what of his life?

She flinched at hearing Belial's voice inside her head. So he had regained some of his strength. She would have to remember that and take more precautions.

"Arina!" Belial cried. "I am so grateful to find you safe. You had me terribly worried."

She exchanged glances with Daemon, warning him with her eyes to play along. "I beg your forgiveness. I didn't mean to cause you worry."

Belial rode his horse over to her. "I trust you weren't harmed?"

She had to crane her neck to look up at him, and she had the distinct impression that he enjoyed making her strain. "Not physically."

He dismounted, knelt beside her and whispered just for her ears. "I suggest you do not try to escape again."

"Don't threaten me, demon," she said, making sure neither Daemon nor his men could hear. "I *know* the extent of your powers."

His smile sent a chill over her. "I hope for your sake that is true, but what if you're wrong?"

"Arina?"

She turned at Daemon's call, grateful that he had startled her out of her fear. Aye, Belial's words were meant to shake her confidence.

Daemon approached them, and though he held himself rigid, no part of him betrayed that he knew the truth about Belial. Pride swelled inside her, and with it hope. Mayhap they could find a way to thwart Belial's plans.

"Is your brother chastising you?" Daemon asked.

Belial shook his head. "Nay, I could never be harsh with my sweet sister."

"Then come," Daemon said, leading Belial's skittish horse toward him. "Let us return."

Though the journey back was uneventful, it wore on her nerves. Even without speaking, she could feel Belial's malevolent intent, his treacherous gaze seeking her out and noting the way she held her husband.

If only she possessed the powers to see inside Belial's mind. Arina sighed, wishing that she could see into the future too.

In little time, they rode into the bailey of Brunneswald Hall. The children broke from their play and ran to greet them, their cheeks rosy and smiles bright. Her heart warming at the sight, Arina waved to them.

Edith paused next to Ganille and smiled. "We made snow angels, milady. Would you like to see them?"

Arina returned her smile, but before she could answer, Daemon spoke up. "Milady is injured, good Edith. It may be a while before she can see your angels."

Edith's face puckered into a worried frown. "Will you be all right, milady?"

"Aye," Arina answered. " 'Tis naught serious."

"Come on, Edith!" a small boy cried. "We've got Creswyn pinned down."

Arina stifled her laugh as Edith eagerly ran to join the other children.

Daemon dismounted, then helped her down, his arms a perfect cradle for her body. Arina wrapped her arms around him, noting the darkening of his eyes as he stared at her lips.

Smiling, she wished they were alone so that she could yield to the part of her that longed for his kiss.

His grip tightening, he carried her through the hall to their chambers and placed her on her bed. He pulled her cloak from her shoulders and folded it.

A strange look crossed his face as he watched

her. "At least I have no worries about you running away. Not until your leg heals."

Arina swallowed and glanced away. "Perhaps it is you who should run away."

He placed her cloak back in the small chest, then turned toward her. "I refuse to run, milady. You know that."

"Aye," she said, her tears clogging her throat. "I do know that."

She watched him leave the room, her heart heavy from pent-up tears. There must be some way to save him.

Chapter Fifteen

Weeks dragged by as if each day were carried upon an old man's shoulders. Arina greeted every dawn with fear and anxiety. Would this day be the day of Daemon's death? And each day, she tried a new way to break the curse, but nothing seemed to work.

Finally, more snow fell, blanketing the land in a pure, white cover that made her wonder how evil could rest so comfortably around them and not at least be touched by the innocence of this world.

She sat outside watching the children make their snow angels while she sipped a cup of warm cider. Their laughter rang in her ears and brought a smile to her lips.

She'd enjoyed these last three fortnights. Daemon always stood near, ready to assist her. She had taught him to play chess, and he had taught her much about human feelings and desires. But their time together only made her greedier for his presence, greedier for a lifetime spent by his side.

Whatever was she to do?

"M'hlafdie?"

She turned at the old gnarled voice and faced the crone.

"I beg your forgiveness for disturbing you," the old woman said, drawing closer.

Arina stared at her. Though she ought to hate the old woman, only pity filled her. "What do you need?"

"I . . ." The crone glanced away. "I know I have no right to ask, but I seek your charity."

Arina frowned at her words, wondering what charity the crone sought. "My charity?"

"Aye, *m'hlafdie.* I need you to forgive me for what I have done."

The crone's request shocked her. How could she even ask such a thing?

"Please," the crone begged. "These days past, I have watched you and regretted all I have done. 'Twas my grief and pain that caused me to seek vengeance. And I . . . I saw my boy last night." She looked away, her old eyes troubled.

"Your son?" Arina asked, a tremor of fear fill-

290

ing her heart. Had Belial been playing with the old woman's dreams?

"Aye," she said, her old voice shaking. "He came to me and told me how glorious his new home was, just as you had said. My boy bade me seek forgiveness so that I could join him there one day. He wants me with him for all eternity."

Arina's chest tightened. Sorrow and regret mingled in the old eyes, eyes that spoke of too much hardship and grief.

How could she deny this woman what she asked? Indeed, her forgiveness seemed a small request. "What is your name?"

"Raida, *m'hlafdie.*"

Arina smiled. "Raida, I do forgive you."

And even as she said the words, she knew them for truth. All too well, she understood human emotions and why the loss of Raida's son would raise the woman's wrath and make her take such actions.

Fear flickered in the woman's eyes and she hugged herself close. "Is it too late for me to save my soul?"

Arina glanced about the yard, looking for Belial. If he learned of this, there was no telling what evil he might visit upon both of them. She could protect herself, but the old woman's frailty would make her an easy victim.

Leaning down, she whispered, "Aye, but 'tis treacherous business should Belial catch you."

Raida swallowed, her eyes wide and fearful. "What must I do?"

Arina thought the matter over. There were several ways to reclaim a bartered soul, provided the pact had not been signed.

No power could break a signed agreement.

"How was your pact set?"

"I renounced the Lord and promised to serve Belial and the devil."

"Did you set your pact in writing?"

"Nay, *m'hlafdie*. I know not how to write, so I took a verbal oath that Lucifer could claim my soul upon my death."

Arina nodded in relief. It would be a little tricky, but not impossible. If only the curse were as easily undone. "Did Lucifer specify when your death would take place?"

"When the curse is fulfilled."

Arina sucked her breath between her teeth. 'Twould seem everything hinged upon Daemon's death. But if she could convert Raida, mayhap she could thwart the curse, or at least make it easier to break. "You must do penance for your sins and pray to the Lord for forgiveness."

"Will He forgive me?" she asked, her voice brittle.

Arina smiled at her. *There's always hope.* Kaziel's words echoed in her head and she chose to believe them. "If you implore the Lord honestly and truly repent, aye, He shall forgive you."

Raida's eyes shone in relief and she started to move away.

Arina grabbed her arm and pulled her back. "One other thing, Raida; your penance must be public. You must show the Lord your sacrifice."

"Thank you, *m'hlafdie!*" Raida cried, falling on her knees and kissing the hem of Arina's kirtle. Clutching it tight, Raida shook all over.

"But," Arina said, pausing until Raida looked up at her, "you must take care. Lucifer and Belial will not take kindly to losing you. Upon your death, they will try to claim your soul. When they appear, you must invoke the name of Azriel. He will come to your aid and banish the demons back to hell."

"Azriel; I shall not forget."

Arina smiled, wishing Azriel and his army could help her.

She touched Raida's hand, and the old woman's eyes turned gentle. "I should never have blamed you, *m'hlafdie.* You are truly kind."

A breeze blew an odor toward Arina and she stiffened, recognizing the stench of hell. She urged Raida to her feet. "Go now and pray."

Almost as soon as Raida left her, Belial appeared, walking from beside the manor as if he were on a leisurely stroll about the bailey. A smile curved his lips as he closed the distance between them.

Once more, a shiver ran down her spine, and she lifted her chin to confront him.

Show him no fear, she repeated silently. But the longer she remained human, the harder it became for her to battle her emotions.

Belial paused by her side, looking down with a chiding glare. "Do you think 'tis that easy?"

"Nothing is easy," Arina said with a small laugh, knowing Raida would have a difficult time saving herself. "You'd do well to remember that yourself."

He laughed, the evil sound grating on her ears. "So you are regaining your spirit."

She narrowed her eyes at his double meaning, but held her tongue. Looking away from him, she watched the children frolicking. She hoped he would take her hint and drift away.

"Do you think you can break the curse?"

His words brought her attention back to him. "Can I?" she asked, trying to act nonchalant, but inside her heart stilled, her senses waited in expectation of his words.

Belial's smile widened. Crossing his arms over his chest, he assessed her with a calculating stare. "If you seek to make me give you that information, you'll have to offer me a tidbit."

This time, Arina smiled, her heart suddenly light. She wanted to laugh, but she squelched her desire. No need to raise his wrath and force a direct confrontation. "Thank you, demon. You've already answered my question. If you are able to barter, then there is a way to break it."

His gaze turned cold. Belial uncrossed his arms and seized her, pulling her up from her seat.

Fear darted up her spine, and it was all she could do not to cower.

"Don't play this game, angel," he snarled, his tone cutting through her. His eyes flashed red and his teeth lengthened to fangs. "You don't know the rules."

A large shadow moved over them. Arina looked up almost expecting Kaziel, but instead she met the displeased frown of Daemon.

He raked a scathing glare over Belial. "I warned you before about touching her in anger."

Belial closed his eyes and tensed. She knew he struggled to regain control over his appearance. Lifting his chin, he opened his eyes and released her. Once more his eyes were blue, his teeth short.

With a smirk on his lips, he turned to face Daemon. "So you have, Daemon *Fierce*-Blood," he said in a slow drawl, clapping him on the back. He lifted his eyebrows. "So you have."

The two men locked gazes. Arina held her breath at the tension that sparked between them, tension that sizzled with heat and scorched her with its intensity.

"Go ahead," Belial said, indicating her with

his gaze. "Take her. You've earned the right." And there was no mistaking the malevolent undertone in his voice.

Belial cast them each one last amused look before sauntering back toward the hall.

"Are you all right?" Daemon asked.

In spite of her fear, Arina offered him a smile. Hope blossomed inside her. There *was* a way to break the curse and she must find it. "Never have I felt better!"

Arina knelt in the small chapel just outside the hall. For hours she had prayed, hoping to receive some clue as to how to thwart Belial and Raida's curse. But all she'd gained thus far were swollen, throbbing knees.

The shuffling of feet intruded on her quiet, and she glanced over her shoulder to see Brother Edred approach. He crossed himself before the altar, then knelt by her side.

"Is milady seeking forgiveness for some sin?" he asked, his voice scarce more than a whisper.

Arina glanced at him. "Nay, Brother. I have no public confession that needs be made."

A frown furrowed his brow, and he ran his gaze over her body as if searching for something. "Then what has kept milady here for all these hours?"

She lifted a brow, amazed by his confession that he had been watching her. She started to take him to task, but all of a sudden an idea formed in her mind. Aye, even with his sins, Brother Edred could be a good ally. "There is a demon in our midst."

"Ah, child," he said, patting her clenched hands. "At last you have seen the truth of your husband's nature."

Arina removed her hands from his grasp and shook her head. "Not my husband, Brother, but another man."

A frown furrowed his brow and disbelief filled his eyes. "And what makes you think 'tis someone else?"

"There have been signs," she said, leaning close as if she whispered a horrible secret.

Arina had always scorned mankind's superstitions, but for once she decided they suited her purpose. "At night I hear weeping and during stray breezes, I smell the devil's sulphur."

His eyes widened. "And you are certain 'tis not at your husband's approach?"

"Aye," she said gravely. "I am most certain. I hear it only when he is away."

Brother Edred produced a small vial from his robes. "Take this milady," he said, pressing it into her hands. " 'Tis the Lord's water. Should evil approach you, this will scatter it away."

"Thank you, kind brother."

He blessed her before moving away. Arina watched him leave, hoping he would begin searching elsewhere for the demon.

With any luck, he would detect Belial of his

own accord. But if she spoke Belial's name in accusation and others learned what he was, she could be tried for heresy and communing with demons.

But once they learned of Belial and realized Daemon had no association with him, then mayhap some of the fear reserved for Daemon would be decreased.

Chapter Sixteen

Belial hovered in the shadows of the stable, his body translucent as he floated around the rafters. At last he could convert to his demon form. He threw his head back and laughed, reveling in his growing power. Just a few more days and he would be back to his old self.

A flash of brown caught his eye. Drifting to the top of the stable so that he could peer more closely out of the crack between the chinks, he spied Edred crossing the yard. The fat little friar cast a furtive glance around as if seeking someone, or mayhap avoiding someone.

Belial frowned, an uneasy twinge settling in his belly. Something was amiss.

He lowered himself to the floor and nonchalantly made his way outside.

"Lord Belial!" the friar cried.

Stifling his smile, Belial feigned surprise and walked over to him. "Greetings, Brother. What duties have you this day?"

The friar seized his arm and quickly pulled him off to the small garden beside the hall. He scanned the garden like a fearful mouse looking for a cat.

Belial longed to claw the tight grip from his elbow, but he tolerated it, knowing that eventually he would find out what had the little man so distraught.

"I have spoken with your sister," Brother Edred said in a low tone.

Belial cocked his brow in expectation. Could the fat little mouse have taken the wrong piece of cheese? "Did you now?"

"Aye," he said, his eyes large and round in fear. "And she spoke of demons among us!"

Belial gave him a patient, chiding smile. "Of course there is a demon among us. Lord Daemon—"

"Nay, she said 'twas another."

"Another?" he asked, making sure to look frightened as he leaned nearer. "Did she name the beast?"

Edred shook his head, his gaze wistful. He wrung his pudgy hands. "I'd give aught if she had, but alas, she said she didn't know who.

Only that she had seen signs and that the beast traveled close by."

" 'Tis a bad sign," Belial said, shaking his head. So Arina had set doubt in the friar's mind and sent Edred out to find *him*. 'Twas a good thing he had already allied with the friar, or she might have succeeded.

Yet he had to stifle a smile at her resourcefulness. Clever little angel. He would have to watch her more closely. Arina was learning his job and ways a little faster than she should have.

A rush of warmth covered his body. He admired a quick learner. But even so, she could not out-think him, and her little ploy with the friar could certainly be turned against her. " 'Twould appear Lord Daemon is gathering his minions."

The friar crossed himself, his entire body trembling. Belial breathed in the sweet bouquet of fear, nourishing his starved soul on it.

"Do you really think demons are gathering here, among us?"

"Aye," Belial said gravely. "We must expose Daemon. Fetch Lord Norbert. Together we may yet outsmart the devil's mind."

Daemon left the hall, but before he took three steps outside, Brother Edred ran up to him and slung water in his face. Daemon cursed, wiping at the drops dripping from his chin. Glaring at the little man, he fought his urge to beat him.

"What is the matter with you?"

"Forgive me, milord," Brother Edred said, his hands trembling. "I didn't see your approach. I beg you humbly for forgiveness."

Daemon narrowed his eyes. From what he'd seen, it had been no accident. Indeed, it looked very deliberate. His rage brewing in his chest, Daemon pushed the man aside with a warning. "I beg you to take better care where you walk. You could hurt someone, mayhap even yourself," he grumbled, making his way to the stable.

Belial pulled Norbert down behind the large shrub as Daemon walked by, his eyes enraged. He nodded to Norbert. " 'Tis as I said."

Norbert clenched his teeth. Aye, Belial had been right. Daemon possessed such power that not even the friar's Holy Water blemished his evil flesh.

Hatred seeped through his veins. If only Harold had survived, then these beasts would not be feasting on the good Saxon people.

Brother Edred joined them, his wise old eyes troubled. "Whatever are we to do?"

Norbert ignored the question and excused himself. He might not be able to defeat the devil, but maybe he could save Arina. Aye, the Norman beast may have brought her back against her will, but with any luck he might be able to thwart this evil and get her away.

*   *   *

"Enter," Arina called. She looked up from her sewing to see Norbert entering her chambers. Frowning at his presence, she couldn't imagine what he might want with her. Never since the night on the battlements had he sought her out. "*M'hlaford*, what brings you here?"

He moved to her side, then paused as he caught sight of Cecile. Norbert watched her weaving path as she made her way across the floor. A strange look crossed his face, and if Arina didn't know better, she'd swear the small kitten frightened him. His jaw twitched as if he longed to say something.

She waited for several heartbeats. When it looked as if he might continue his silence, Arina gave him a patient smile. "Is there a vexing matter on your mind, *m'hlaford?*"

He looked back at her, and she struggled to read him, but his emotions eluded her. "*M'hlafdie*, I wanted to tell you that my brothers and I intend to leave within the hour."

She looked back at her sewing and took a careful stitch. "Then I bid you godspeed and safety."

He knelt before her and took the needle from her hands. Staring up into her eyes, he reminded her of a supplicant seeking Divine aid. "*M'hlafdie*, if you wish, we can take you with us."

Arina started at his words. Why would he ask such a thing? "What do you mean?"

He took a deep breath and touched her knee. "I know you ran away and that the Norman brought you back. If you still wish to flee him, we can take you. I assure you this time he will never find you."

Arina stared at him, part of her wanting to accept and part of her unable to. If she left, Daemon would be safe, but her heart cried out in denial.

How could she leave him?

She looked down at Daemon's tunic in her lap. Tracing the fine linen with her finger, she could almost feel his muscles beneath it. Excruciating pain ripped through her, and though she knew she should leave, she just couldn't accept Norbert's offer.

Indeed, no mishap had befallen him in all these weeks. Mayhap one of her prayers had worked. Or Raida's penance.

She must believe that all would be well. "I can't leave," she whispered.

Norbert took her hands into his. Startled by his touch, Arina stiffened. "Please, *m'hlafdie*. Let me help you."

Just as she opened her mouth to reply, a loud crash sounded from outside. A gasp lodging in her throat, she tossed the tunic aside and ran to see what had happened.

As she entered the hall, she stopped, her heart pounding ever more. Daemon lay in the center of the floor, a large, broken rota by his side.

Wace stood over him, staring up at the ceiling.

A group of servants stood nearby, none moving. 'Twas as if they were too scared to breathe.

Crying out in fear, Arina rushed to her husband. "Milord, are you all right?"

"It almost crushed him!" Wace said before Daemon could answer her question. "Never before have I seen such."

Arina scanned the splintered wood and twisted iron that littered the area around Daemon.

"Pardon us, *m'hlaford*," one of the servants said, wringing his hands in nervousness as he finally came over. "But the rope slipped from poor Aldred's hands while we were trying to replace the candles. 'Twas an accident, I swear it!"

Daemon pushed himself up and brushed debris from his tunic. For a moment, suspicion darkened his eyes, but as he looked from the old man before him to the younger men huddled by the wall, his gaze lightened. "Fear not; no damage done."

"No damage!" Arina gasped. "You could have died."

As soon as she said the words, she realized what had happened—the curse.

She had been foolish to think it had been broken. Cold rushed over her body, dimming her sight.

She backed away from him, Raida's all-too-familiar, hate-filled words echoing through her head. *You must watch him die.* Terror blinded her, and she turned around and ran from the hall.

Returning to her chambers, Arina scanned the room, her body quaking with fear. Her chest burned and her breath came in short, sharp gasps. She felt as though she would pass out, or die herself.

"Nay," she whispered. He couldn't die. Not because of her. Why, why had she stayed? How could she have thought for one moment that she might break the curse and free them?

"Milady?"

She turned at Daemon's voice. He pulled her into his arms and she shivered in fear.

" 'Twas nothing more than an accident," he said, his voice tender.

"Nay, 'twas the curse," she whispered, reveling in his touch, and afraid the next moment might rob the strength from his arms, the breath from his lungs.

An image of the young Saxon boy dying crept into her mind and she stiffened. Tears gathered in her eyes. She didn't want to see Daemon that way. To watch his life drain out, his eyes turn dull.

Daemon shook his head. "If it was the curse, then I would be lying dead," he said, stepping away from her. "Do I look like a phantom?"

She shook her head, her tears spilling down her cheeks. " 'Tis the curse, I say."

Daemon wiped her tears from her face, his warm hand only making her fear grow. He stared at her with wonderment, and she saw the pain lurking in the odd-colored depths. "No tears, milady. I am still here."

Arina nodded and he pulled her back in his arms. He held her for several minutes. Each one seemed suspended in time, and she savored every beat of his heart against her chest. And with each beat, she knew what she had to do.

Heaven help her, but she had to leave him.

A knock sounded on the door an instant before Wace opened it. "Forgive me, milord, milady," he said, his cheeks flushing. "I was—"

"I know, Wace," Daemon said, interrupting him. "Wait by the horses."

Wace nodded and left them alone.

Daemon rubbed his hands down her arms. "No more fretting, milady. All shall be fine."

She nodded, her throat too tight for her to speak. With a heavy heart, she watched him strap his sword to his hips.

Arina followed him through the hall and out into the yard. He swung up onto his horse, and she admired the handsome figure he made.

She would never see him again. The thought ravished her heart, her soul.

Arina stared at him, committing every line of his body and face to her memory. That memory would be her only comfort in the years to come. Hollow, empty years spent wishing for a man

307

she knew she could never have.

Lifting the reins, Daemon gave her one last, tender look.

Arina waved at him.

The heated look in his eyes stole her breath. Daemon kicked his horse and sped out the gate. She clenched her hand into a fist and lowered it to her side. "Take care, my precious Norman," she whispered.

Closing her eyes, Arina wished the rota had fallen on her. At least then her misery would be over. Her heart heavy, her throat tight, she turned around and saw Norbert standing with his brothers.

She approached them.

"Have you changed your mind, *m'hlafdie?*"

"Aye," she said, her voice shaking.

Don't leave, her mind warned, but this time she ignored it. "I shall go with you."

Chapter Seventeen

Daemon entered the hall and breathed a weary sigh. After spending the entire afternoon at the ramparts listening to Master Dennis instruct him on how many men they would need come spring, list all the different supplies he would need to order by then, and explain why they must redesign some of their earlier plans, Daemon wanted nothing more than to find his wife and enjoy a quiet evening in solitude.

He pushed open the door to his chambers and froze. The tunic Arina had been mending lay folded on his bed, but no other sign of her existed. Cecile ran out from under the bed, collided with his legs, then proceeded to circle his feet.

Daemon placed his helm and gloves on the table beside the bed and stooped over to gently rub the kitten's head.

"Where is our lady?" he asked, but his only answer came as a soft meow.

Where could Arina have gone? Frowning, he left the room and went to find her.

A quick search of the hall and bailey yielded nothing. As he entered the stable, a disembodied voice stopped him. "If you seek my sister, then I fear you are out of luck. Once again you have allowed her to escape."

He turned toward the voice. "What say you?"

Belial stepped out of the shadows, his face grim, his eyes hollow. Daemon held the distinct impression the demon's anger had reached its shattering point.

The demon shook his head, disbelief flickering in his light gaze. "She rode off with Norbert and his brothers. She told me she was riding to join you, but now I realize she must have lied." He looked away, his gaze troubled.

"An unbelievable action really," Belial whispered. "I never thought her capable of such."

Daemon's blood ran cold. She'd left with Norbert? "Do you know in which direction they rode?"

Belial snorted, his eyes bitterly amused. "They rode to the north when they left here, but they may have altered their direction."

Clenching his teeth in fury and pain, Daemon

grabbed a fresh horse and saddled it. With practiced ease, he worked the leather straps around the horse's belly.

Had Norbert taken her, or had she left of her own accord?

But why had she left him voluntarily? And as soon as the question flicked across his mind, Daemon knew. Because of the rota.

Why had he left without easing her fears more? He should have known she would do something foolish.

Daemon tightened the cinch with one last tug, then swung himself up on the horse.

"Do you not wish for supplies?" Belial asked, a strange glow in his eyes.

"Nay," he said, his chest tight. "But I do wish to know how long they have been gone."

"They left not long after you."

Most of the day. Anger coiled in his belly at her foolishness, her abandonment. The rational part of him begged him to leave off and let her go, but his heart shouted in denial, reminding him of what his life would be like without her precious touch, her tender smile. Nay, he could not let her go, not without a fight.

But would he have time to find them? If he rode through the night, he should overtake them. Provided they stopped to sleep. Surely they wouldn't travel without stopping.

"My thanks," he said to the demon, then

wheeled his horse about and kicked it into a run.

Arina stared at the flames of the fire, her mind traveling back to the blizzard and the night she'd made love to Daemon. The fire before her warmed her cheeks, but did nothing for the coldness inside her, the coldness that needed her husband's touch.

Arina closed her eyes against the agony that tightened her throat. Saint Peter help her, all she wanted was to go back to him. But how could she? He would die and it would be her fault!

"M'hlafdie?"

She looked up at Norbert, his face shadowed by the darkness. He extended a bowl of porridge to her. "I thought you might be hungry."

"My thanks," she said, taking it from his hands even though her cramped stomach protested the smell.

Norbert squatted by her side and tossed more wood on the fire. After a silent minute, he looked back at her. "He won't find us. You're safe now."

Safe. Dare she even hope for that? But it wasn't her safety she longed for, or cared about. It was Daemon's safety she sought.

Would he understand what she had done and why? Or would his pain be so great that he wouldn't even care about the reasons? Pain squeezed her heart in a brutal grip that stole her breath.

"M'hlafdie?" Norbert asked, his concerned tone doing nothing to alleviate the misery inside her. He touched her arm, and it took all her control not to flinch or flee. He had been so very kind since they left, but he wasn't Daemon and she wanted no other man to touch her in any way.

"I am fine, *m'hlaford*," she said, then tasted some of the porridge.

Norbert nodded, but his doubt reached out to her and she sensed he wanted to say something more.

The younger of his brothers—Arthur, if she remembered his name correctly—stepped forward with a blanket. Norbert rose and took it, then wrapped it around her. "You should rest yourself and try not to worry overmuch," he said, patting her arms. "I'll not let the Norman harm you. I swear it."

Arina set the porridge aside and settled down by her fire. Drawing the blanket up to her chin, she gave a weary sigh, grateful for Norbert, but wishing she had never been forced to leave.

Norbert and his brothers had dug through the snow to make her a pallet on the ground, but still the cold dampness seeped through her body. Watching the flickering flames, she allowed her thoughts to drift.

For awhile she remembered her heavenly

home, the friends who waited there for her. And though the memory filled her with happiness, it didn't compare to the warm thrill that shot through her when her thoughts turned to Daemon.

"Arina?"

She opened her eyes, her heart pounding. 'Twas Belial's voice! Scanning the campsite, she tried her best to find a trace of the beast, but only Norbert and his brothers talking by the fire met her eager gaze.

A chill set her hands shaking and she smelled his demon odor.

"Here you are," the disembodied voice said, and she turned to see the winged shadow beside her.

"You wager much appearing this close to humans," she whispered.

He laughed, his voice ringing through the trees, but she knew its pitch was higher than that which the human ear could hear. Yet the night animals screeched and moaned from the insidious sound.

Norbert and his brothers unsheathed their swords and looked about the forest.

"*M'hlafdie,*" Norbert said, returning to her side. "Harald is going to check on the noise we heard."

She nodded. His brother clapped him on the back before heading into the woods.

"Pathetic beasts," Belial said with a laugh.

"Do you think I should gather wolves to feast on his hide?"

"Nay!" she gasped.

Norbert looked at her with a frown. "You don't want him to go?"

Arina cast a heated glare at Belial, then looked back at Norbert, her temper carefully shielded. "It wasn't your brother's search that I spoke of, *m'hlaford*, but rather a response to the sudden cold that bites my flesh."

Norbert offered her a knowing smile. "I shall get you another blanket."

Belial brushed a cold, shadowy hand against her cheek. "What a liar you have become. I am impressed by your abilities."

Arina slapped at his hand, and a fierce jolt shot through her arm.

"Come angel, you know better than that. You cannot harm me now."

Arina trembled. He was getting ever stronger. Soon she would be no match for his powers and he would have the strength to brew whatever evil he wanted.

What would she do then?

Norbert returned with the promised blanket. He offered her a timid smile as he draped it over her. "Rest easy, *m'hlafdie*. I'm sure the noise was nothing serious."

"Thank you," she said, returning his smile.

When he had left her once more, she turned toward Belial. "Why are you here?"

315

"I wanted to find you."

A chill set her hands shaking, and this time it had nothing to do with the winter frost. "Why?"

Before Belial could answer, she heard a horse approach. Dread feasted in her heart.

"Nay," she whispered, knowing the rider even without seeing him. Panic consumed her.

Daemon entered the clearing, his horse prancing. Arina scrambled from her pallet, her heart pounding as she rushed toward him.

"Nay, you evil bastard!" Norbert shouted at Daemon as he unsheathed his sword. "You'll never take her."

Arina's body running cold, she looked back toward her husband.

Daemon had reined to a stop. His spine rigid, he stared down at Norbert. A sudden gust of wind caressed the blond braid he wore draped over his right shoulder and billowed his cloak out behind him.

Even from a distance, she could see the malice shining in his eyes. "Don't make me kill you, Saxon. 'Tis my wife you have taken. Give her over and you may leave in peace."

She held her breath as Norbert charged forward. Daemon's horse reared, dancing away from Norbert's sword. "I'd rather send you to hell first!"

Daemon brought the prancing horse under control, then slid from his saddle and unsheathed his sword. Tears sprang to her eyes and she feared she might faint. They couldn't fight! Not with the curse and not with her present to witness the event. 'Twould be Daemon's death!

Daemon and Norbert doffed their cloaks.

"Nay!" she screamed, running toward them and placing herself between them before they could engage in swordplay.

She grabbed Daemon's brown, woolen tunic and held tight. "Milord, please, for my sake do not do this."

The look in his eyes tore through her. She ached to ease the agony that stole her breath, but she couldn't—not at the expense of his life.

He wrapped his arm about her and held her close to his beating heart. "Return with me."

"I can't," she said, choking on a sob, feeling his heartbeat race beneath her fingertips. She couldn't stand the thought of touching his chest and not feeling that steady throb. "There's no chance for us."

His jaw tensed and he glared at her. "Don't you say that! 'Tis not so."

"Aye, milord, but it is," she sobbed. "I beseech you to leave while you still can. You must live for me."

He opened his mouth to reply but before he could, Norbert grabbed her and shoved her into his brother's arms. "Hold her, Arthur."

"Nay!" she screamed again, trying to break free, but Arthur's hold didn't lapse.

"This is between us, Norman. 'Tis time for you to pay for the souls you have taken, the lives you have destroyed." They crossed swords. "Give your hellish master my best!"

Metal clanked against metal, the sound blistering her soul, her conscience.

"Please God, no!" she cried, the words searing her throat. Pain echoed in her body and she sobbed, unable to stand the sight of the two men who sought to kill one another.

All her senses dulled, save her hearing. With crystal bright clarity, she heard every time the swords hit, every grunt made by Daemon, and she held her breath, terrified of hearing him groan from a deathblow.

Suddenly, a light broke over their heads.

Arina looked up through her tears and gasped. Invisible to the men, Kaziel descended and joined the fight. She drew a deep, ragged breath. Kaziel caught hold of Norbert's sword and sent it flying.

So Kaziel was Daemon's guardian. Arina looked heavenward and gave a silent prayer of thanks.

Belial flew forward with a snarl and pulled the angel away from the men. "Nay!" he shouted. " 'Tis not for you to interfere!"

Kaziel turned in Belial's arms. " 'Tis not Daemon's time this night, demon. *You* would do well to remember we are not to interfere!"

Arina sagged in relief. *'Tis not Daemon's time*

this night. The phrase lightened her heart as she repeated it over and over, reveling in its sweet sound.

But even so, Norbert rushed toward Daemon and caught him about his waist. Daemon tossed his own sword aside and the two fought with their fists.

Belial flew to her side, his cold fingers biting into her chin as he forced her to look up at him. "He might be safe for this night, angel. But he will be mine. Do not take comfort so soon."

She swallowed, fear once more claiming her. Belial meant his words. She only hoped that she could prevent him from fulfilling them.

The fight continued for a few minutes more until Daemon knocked Norbert to the ground. Retrieving his sword, he held it to Norbert's throat. "Leave off this fight, Saxon," he said, his breathing labored.

Norbert lay back on his elbows and glared up at Daemon, his gaze harsh and damning.

His sword never wavering, Daemon looked to her. "Arina," he called. "Come here."

Arthur released her just as Harald returned to the clearing. Rebellion glowed in both their eyes, but Daemon pressed his sword tip closer to Norbert's throat. "Don't," he warned them, his tone lethal.

Harald dropped his sword and moved to stand beside Arthur.

Still apprehensive and uncertain if what she

did was right, Arina joined her husband.

Daemon wrapped a protective arm about her and gave her a fierce squeeze that nearly cracked her ribs.

Releasing her, he forced her to stand behind him. He removed his sword from Norbert's throat and sheathed it. "I suggest you be on your way. Neither you nor your brothers are welcome on my lands."

Daemon helped her up on his horse, then mounted behind her. Norbert didn't move from his place on the ground, but his glare was such that she almost expected him to rise and again attack Daemon.

Kicking his horse forward, Daemon held her close and they left the Saxon camp. In spite of the fact he said nothing, Arina sensed the pain inside him and she longed to soothe it.

Leagues flew by before Arina found the courage to speak. "I had to leave."

"I know," he said, his voice bitter.

"Then why did you come for me?"

Anger mixed with tenderness in his eyes and his arms tightened about her waist. "I will always come for you, milady."

Though his words brought a warm rush to her heart, frustration claimed her and she wanted to shout at him to see reason. But she bit her tongue. Daemon would never agree with her side of this matter.

* * *

Belial grimaced. Once more the internal pull tightened his gut. "Damn," he cursed, unable to ignore its insistence. Whether he wanted to or not, he had to heed its call.

He closed his eyes and allowed it its way. Light shot around him as he fell through the dimensions of time and space. His body aching, he soon found himself in hell, the pungent odor choking him.

Just as he'd expected, he landed in the main throne room. Orange lights danced along the sulfur-laced walls. Screams echoed around him, and he looked up to his master's chair.

Mephistopheles sat on Lucifer's golden throne, staring at him as if he'd like nothing better than to rip his demon flesh apart. He stroked the black warthog chained to the throne's arm and raked a hostile glare over Belial.

Though Belial had never cared for Mephistopheles even when they'd been true angels, he had to admire the job God had done on Mephistopheles' once beautiful form. As every year passed it seemed more horns grew from his head, more fur on his body, and more mold upon his teeth.

"Greetings, Brother Belial," Mephistopheles said, saliva dripping from his fangs.

Surprised by Mephistopheles' presence, Belial pushed himself up and faced his greatest rival. "Where is Lord Lucifer?"

Mephistopheles shrugged. "Amusing himself

Sherrilyn Kenyon

with the damned, no doubt."

"Then why was I summoned?"

An evil smile curved Mephistopheles' lips and a tremor of fear chilled Belial's spine. Since the day of their fall, Mephistopheles had coveted Belial's place as Lucifer's second-in-command, and Belial recognized the familiar envy and hate burning in Mephistopheles's red eyes. "Lucifer wanted me to inform you of his displeasure."

"His displeasure?" Belial asked. Fear coiled in his belly and he swallowed. Lucifer's temper was not something he wanted to provoke.

"Aye, *dearest brother*," Mephistopheles said, scratching the warthog's ears. " 'Twould seem you have been wasting time and Lucifer is eager for the promised souls. When can we expect them?"

"I'm doing what I can."

Mephistopheles laughed, balling his fist up in the beast's fur. His hand froze and a gleam lightened his red hue. "You want me to carry such a message to Lucifer?"

A dread shiver raked his spine. "Nay. Tell him they will be here soon."

Mephistopheles left Lucifer's throne and approached Belial on his cloven feet. He grabbed him up by his neck and held Belial before him. "For your sake, they'd better be. You know how much Lucifer hates to be disappointed. Indeed, he has already prepared a special pit for you should you fail. Would you care to see it?"

Terror claimed Belial. He'd spent enough nights in Lucifer's pits to know the type of pain they yielded. Even at the mere thought, his body contracted violently.

"Lucifer grows weary of the wait," Mephistopheles spat, shoving him into the arms of a waiting demon. "I suggest you hurry."

A whip cut through his back. Belial gasped at the fire that erupted along his spine. He fell to his knees, his legs too weak to hold him.

"Don't fail, Belial."

Suddenly, he found himself back in the forest. He reached behind him and touched his aching spine. When he pulled his hand away, he saw the blood.

Groaning, Belial stretched out on the ground, needing time to regain his strength.

What was he going to do? He couldn't take Daemon's soul before 'twas his time to die. If Kaziel continued to interfere, what *could* he do?

Belial shuddered, his mind torn between displeasing Lucifer and crossing the will of God.

What a choice to make. God's wrath or Lucifer's?

Fear seized his chest. Why had he ever followed Lucifer? He should have known better than to believe Lucifer's lies.

What a damned fool he'd been.

Belial curled his lip. How he hated being ordered about. Since they'd fallen, Lucifer had done nothing save tread upon him and Belial was weary of it.

When he had agreed to join Lucifer, the bastard had promised him an equal share of their kingdom. But the only equality Belial shared was with the other poor damned souls Lucifer tortured. Aye, Lucifer would gladly give *him* what Lucifer gave them.

Closing his eyes, Belial allowed his impotent fury to wash over him. But in the end, he knew he had no choice.

Regardless of God's laws, he must press the curse forward and claim Daemon and Arina.

Chapter Eighteen

The ride back to Brunneswald was arduous. Arina managed to doze fitfully during the ride, but Daemon's angry silence wore on her. Her attempts at conversation had all ended in failure.

Dawn had broken a short time ago, and Arina marveled at the beauty of the pink and blue-laced sky. The morning air was crisp and fresh, its breath stinging her cheeks with cold as they rode.

What she wouldn't give for a lifetime spent witnessing such moments in Daemon's arms. She stiffened at the thought—Daemon's mortal arms, attached to a mortal body that was destined to perish.

She closed her eyes against the wave of grief

that swallowed her heart. Were she human, they would have a future to plan for, a future filled with real hopes and dreams, and children born of their love. Oh, to have one precious moment when she might hold a child in her arms, a child that united her and Daemon forever. Why was that dream impossible?

Arina ignored the voice in her heart that answered, and for the first time since her creation, she despised angels. She despised anything that stood between her and her husband.

At long last, they entered the bailey. Daemon slid to the ground with her in his arms. Embarrassed by his continued embrace, she tried to squirm from his hold, but he tightened his grip.

"I can walk, milord."

"Aye, and run as well."

She stopped moving and stared at him. His gaze blank, he said nothing more as he carried her inside. The people were just waking, and they paused in their morning routines to stare at them.

Arina averted her gaze, embarrassed by the speculative gleam in the few sets of eyes she'd noticed. Heat crept up her cheeks and despite her wish that Daemon release her, she kept her silence.

At last Daemon entered their chambers and deposited her on the bed. "I should chain you," he said, his voice as empty as his eyes.

She swallowed. He would never do such to

her. 'Twas only his pain that made him threaten, pain *she* had given him. "I didn't mean to hurt you."

"Indeed."

Arina flinched at the sarcasm underlying his tone.

"If milady did this much damage unintentionally, then I would hate to see what you could do if you applied yourself." Fury darkened his eyes, and he turned away as if he could no longer stand to look upon her.

Tears gathered in her eyes, but she refused to let them fall. He had a right to be angry.

When he spoke again, his voice was barely more than a whisper in the quiet room. "I thought after your last escape you had decided to stay."

She had to make him understand that she left *for* him, not because of him. "I was trying to find a way to break the curse, but when the rota fell, I realized I was tempting fate by staying here. I only wanted to protect you."

Daemon shook his head and braced his hands against the back of the chair in front of him. Still facing the wall, he sighed. "I don't want your protection, milady. I only want you."

Arina closed her eyes against the warmth his words brought to her heart and the accompanying desire that made her want to stay with him forever.

She couldn't feel this way, not if she were to save him.

Whatever she did, she must keep her mind unclouded by emotions. "Please, Daemon, understand that I cannot stay here and be responsible for your death. I just can't."

She crossed the room and placed a hand on his rigid shoulder. His muscles bunched beneath her fingertips, but he made no move to pull away. "When the rota fell, I realized there's no time or place for us. You have your world and I have mine. *We* are not of the same flesh."

He turned about and held her by the arms. His angry gaze searched hers. And beneath his rage, pain flickered in the odd-colored depths, stealing her breath, her will. "How can you say that? 'Tis your flesh I feel next to me, *human* flesh."

She shook her head. " 'Tis a temporary delusion."

His grip tightened on her arms, and she sensed his desire to shake her. "As is my body, as is everyone's."

"Nay, 'tis different," she insisted. "You were created to live as human."

"Was I?" Bitterness replaced his anger. "I have never lived as others. All my life, I have lived alone, without family, without friend. Is that the way of humans?"

Arina swallowed, her chest tightening in fear and apprehension. "I don't want you to die."

"And I don't want to live, unless I have you."

She closed her eyes, unable to face the sincerity of his gaze. Why was Daemon doing this? Why was he being so stubborn? "Are you willing to damn yourself for a moment's pleasure?"

"For one sweet moment with you, aye," he said, his voice rich and sure. "Never once in my life have I expected to grow old, and I would rather live one day held in your arms than to live out the rest of my life in the empty void that has been my lot since birth."

Arina pulled away from him, his words branding her, thrilling her. It would be so easy to stay, so very easy to give her pledge that she would remain with him for whatever time fate had set aside for them. But the price was too high and she was unwilling to pay it.

Her thoughts whirled through her head as she sought some argument that would make him understand her side of the matter. If only he could see things as she did.

Aye, that was it. She must show him.

Lifting her chin, she turned around. "And what if the curse said that I was the one destined to die in *your* arms, milord?" she asked, stepping closer to him.

Arina touched his cheek, his whiskers gently scraping her palm, and she wished time would befriend them. But time worked against all mortal beings. "Would you be willing to take your pleasure in the present if you knew that any day my life would end and that you might have to live out the whole of your life without me? Could you stay by my side knowing that was the price?"

Daemon started at her words. He'd never once thought of it that way.

She nodded. " 'Tis as I thought. You would never take such a risk. Yet you expect me to."

" 'Tis not the same," he said, his throat tight.

"Aye, it is and you know it."

Daemon clenched his teeth, the knot in his stomach tightening even more. Aye, he did know it, knew it and cursed it. "Then what is left?"

"I know not," she said, her eyes dimming. "I only know that I can no longer put your life at risk." She walked away from him, her shoulders slumping while she wrung her hands. Her obvious misery brought a painful burning to his gullet.

Indecision racked him. Life had never been more than a bothersome burden and he would gladly put it aside. Yet he could not allow his death to haunt Arina. The guilt from it would tear her apart.

But to leave her would destroy his heart. Daemon sighed, uncertain what to do. He clenched his teeth and cursed himself. He was a selfish bastard, but not so selfish that he would hurt her.

So be it. He'd had his time with her. He

wouldn't ask for more. Since death was his sentence, he would meet it bravely. But he'd meet it away from his Arina.

"Very well," Daemon said at last. "You stay here where you are safe. I shall make terms with my brother for your welfare. I'm sure he will appoint a steward loyal to him, but you will retain final say." Clearing his throat, he pulled his gloves from his hands. "I shall leave for London on the morrow."

Arina gasped. 'Twas what she'd wanted, so why did her heart ache as if it were breaking?

"Come, milady. Neither of us has rested. I doubt I shall die in my sleep, so let us take our slumber."

Arina nodded, her throat too tight for her to speak. Inside, her heart shriveled. She bit her lip to keep her tears from falling. It must be this way.

And yet she cursed their fate.

Fully dressed, she lay upon the bed, her soul crying out for her to keep him near. Daemon pulled his tunic from his head and joined her. His strong arms reached around her and drew her closer to his warmth, his hard chest.

She shivered, wanting nothing more than to stay like this forever, but knowing how impossible a dream it was. His breath fell against her neck and she trembled. Was there truly no way to break the curse?

Perhaps in his absence, she might find some

way; then she could send for him. Aye, that was what she'd do. 'Twas only a temporary separation. As soon as he was away and safe, she would do whatever she must to dissolve the pact and then they would be together.

Holding that thought dear, she closed her eyes and allowed herself to succumb to sleep.

Daemon came awake to Wace's insistent shaking. "Milord, forgive me," he whispered, "but a sickness has come over Ganille. The groom bade me fetch you."

With a frown, Daemon pushed himself up, careful not to wake Arina. Retrieving his tunic, he frowned. What could have happened to his horse?

He pulled his tunic on and excused Wace. Ganille had been fine this morning when they'd returned. What ailment could have come upon the destrier so suddenly?

Narrowing his eyes, he knew the answer. Belial. The beast had probably poisoned Ganille to keep him at Brunneswald. His anger rising, Daemon made his way out of the hall and to the stable.

As he pushed open the door, his anger dissipated. How would Belial know he planned to leave? Arina had said Belial couldn't read minds. Yet what else could have tainted the stallion if not Belial's wickedness?

The avener met him in Ganille's stall, his face

grim. "Must've been bad oats, *m'hlaford*."

Sweat covered Ganille's body and the horse struggled for breath. Daemon stroked his velvet nose, wishing he could alleviate some of the horse's obvious pain. "Will he be all right?"

"Hard to say," the avener said, wiping his nose with a grimy hand. "Don't know exactly what ails him."

Daemon nodded. "Keep an eye on him and do your best."

"Aye, *m'hlaford*."

Daemon sighed. Ganille's illness was not enough to stop him from leaving. In fact, 'twas nothing more than a mere nuisance. He could easily use another horse to reach London, and once there buy another destrier. But he had been through much with the stallion, and hated to lose such a well-trained animal.

With one last pat to the horse's head, he started to leave the stall, but something solid struck him across the back of his head.

Pain exploded through his brain and he stumbled to the ground. Shaking his aching head to clear it, he tried to rise, but another strong blow knocked the air from his lungs. What was happening?

Rough hands seized him and tied ropes to his wrists. Anger burning through him, Daemon struggled against his attacker. But his fuzzy vision and disorientation left him too vulnerable.

"Hold him!"

Daemon frowned at Edred's voice, and he suddenly realized there were several men around him. Two large, burly Saxons pulled him to the front of the stall. There they tied his hands to the wooden posts and forced him to kneel before the friar.

Edred stepped forward with a vial of water and splashed his face and tunic with it. His voice rang out, the words of exorcism all too familiar even to Daemon's dazed senses. "Let evil bow before the good; and the wicked at the gates of the righteous."

"What do you think you're doing, friar?" Daemon growled, his sight still hazy from his blows.

"Watch the door," Edred called to one of the men next to Daemon, ignoring the question. "He might summon one of his minions to save him."

Edred turned back to face him. "I saw you last night in my dreams and I know you for what you are!" Again he slung water across Daemon's face.

Whoever stood behind Daemon slit his tunic and exposed his back. Fury boiled inside Daemon's veins. Memories surged through him and without being told, he knew what would follow.

Daemon snarled, pulling against the ropes until his wrists burned. "Release me!" he shouted and lunged at the friar before him.

Edred stumbled out of his reach. "Gag him,"

he instructed the man behind Daemon.

Daemon did his best to prevent the orders from being carried out. He shouted for Wace, but before he could get the sound out, cloth covered his lips.

Once more, Edred began reciting his call to God. "Lord, open their eyes that they may turn from darkness to light and from the dominion of Satan to God; that they may receive forgiveness of sins and an inheritance among those sanctified by faith." He paused and nodded to whoever stood behind Daemon.

Once again, Daemon craned his neck to see whom Edred addressed, but before he could, pain ripped through his back and he recognized the familiar strike of the lash.

As hard as he could, he pulled against the ropes and once more they held fast. Over and over the whip crossed his back, pain exploding through him until Edred's voice died out and all around him faded.

Arina stretched and yawned. She reached out for her husband, but found only emptiness. Where had he gone?

Yawning again, she stepped from the bed, opened the shutters and realized it was late afternoon. She scanned the yard and spied children playing and people bustling with chores and duties. Not seeing Daemon among them, she left her chambers and entered the hall.

Wace sat in one corner carefully wiping Daemon's armor with an oil cloth. If anyone knew where Daemon had gone, 'twould be Wace.

"Good day," she called, drawing near.

Wace looked up from his task with a smile. "Good day, milady. I trust you slept well?"

She nodded, returning his smile. "Have you seen Lord Daemon?"

"I wouldn't seek him if I were you."

She stiffened at Belial's voice. How had she missed noticing his stench? "And why not?"

Belial paused by her side, his hands held behind his back. "He was terribly angry at you when he found you gone. Wasn't he, good Wace?"

"Aye, milord," Wace said, his hand pausing as he looked from her to Belial.

The demon gave a wistful sigh. "He even swore he'd beat you for your actions."

Arina lifted her chin. "He didn't seem so angry when we went to bed."

A crude smile curved Belial's lips and he raked a snide glare over her body. "Few men hold their anger when a beautiful woman lies in their bed."

She clenched her teeth, disgusted by his crudity. "Where is he?"

Belial shrugged. "How would I know?"

"Milady?"

She faced Wace.

"He went to the stable nigh on an hour ago to

check on Ganille. I haven't seen him since."

"Thank you, Wace," she said.

Turning around, she found Belial blocking her path. "Excuse me." She tried to step past him, but he refused.

A tremor of fear shook her body. Why was Belial doing this? Something must be amiss. A knowing light glowed in his eyes. "Remember, he can't die unless he does so in your arms," he whispered.

How could she forget?

Suddenly, she caught his meaning. Daemon was in danger! Arina started to leave, then paused. If she sought him, would that cause his death?

And yet she felt a pressing need to find him and make certain nothing had happened to him.

A new fear seized her breast. Could Daemon die even without her present? A chill crept over her. What if he was merely injured? By not going, would she cause his death?

Go to him.

She blinked, recognizing Kaziel's voice. "Wace, come with me," she said before lifting the hem of her kirtle, and running for the stable.

She pushed against the stable doors, but they held fast. Panic ripped through her. Something was wrong, terribly, terribly wrong.

Wace joined her, and he too tried to open the doors. "They're locked?" he asked in shock.

"Is there another way inside?"

"Aye, milady. There is a small door in the rear."

Determined to find it, she hurried around the stable, Wace one step behind. Wace rushed ahead and opened it. He waited for her, and together they entered.

Arina stopped. Unable to believe the sight before her, she went numb for the flicker of a heartbeat; then anger pounded through her.

"Nay!" she cried.

"Holy Mother," Wace breathed. "I shall get help!"

Arina barely understood his words through the horror filling her. Dazed, she raced toward her husband.

Brother Edred looked up and caught her before she reached Daemon's side.

"Milady, please," he said, holding her away. "You must not interfere. 'Tis God's business we are about. He must do penance for his evil if we are to save his soul."

She twisted out of Edred's arms. " 'Tis you who are evil!" she said, reaching for Daemon. He rested on his knees, his entire body soaked in blood. She cupped his face in her hands and raised his head.

His fevered skin burning her, she recoiled in horror. A filthy gag covered his lips.

"Milady, do not interfere!" Brother Edred said.

The main doors burst open. She looked up to see Wace leading a group of Daemon's men. They seized the three men with Brother Edred.

"You've damned his soul with your actions."

Ignoring the friar, Arina pulled the gag from Daemon's lips. His breath came in shallow, pain-filled gasps. Agony and fear swelled inside her. " 'Tis you who are damned, friar. The Lord would never sanction this."

Wace came forward and sliced the ropes holding Daemon up. He fell into her arms and she held him close, her entire body shaking in fear of losing him.

"He is the son of Lucifer!" Brother Edred insisted. "I can prove it to you, milady."

She looked up at him, her rage dulling her sight. She wanted to cut out his heart for what he'd done. "You can't prove what isn't true," she said between clenched teeth.

"Aye, 'tis true," he insisted. "Look beneath his hair and you'll see the devil's mark. Why do you think he wears it long while others of his kind wear their hair cropped?"

Her anger doubling, she grabbed the friar by his sleeve and forced him to kneel beside her. Cradling Daemon's head against her breast, she pulled his hair back and showed Edred the mark it hid. " 'Tis the mark of our Lord he bears, Brother, not the devil's."

Brother Edred's jaw dropped and shock darkened his eyes.

" 'Tis an innocent man you have punished."

Arina reluctantly released her hold on Daemon and allowed his men to carry him out of the stable. Rising to her feet, she stood before the friar. "Were I you, Brother, I would worry about paying penance for my own soul."

She left him gaping, and followed after Daemon.

Hours sped by as Arina tried to staunch the flow of blood and brewed poultices to fight infection. Daemon remained unconscious and she prayed for his survival. He couldn't die, not like this.

Long after the hall had settled down to sleep, Arina left Wace to watch over Daemon while she went to seek Belial. During the last hour she had tended her husband, a new way to break the curse had come to her; one she had never thought of.

Though the mere thought of it terrified her, she realized this price was one she could afford, one she would gladly pay.

Arina found Belial in the little garden outside. She drew her cloak tighter about her, amazed he could stand the coldness as yet another chill wind blew across her face and took her breath.

Without a cloak for warmth, he sat on a wooden bench, staring up at the sky. " 'Tis a lovely view, isn't it?" he asked as she drew near.

Arina glanced up. "I have no care for the view this night."

"Nay, I suppose not." He looked at her, his red, glowing eyes unreadable. "How is he?"

She stiffened at his audacity. "Why do you even ask?"

He shrugged and looked back at the stars. "Daemon is an exceptional opponent."

"Is that all people are to you?" Arina asked, almost pitying his foul existence.

He laughed, and tilted his head back. "Oh, look who is accusing *me* of callousness." Sitting up straight, he pierced her with a malicious glare. "At least I don't dump their miserable souls in hell. I am not the one they cling to and *beg* for forgiveness. How many souls have you left to final agony?"

She swallowed, his words tearing through her. "I have no choice about what I do."

"And neither do I."

Arina approached him and despite the part of her that urged her to flee, she sat down beside him. "What is it like to be damned?"

"You cannot imagine." The bitterness in his voice caught her off guard.

"Why not?" she whispered, wondering what it would feel like to experience Lucifer's kingdom.

"Because there is nothing like it in this world or in yours."

She nodded, her heart pounding in fear and remorse. "Do you regret what you've done?"

Belial looked at her, his red eyes haunting in

their pain. "I regret every decision I have ever made." He stiffened as if suddenly aware of her for the first time, and again he looked up. "What brings you out here?"

Arina drew a deep breath for courage. "I have something to ask of you."

"Of me?" he asked incredulously. "I find it hard to believe you would deign to ask me for a favor."

"Believe what you will, but I am here."

"So you are, angel." He chewed his lip and glanced her way. "What is it you want?"

"A trade," she said, then rushed on with her practiced words before she lost the courage to utter them. "If I give you my soul, will you spare Daemon's life?"

Chapter Nineteen

Belial sat straight up, his attention finally on her. "You jest."

"Nay," she said, a shiver moving over her at the mere thought of her sacrifice, a sacrifice she must never let Daemon know of.

The demon's eyes blazed. "Does the mortal mean so much to you?"

She lifted her chin, refusing to answer the question. He knew her response, and she feared uttering it might somehow give him more strength.

Shaking his head, Belial gave a small laugh. "You are a fool."

Her cheeks warmed at his mockery. Aye, 'twas foolish, but she had no choice. She refused to see Daemon punished for something she'd done. "Is it agreed?"

He nodded. "Aye."

Arina closed her eyes, relieved and yet terrified. But she would rather lose her own soul and give Daemon life. "Thank you," she whispered, rubbing the chills on her arms. "When will you claim me?"

Belial opened his mouth, then shut it. A strange look hovered in his eyes. He leaned his head back and yielded a heavy sigh. "I can't do it," he whispered in such a low tone she wasn't even sure she'd heard it.

He met her gaze. "Lucifer help me, but I have to tell you the truth."

She frowned at his tortured voice, wondering what he meant. "The truth?"

"Aye, I lied," he whispered. "I can't take your soul and spare him. You know I have no control over his current condition."

"But you can break the curse!" she insisted, afraid he would back out of the agreement. He couldn't. Surely not even Belial was that vicious. "If you take me now, he stands a chance of survival."

Belial snorted. Then, before she could move, he pulled out a dagger and sliced her throat.

Arina gasped and touched her wound, but where blood should have been pouring out, there was nothing save smooth skin. She looked at him in horror. "What is this?"

He replaced the dagger in his belt and shrugged nonchalantly. Looking away as if the matter bored him, he sighed. "I can't claim your soul until you die, and you cannot die until after he does."

"I don't understand," she said, her mind racing. She was human, she had to be. And if she were human, then she should be able to die before Daemon. "I have hurt myself since I've been here. I have—"

"But you've never once bled."

She opened her mouth to protest, then clamped it shut. He was right. When her mare had thrown her in the snow, she had been bruised, and no blood had fallen.

Agony and hopelessness invaded her heart, her soul. Was there truly no way? No hope? "You told me the curse could be broken."

"Nay, you told yourself that. I merely offered to barter. You drew your own conclusion. Nearly every word out of my mouth has been a lie of some sort and you fell for each and every one. You, my angel, are far too naive."

Stiffening at his insult, she narrowed her eyes. "Why are you telling me this?"

Belial sighed and studied his hands. "I'm an evil bastard but even I am still capable of feelings. I have never minded claiming humans like Edred who bring their damnation on by their own actions, or even the ones who were stupid enough to fall to my temptations, but you . . ."

He paused and started to move away.

"What about me?" she asked.

Belial turned toward her. Emotions played across his face and she longed to call them by name, but their source eluded her. Finally he sighed again. "You are truly unselfish, and no matter how much I would love to hand you over to Lucifer, I can't."

Belial stared at her, and his heated look sent a chill down her arms. "Daemon's heart is not the only one you have claimed."

Stunned, she could do nothing but stare. How could he say that? Was it merely another of his lies he used to manipulate her? "And I am supposed to believe you?"

He shrugged. "Believe what you will. Just leave me in peace."

Arina hesitated. What should she believe?

When she didn't move, Belial shoved her away from him. "Get back to your husband, angel."

By the look in her eyes he could tell she wanted to argue, wanted to call him liar, but she said nothing. Instead, she turned around with unmatched dignity and grace and walked back toward the hall.

Sitting down, Belial leaned forward and hung his head in his hands. Perhaps it had been the peaceful night that had weakened him. Arina had caught him in a weak mood and he had confessed to her. Damn him for his stupidity!

"You already are."

He looked up at Mephistopheles. "I'm in no mood to deal with you this night."

Mephistopheles lashed out with one clawed hand, catching him against his jaw. Belial recoiled from the blow, his face burning. He changed to demon form and lunged for Mephistopheles, but it did no good.

"I have always said you were too tender-hearted for your missions. But Lucifer wouldn't listen. Nay, he liked your pranks too much. Thank you for finally proving to him what you really are."

Belial tried to loosen the grip on his throat. "Release me!"

Mephistopheles shook his head, his grip tightening even more. "I have come with a directive from Lucifer. Kill the Norman and bring him the angel or you will be enslaved to me."

Mephistopheles dropped him. Belial choked and coughed, his throat burning.

"Personally," Mephistopheles said, flying above him, "I care not which you choose. Either way, I have won Lucifer's trust. You were a fool, Belial. You had his favor and you traded it for *them!*"

Belial reached for him, but Mephistopheles vanished into the night. Leaning his head back against the ground, he listened to the gentle sounds of the night, the breeze drifting through leaves. So much for compassion.

Clenching his teeth, he ran through a list of his accomplices. Norbert was gone, Raida had converted and Edred had failed. All his pawns had been effectively neutralized. Where did that leave him?

Between Lucifer's fist and his palm. Sighing, he knew he had no choice. "Forgive me, angel," he whispered.

For three days, Arina stayed with Daemon while his fever raged. Since his injuries covered his back, they had been forced to lay him on his stomach, which made it almost impossible to feed him. She prayed for his recovery before starvation took his life.

Raida stood at the table, mixing herbs and uttering her own prayers.

"Here, *m'hlafdie*," she said, handing Arina a goblet. "This should break the fever."

Arina forced it down his throat as best she could. "Oh, Raida, what are we to do?" she asked, her heart aching.

Raida shook her head and sighed. "I know not, *m'hlafdie*. I have tried to find some way to break the curse, but nothing has worked."

A soft knock interrupted them.

"Enter," Arina called.

The door opened and Brother Edred stepped in. She cocked her brow in surprise, and the bitter taste of hatred scalded her throat. "What brings *you* here?"

He swallowed, his fat jowls flopping. Clearing his throat, he gave her a baleful look. "I have come to make peace. I have been fasting and praying and finally a voice told me to come here. I made a mistake, *m'hlafdie*. I falsely accused an innocent man and now he may die because of it."

Arina opened her mouth to order him from the room, but she paused. Over Brother Edred's shoulder, she saw Kaziel. He reached out and pushed Edred forward.

Edred took a step and gulped. "Please forgive my error, *m'hlafdie*."

"You are forgiven," she said softly, realizing Brother Edred must have won a higher forgiveness than hers.

Nodding at her, Kaziel curved his lips into a gentle smile, then vanished.

A sudden, deep, ragged breath drew Arina's attention back to the bed. Daemon shifted, and slowly opened his eyes.

Arina gasped, rushing to his side. Her heart hammered, and she reached a shaking hand to touch his fevered cheek.

"Milord?" she asked, relief pouring over her. Nothing had ever been more beautiful than the sight of his open eyes, their lucid intelligence shining brightly.

She heard the door close. Looking up, she realized Brother Edred had left quietly.

Daemon tried to push himself up, but Arina

stopped him. "Please, milord. You'll hurt yourself."

He dropped back to the mattress and released a weary sigh.

She knelt beside him so that he wouldn't have to strain to look at her. "How do you feel?"

He answered her with a grimace. Arina smiled, and brushed a lock of hair out of his eyes.

"What happened to them?" he asked, his voice weak and hoarse.

Anger mixed with pain and set her heart pounding. She didn't need Daemon to explain which *them* he asked about. "The two who guarded the door were fined. I had the one who wielded the lash beaten, and Brother Edred . . ."

Arina paused, unsure how to tell him.

"You released him."

Swallowing, she nodded. "I thought it best to allow the Lord and Peter to hand out his sentence."

Daemon reached out a hand and took hers. His weak grip brought a wave of guilt to her that she hadn't done more. But she couldn't.

" 'Tis well, milady. Our laws are such that we are not to harm the clergy, and my brother would have been sorely vexed had you broken that law—even for me."

"Then you're not angry?"

A light came to his eyes, and if Arina didn't know better, she'd swear he smiled. "I'm not angry. At least not at you."

She shook her head, her throat tight. " 'Tis not the Lord you should—"

"Milady, please," he whispered, interrupting her. "I am already acquainted with your lecture on how the Lord is not responsible for the actions of His followers."

"Yet you blame Him still?"

To Arina's utter astonishment, he shook his head. "Nay, milady. I find no fault with the one you worship. My anger is reserved solely for the friar."

She stared at him, unable to believe his words. Words that must have caused him much pain to utter and words that gave her more hope than she'd ever had before. If Daemon could suffer what he had and not lash out at the Lord, then anything was possible.

Weeks sped by and Arina waited in fear and hope. She and Raida had tried everything they could to break the curse. The worst part was that they had no way of knowing for certain whether or not the curse had been broken.

Several times Arina had tried to consult Belial, but he refused to speak further to her. She decided the curse must still be holding; otherwise he would have left them.

Daemon's back healed rather quickly, but even so he was in no condition for travel to London. And though she wished them apart, she also reveled in their days together, grateful for every touch and glance he gave her.

Now Daemon sat before her in a large tub the servants had brought into their chambers and filled with steaming water.

As carefully as she could, she sponged his bruised back. Most of the cuts had healed, but fresh scars attested to the brutality of his attack. Arina traced one of them with her finger, her heart aching at how many times he had been so abused in his life. She would give much to remove every such vicious scar and memory from him.

Running her hand down his back, she marveled at his hardened muscles. Chills sprang up beneath her caress and she smiled at his reaction.

"Careful, milady," Daemon said, turning his head to look at her over his shoulder. "You are tempting me beyond endurance."

Her smile widened. "Milord should not make such empty threats."

"Empty threats?" he asked, his face aghast. "Madame, I assure you 'tis not empty."

She cocked an eyebrow at his double meaning and pleasure rippled in her stomach. Before she could move, he ran his hand under her hair and pulled her forward until his lips claimed hers.

Arina moaned with pleasure, delighting in the feel of his soft mouth. She opened her lips and drew him in. Nothing had ever tasted finer, ever felt better.

His kiss deepening, he again pulled her and before she could protest, he had her in his lap. She stiffened with a cry of protest. "You've soaked me!"

One corner of his mouth turned up. "I thought you would gladly hurl yourself into a lake for my attentions."

Arina laughed at his memory and thought about the night she had uttered that statement. Her blood warmed. He had changed so much since then, as had she. But she decided she liked the difference in his personality.

"Mayhap I have changed my mind," she said, trying to ignore how pleasant he felt beneath her.

"Have you now?" he asked, his voice deep with desire.

She opened her mouth to respond and once more he kissed her. Arina wrapped her arms about his shoulders, sliding her hands down his spine. A thousand flames ignited in her stomach and her body throbbed. He felt so good in her arms.

With a tight groan, Daemon lifted the hem of her kirtle and ran his hands over her bare buttocks and hips. Fire ran through her veins. His wet caresses sent shivers over her and her body demanded him. Arina gasped and adjusted her legs until she straddled him.

Her heart pounded in her ears as her lower body came into contact with his heated arousal. Daemon sucked his breath between his teeth and closed his eyes.

Arina smiled at his reaction, reveling in her power over him. She buried her lips in his neck, tasting the salty stubble of his throat, and pressed herself closer to him.

He tugged her kirtle off and tossed it to the floor, where it landed with a splat. Arina laughed at the sound, but her humor fled as he touched her breast. Leaning her head back, she bit her lip as his mouth played upon her, and the throbbing increased. She held his head in her hands and moaned with pleasure.

Suddenly, he filled her. Arina gripped the sides of the tub, her body afire. Her breathing labored, she looked into his eyes, and the love that shone there sent another wave of chills over her.

He dipped his hands in the water and caressed her lower hips. "Stay with me, Arina," he whispered, leaning forward until he kissed the flesh just below her ear. His warm breath on her neck sent shivers down her arms. "I know I have no right to ask, but I can't let you go."

Arina closed her eyes against the agony his plea brought.

He moved his hips against hers, and she clenched her teeth at the searing pleasure that overshadowed her sadness. She wanted him, longed for his presence.

How could she deny his request when 'twas her own fondest desire that she stay by his side?

She couldn't. May Peter forgive and protect her. "I shall stay with you, milord. No matter what comes on the morrow, I shall remain by your side and not force you to leave."

Daemon pulled back, his body rigid. "Milady?" he asked, blinking as if he couldn't believe he'd heard her correctly.

Arina laid her hand against his cheek. "You heard me aright, milord."

Cocking his head, he gave her a suspicious look. "Is it your intent to leave?"

She shook her head. "Nay."

He pulled her back into his arms and crushed her with a hug until she was forced to cry out. "Milord, please. You're halving me!"

Suddenly, he rose from the tub. Apparently oblivious to the water dripping from them, he carried her to the bed and laid her on it. Arina stared up at him, her heart pounding.

His hair cascading over her like a wet cloak, Daemon pulled her legs around his waist and again slid inside. Arina trembled, needing him, afraid that on the morrow he would perish.

But she had given her pledge and she intended to stand by it. She took him in her embrace and held him close to her heart. Arching against him, she gripped his arms.

All her worries fled and she concentrated on the smell of his sweet skin, the taste of his flesh. Over and over he thrust against her and she raised her hips to meet him. Her body tingled and throbbed and before she could beg for more, she found her release.

Crying out, she tightened her hold on his arms.

With two more thrusts, he joined her. His breathing labored, he collapsed on top of her.

Arina moaned in satisfaction, her body still pulsing. Running her hand over his back, she smiled.

Daemon nibbled her neck, his teeth raising chills along her body. "I love you, milady," he whispered, then nibbled her earlobe.

Cold terror seized her and Arina stiffened at his words. He pulled back and stared down at her. "Does that displease you?"

Tears gathering in her eyes, she shook her head. "Nay, milord," she whispered, her heart torn between pleasure and agony.

Why had he uttered the words? Would they activate the curse? Closing her eyes, she prayed for time.

Norbert reined his horse at the ramparts, his anger charged by the half-finished wall before him. A wall that further reminded him of the Norman pestilence feeding on his people. And 'twas time they rid themselves of the rats.

He had gathered Saxons all the way from his sister's home to Brunneswald. Good Saxon men chased from their homes by the Norman filth.

Though they scarce numbered a few score, they were still numerous enough to finish the task ahead of them.

Norbert scanned their dour faces, and he thought of what all of them had been through.

Suddenly, an image of his sister's sweet, innocent face swept before his eyes. His stomach tightened in grief and rage. She had died because of *them*. The Norman dogs had taken her home and killed her husband; then their leader had forced her to live as his concubine. Degraded by her position, she had slit her wrists.

Norbert tightened his grip on his reins. He hadn't been able to rescue his sister, but he vowed to save Arina.

Come the morrow, he would take the Norman's head and use it to decorate his home just as his forefathers had done!

Chapter Twenty

Daemon watched his men training. He had tried for a time to exercise himself, but his back was still stiff and sore. Too sore for him to make more than a few strokes of the sword.

A flutter of red caught the corner of his eye. He turned his head and watched Arina cross the yard. A group of children ran around her and she laughed with them, her face more beauteous than any creature ever born.

Heat rushed through his body, inflaming his loins. Daemon took a step toward her, intending to seize her in his arms and carry her back to their chambers.

But before he could cross the distance, an unfamiliar rider came through the gate. Frowning, he stared at the serf astride a jackass. He remembered seeing the boy tilling a field with his father, who lived not far away.

Daemon paused as the youth stopped before one of his servants and leaned down to talk. The servant gestured toward Daemon, and the boy followed the line of his arm and nodded.

What could the boy want with him? Daemon waited for his approach.

The boy kicked the mule forward and drew to a stop by his side. "Are you *hlaford* Daemon?"

"Aye."

"My father sent me to fetch you, *m'hlaford*. There are men destroying the castle wall on the hill and setting fire to our fields. My father begs you come quick!"

His sight dimming in rage, Daemon called to his men to assemble.

He ran toward the stable, but before he could enter, Arina caught up to him. "Milord, what is it?"

Daemon opened his mouth to speak, then paused.

Masking his emotions, he realized she would do naught but worry if she knew the truth.

His mind racing, he searched for a quick lie. What could he tell her to keep . . .

An idea struck him. With any luck, she wouldn't know construction of the castle had stopped for the winter, nor how things such as castles were built in this world. 'Twas at least worth trying. "Master Dennis needs assistance with his work. I am taking some men to see if we can help."

"Should I keep supper for you?" she asked, and her ready acceptance of his lie brought guilt to his heart.

Daemon shook his head, reminding himself that he must mislead her. 'Twas for her own good. "Nay, milady, I may be late getting back."

She nodded. "Then take care, milord. I shall see you anon," she said, reaching up to kiss his cheek.

Daemon watched her walk away, his face tingling, and again he wanted her. Clenching his teeth, he forced his mind to the coming task and promised himself that on his return, he would carry out what he had originally intended.

After the midday meal, Arina decided to take Daemon and his men a bite of food. She didn't know what kind of provisions they had up on the hill, but they probably were not enough for all the extra men Daemon had taken.

The cook wrapped provisions in plain pieces of cloth and Arina packed her saddlebags while the groom saddled a palfrey.

Arina handed the saddlebags to the groom and he placed them at the rear of her saddle. With a smile, she thanked him.

Whispering to the mare to take care and not frighten her, Arina urged the small horse across the yard and out the gate. The weather was pleasant, and she decided she couldn't wait to see the coming spring and what new beauty it would bring to the land. Smiling, she hummed to herself.

It didn't take long to reach the hill. Strange, foul-smelling black smoke drifted around the area, and she wondered what they had burned.

A breeze whipped her cloak out from behind her and she heard the groans and strains of men at work.

Arina dismounted and led her palfrey up the hillside. Rounding the side of the wall, she froze, her body numb from fear and panic. 'Twas no work they were about! Fierce battle raged all around her.

Though her mind screamed at her to run, she couldn't move, couldn't take her eyes off the horrifying sight before her.

"Milady, why do you come?"

Daemon froze at the familiar voice, a voice he hadn't heard since he'd found his angel. His heart pounding, he turned in his saddle and saw Arina rising out of the billowing smoke and standing on the hill, looking down upon them. Wind whipped her cloak and pale hair around her, and she appeared just as she had all those times when she'd visited his dreams.

A group of Saxon men rallied around her as if they sought to protect her. His stomach tightened and again he remembered his dream.

Daemon whirled his horse about, trying to reach her, but the men around him prevented it.

A shadow passed over his body. Daemon turned in his saddle, expecting the sword to slice his thigh as it had always done in his dream. Save this time, it wasn't his thigh. His attacker's sword bounced off Daemon's blade and into his chest.

Daemon gasped at the sudden pain that seeped through him. His sight dulling, he slid from his saddle.

"The Norman is dead!"

Arina flinched at the cry that went up among the Saxon men as they raised their swords in victory. Pain racked her body, but she had to make sure. . . .

"Nay!" she screamed, knowing who must have fallen.

She picked up the hem of her kirtle and ran across the field. Men scattered from her path, staring at her as if her presence frightened them.

"M'hlafdie!"

She heard Norbert's call, but paid no heed as she continued to race across the fallen bodies, searching for the familiar form of her husband.

Mayhap he hadn't fallen. Mayhap he was . . .

Suddenly, she saw him, his light blond braid

363

coated with blood, his helm and sword lying next to him. Screaming in denial, she ran to his side. Anguish twisted through her body as she collapsed on the ground beside her precious husband and pulled him into her lap.

Tears filled her eyes and her heart shattered. This couldn't be happening. Nay, please, just one more day with him, just one more moment.

"Arina?" Daemon asked, his voice hoarse.

"Hush, milord," she said, choking on the words and using a corner of her cloak to wipe the red blood from his lips, his pale cheeks. "You must save your strength."

"Nay, 'tis mortal." His accepting words ripped her soul asunder. He reached his hand up and touched her cheek. A slow smile spread across his face. " 'Tis as wondrous as I thought."

She frowned at him and the misplaced happiness in his gaze. "What is?"

"Dying in your arms."

Closing her eyes against the sudden wave of agony, she held on to him, willing him to live. "You can't leave me," she whispered. "I won't let you."

His smile widened and he dropped his hand. "I . . ." The light faded from his eyes.

"Nay!" she screamed, unable to believe he was gone, unable to accept this fate.

All around her, angels appeared claiming souls.

Arina looked up and met the sad eyes of Kaziel, who hovered over them. Gripping Daemon tight, she willed his soul back into his body.

But it did no good. Against all her prayers and pleadings, his soul rose.

Arina shook her head, unwilling to let the curse end this way, stealing the life and soul of an innocent man. "Nay!" she shouted again.

Pain spread through her like fire.

Suddenly the pain stopped. She floated free of her body, and once again her angel's wings fluttered against her spine.

Arina stared down in amazement. She saw Daemon's body, and next to it her red kirtle and cloak. Emptiness filled her. So she had never truly been human. Only an image, an illusion.

Swallowing, she looked back at Kaziel, who took Daemon's hand. Anger washed over her and she vowed to set this matter right.

"Don't interfere," Kaziel warned.

Arina shook her head, her stomach pitching at what she intended. "I must."

And before Kaziel could stop her, she broke his hold on Daemon. She grabbed both of Daemon's wrists.

"Arina?" he asked, amazement lighting his eyes at her appearance.

Biting her lip, she touched his face; only this time she felt nothing beneath her fingertips. "I'm sorry, milord. But 'tis better this way."

"Nay, Arina!" Kaziel shouted.

Ignoring him, she pulled Daemon back toward the ground. "I love you, Daemon Fierce-Blood," she whispered as she coaxed his soul back into his body.

"That was foolish, Arina. You know the rules."

Relief and fear knotted in her throat and she nodded her head. "Aye, I do." She held her hands out for Kaziel. "Take me to Peter. I am ready to receive my eternal fate."

Daemon jerked awake, his body aching.

" 'Tis a miracle!" Wace shouted, his youthful face beaming. "I thought you were dead."

Shaken and uncertain, Daemon ran his hand over his chest. His mail was torn where the sword had pierced his chest, but no other mark existed to prove he had ever been wounded. Had he just fallen from his horse and struck his head?

Wace ran off to tell the others he had survived.

Looking around him, Daemon realized his men had defeated the Saxons. And a few feet away, he spied the body of Norbert. He shook his head and sighed. Though he held no great love for the Saxon, he regretted the end the poor man had come to.

Moans filled his ears, and he watched as his men searched dead bodies and gathered the wounded.

Daemon frowned. How long had be been unconscious? Had seeing Arina been another dream?

Suddenly, his gaze fell to the red kirtle beside him. Excruciating agony ripped through him, piercing his heart and scalding his soul. Reaching over, he brought the cloth to his face and inhaled the sweet rose scent.

'Twas no dream.

Arina was gone. The words circled his mind like beasts of prey seeking to bring him low. And bring him low they did. Raw, brutal grief ripped through him. His precious angel was gone.

I love you, Daemon Fierce-Blood, her gentle words whispered in his mind, slicing his soul with pain.

Daemon clutched her kirtle tight, willing her body back into it. Their marriage couldn't end, not like this!

He looked up at the sky, his pain burning deep inside his heart. "I know You are up there, Lord, and that You and I are strangers. But please, please grant me one favor."

Daemon clasped his hands together and forced himself to his knees. "Never once in my entire life have I asked You for anything. But I'm doing it now. Please, don't take her from me."

Daemon didn't know what he expected, a flash of lightning, Arina appearing out of nowhere. Yet he waited anxiously, his heart pounding.

Only a breeze stirred and only the cries of the wounded filled his head.

Arina was gone and there was nothing he could do.

Clenching his teeth, Daemon longed to curse the callous God who had torn her from his side. But he couldn't bring himself to dishonor the being Arina served, the being she had believed in so strongly. It would be like cursing her.

Pulling her kirtle to his chest, he allowed the tears gathered in his eyes to flow down his cheeks.

Arina stood before Peter, her head bowed. By the stern look on his face, she knew she had long outworn his patience.

"You know we are not to interfere with human life," he said, circling around her.

"Aye, Lord Peter."

"Then why did you put his soul back into his body?"

Arina swallowed. Though her emotions were now muted, she could still feel a twinge of remorse over breaking their strict rules, but as she thought of Daemon, all guilt vanished. For him, she would do it again!

Her thoughts centering on Daemon, she waited for the familiar thrill to consume her, but nothing of the kind happened. She sighed.

Her emotions, like her precious Daemon, were gone. And as she stood before her heavenly judge, she found herself missing the vitality her human emotions had given her, the richness her special love for Daemon had added.

"Arina?"

She started at Peter's voice.

"You haven't answered me."

"I couldn't let him die for me, Lord Peter."

Peter sighed, his eyes weary.

Arina moved forward and again bowed her head. "I am ready for my punishment."

"Wait."

She looked up as Gabriel appeared and frowned at the stern look on Gabriel's face. He pulled Peter aside and the two of them spoke in low tones. What were they discussing? Could they be planning something worse than sending her to hell? She shivered at the thought.

After several terrifying moments, they returned.

Gabriel stepped forward and Arina flinched, half expecting him to take her. Turning around, she drew a ragged, fearful breath. What would Peter do with her?

"Arina?"

She blinked at Kaziel's voice. He appeared beside Lord Peter.

With a nod from Peter, he took her by the arm and her wings dissolved. Arina gasped, her throat tightening in fear. "I am being banished?"

"For a time, or for eternity, depending on the choices you make," Peter replied, turning his back to her.

Arina bit her lip to keep from pleading for mercy. She'd known the consequences of her actions and the least she could do was accept them bravely.

"Where are you taking me?" she asked Kaziel, needing to know but afraid of his answer.

Kaziel faced her, his eyes grim. "You shall see."

Daemon sat in his chair, holding Cecile in his lap. She purred contentedly and he wished he could be so easily soothed. Once again pain enveloped his heart. Over and over he saw his Arina in all her beauty and kindness reaching out to him.

Why had she forced him back into his body? Why had she not just let him die?

"Milord?"

He froze at the sound. When he heard no more, he sighed. "Now I am even hearing her voice," he said, his throat tight.

"Can you feel my touch?"

A hand brushed his cheek. Daemon sprang from his chair and he swung around with a gasp. Cecile let out an indignant yowl as she fell.

His heart pounding, Daemon blinked, unable

to believe his sight. "Arina?"

A smile curved her lips and she reached for him. "Aye, milord. 'Tis I."

Seizing her in his arms, he held her tight. "Are you truly here?"

She laughed in his ear, the sound sending waves of joy through him. "Yes, Peter ordered me returned."

"But how? Why?" he asked, pulling back.

Her smile melted his heart. " 'Twas your faith, milord. You brought me back. When Gabriel told Peter of your call and faith, Peter decided I had acted nobly." She touched his cheek, and he marveled at the warmth of her flesh.

A sudden pain replaced his joy. "But for how long?"

Sighing, she shrugged, her face puckering in thought. "I am human now, milord. Like any other I have no way of knowing how long my life will be. So you may have to tolerate me for a very long time."

"Gladly, milady," he said, his heart light. "I'll be terribly upset otherwise!"

Epilogue

Arina stood before the altar and held her son out for Brother Edred. His voice rang in the chapel as he performed the baptism. Her heart filled with joy, she smiled.

At last, she had everything she'd dreamed of. Looking up, she met Daemon's proud gaze.

"I christen thee Peter," Brother Edred said, and marked the sign of the cross on Peter's forehead.

The baby cried in protest, and Arina gently rocked him. "He has his father's lungs," she whispered to Daemon.

Daemon smiled, and she longed to place a kiss upon his lips.

Once finished, Brother Edred clapped Daemon on his back. "Mayhap next time you'll have that daughter you wanted."

Arina watched Edred leave, then turned to hand her son to his father. Brushing Peter's hair, she smiled. " 'Tis truly a miracle," she breathed.

"Nay," Daemon said. "You are the miracle." He shifted Peter to his shoulder. "But 'tis a pity you have no angelic powers left."

She raised a brow, curious about his words. "And why is that?"

"I have a feeling our Peter will need more than one guardian angel to watch over him."

Arina laughed and followed Daemon from the chapel. "If he is anything like his father, 'twill take an army of angels to guard him."

As they entered the hall, Raida joined them and took Peter from Daemon's arms. "Methinks his swaddling needs changing."

As Daemon turned toward her, Arina caught sight of Cecile cleaning herself in a corner of the room. "Milord?"

He lifted a brow. "Yes?"

"Why don't you and Raida take Peter to our chambers. I have a quick matter to attend."

Daemon brushed a tender kiss on her lips. The gentle touch set her heart pounding. "Don't be long."

Arina nodded, then waited until she was alone. Checking around, she made sure no others were about. With a rush of courage, she seized Cecile and placed her hand over the cat's eyes.

Arina's body warmed and her hand glowed. Cecile hissed. "Ssh," Arina soothed. Then, stroking the cat on the ears, she smiled down at the animal. Cecile gave a yowl and her uncrossed eyes sparkled.

"There you go," Arina said. She gave a small laugh and looked up at the ceiling. "I only interfered a little. Besides, 'tis not a *human* life."

She heard Kaziel's laugh, and even though she no longer possessed the majority of her powers, she knew she still had enough left to keep her husband and son out of too much harm. But then, as Daemon had said, if Peter took after him she would extend all her powers just trying to keep up.

A smile curved her lips. 'Twas one challenge she eagerly looked forward to.

Author's Note

The song that I used in Chapter 5 comes from the medieval crusade song *S'onques Nuls Heom,* and both the majority of the translation I used and the song appear on the compact disc *Ensemble Alcatraz Danse Royale;* the song is performed by the group *La Corte Musical.*

The song Arina sings in Chapter 7 is one written by a famous French female troubadour, Comtessa de Dia. The translation used is from the album *Lo Gai Saber: Troubadours et Jongleurs 1100–1300* by Joel Cohen.

Though both songs are just slightly anachronistic, I still chose to use them since they seemed to capture best the mood and meanings I wanted for the story. I hope you'll forgive me for the extravagance.

Dear Reader,

I hope you've enjoyed reading *Daemon's Angel*. Studying the Middle Ages has been a labor of love for me since the day my mother brought home a suit of armor and set it in our den. I spent many childhood afternoons studying each and every piece of plating and pretending a knight stood ready to defend me should any intruder threaten my safety.

The story of *Daemon's Angel* came to me while working on my nonfiction book *Everyday Life in the Middle Ages*. As I covered the Conquest of England, a startlingly real image came to me of a lone warrior astride a panting steed, surrounded by fallen bodies. His attention was riveted on a small rise in the landscape where a woman drew ever closer. From there, the entire story blossomed.

I hope you've enjoyed reading my book. Thank you for your support, and I'd really like to hear your valuable opinion. My address is: 3520 Terry Road, Suite 186, Jackson, MS 39212. Please enclose a business-size, self-addressed stamped envelope for my reply and an autographed bookmark.

Sincerely,
Sherrilyn Kenyon

An Angel's Touch

Forever Angels

TRANA MAE SIMMONS

Tess Foster is convinced she has someone watching over her. The thoroughly modern woman has everything: a brilliant career, a rich fiance, and a glamorous life. But when her boyfriend demands she sign a prenuptial agreement, Tess thinks she's lost her happiness forever. Then her guardian angel sneezes and sends the woman of the nineties back to another era: the 1890s.

At first, Tess can't believe her senses. After all, no real man can be as handsome as the cowboy who rescues her from the Oklahoma wilderness. And Tess has never tasted sweeter ecstasy than she finds in Stone Chisum's kisses. But before she will surrender to a marriage made in heaven, Tess has to make sure that her bumbling guardian angel doesn't sneeze again—and ruin her second chance at love.

_52021-4 $4.99 US/$5.99 CAN

An Angel's Touch

Time Heals
SUSAN COLLIER

Tired of her nagging relatives, Maeve Fredrickson asks for the impossible: to be a thousand miles and a hundred years away from them. Then a heavenly being grants her wish, and she awakes in frontier Montana.

Saved from the wilderness by a handsome widower, Maeve loses her heart to her rescuer—and her temper over the antics of his three less-than-angelic children. As her angel prods her to fight for Seth, Maeve can only pray for the strength to claim a love made in paradise.

_52030-3 $4.99 US/$5.99 CAN